I0747603

READERS' CHOICE
BOOK AWARDS
SILVER WINNER

THE
BOOKFEST®
AWARD
WINNER

FIREBIRD
BOOK AWARD WINNER
SPEAK UP
TALK RADIO

READERS' FAVORITE®
FIVE STARS

PRAISE FOR THE KALANOSI
CHRONICLES

"*Where the Valley Meets the Sky* is a wonderful tale... The characters are well-written, the setting is vividly drawn...Ben Merrick establishes himself as a great storyteller, crafting a tale that explores the human spirit and the bonds that hold a clan together, even in the most challenging of times."

— FIVE-STAR AWARD, *READERS' FAVORITE*

"A captivating coming of age story...that packs more than a punch. A must-read for any fantasy fiction enthusiast."

— FINALIST AWARD, *READERS' CHOICE*

"The writing is superb..."

— AWARD-WINNING AUTHOR JULIET ROSE

"A rollercoaster of a story...this reminded me of Guy Gavriel Kay's *The Sarantine Mosaic.*"

— ANNIINA MOILANEN

"I am so grateful for the experience of having felt the soles of my feet in another world. *Where the Valley Meets the Sky* is a wonderfully told story."

— ERIC DICARLO

"...a fusion between literary and commercial fiction... [Merrick] managed to capture elegance and sophistication."

— NICOLE BOCCELLI-SALTSMAN

BOOKS BY BEN MERRICK

Where the Valley Meets the Sky

Where the River Goes

WHERE THE RIVER GOES

THE KALANOSI CHRONICLES
BOOK TWO

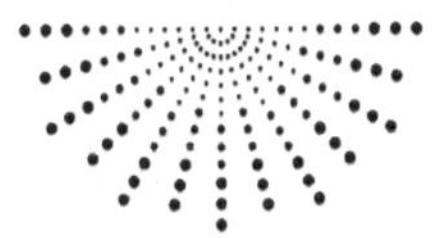

BEN MERRICK

This is a work of fiction. All of the characters, organizations, and events portrayed in this novel are products of the author's imagination and fever dreams.

Copyright © 2023 by Ben Merrick

All rights reserved.

No part of this book may be reproduced in any form or by any electronic or mechanical means, including information storage and retrieval systems, without written permission from the author, except for the use of brief quotations in a book review.

benwritesbooks.com

To the people I can always come home to.

And also dogs.

"Summer grasses;
    All that remain
    Of brave soldiers' dreams."

— MATSUO BASHŌ

1

THE PINES AT THE EDGE OF THE WORLD

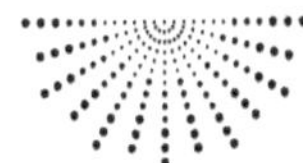

How do we escape the sky's bright hate?
Burrow! Burrow!
The river runs low; below we must go!
Swim! Swim!
A hungry lion, an angry wind—
Hide! Hide!
To father's arms and mother's flint,
Run! Run!

—CHILDREN'S SONG OF
SUMMER

The smoke spoke in two voices.

Playful knots of ether spun to the southwest, swept them-selves upward in patternless twists before vanishing politely in the day's twilight. There was a warmth to their dancing friction that would escape those who did not know to seek it.

At the ankles of the specter were fettered pinions of black, hung inertly in forbiddance, hung laden with something to come. The shapes were difficult to see in the growing shadows of sunset. Cold. Ice on raw skin.

"Promising signs at the shoulders," I muttered to myself. I raised my voice to my waiting companions. "We'll find him to the southwest. I do not think his recapture will be difficult; he moves at a drifting pace. Overconfident, perhaps...no, not overconfident," I corrected, looking again to the knots in the smoke. "I believe he is lost."

"Idiot Rucosti," spoke Callisgrim, her insult the pop of a pine log in fire. A quarrel of short black hair sat atop her reddened face, framing charcoal eyes that sought always for a bellows.

The other of my companions, a man named Barim, met my eyes patiently and studied them before speaking. He was built like the knolls of the area, with wide, sloping shoulders and a thick neck. His hair was long and graying at the temples. "Good," was all he said.

"Let's cover some distance before the sun sets complete-ly," I told them. I felt the wave of torpor that is to be expected after reading the smoke. "We'll likely spot his fire from higher ground."

"What makes you certain he'll start a fire? Just because he's Rucosti doesn't mean he'll be so stupid as that." Barim was fair in his rebuttal.

"They're *all* stupid," interjected Callisgrim. "He didn't even steal a horse."

"They wouldn't have gone with him," rumbled Barim.

"Stupid? Perhaps," I said. "He's alone. He's frightened. But more than anything, he's hungry. And since he took a freshly-killed hare instead of the salted venison..."

Barim understood and nodded. "You're an expert tracker, no? Where do you think a man like Haston Corde would feel safe enough to stop for the night?"

"Traveling southwest?" I thought aloud, turning in that direction. I sensed, as I had several times with the man, that he was testing my competence. As I stood, the dog came to attention. He'd been a fierce traveling companion since that night with Malik a year ago, after I'd buried a scouting party under the hooves of a hundred bison. "He's not quite as stupid as we'd like to believe," I continued, "but he's inexperienced. I bet he'll hunker down in that sizable copse we saw a few miles back. He'll think it'll keep his fire hidden. Let's curve to the north a bit, let him get comfortable, and climb the hills to the east of his position. We'll look for a fire, and if we see one, we'll split up and comb the trees from west to east, since he'll expect the opposite."

Barim and Callisgrim accepted the plan. We mounted our three horses and rode west.

I couldn't shake the way Barim had looked at me after I read the smoke. His was a powerful insight, and I feared I could not lie to him.

Though I didn't exactly lie. I just didn't tell them the entire truth. I shook my head, remembering the conversational acrobatics Avid used to employ when he wanted to justify something to himself.

The voices of the smoke were thoroughly separated. The shoulders certainly spoke auspiciously, and if there were any coming misfortunes in my approach to Haston Corde, the *shoulders* would have said so. But the ankles of the smoke, rolling just at the precipice of the fire, carried an omen of ill fate. While this was disparate from Haston Corde — extraneous regarding his recapture — only a fool would follow a path so cursed.

But if it took becoming a complete fool to earn passage into the Turin homelands, then a complete fool I would become.

They rode with me in the faith that all would be well.

~

IT WAS A SHORT CLIMB TO THE SHELF UPON WHICH WE HID. THE hill continued to the east of our position, ensuring a shadowed cavity to shield us from the last rays of the sun. The pines stood resolutely underneath our camp, and though we couldn't see through them completely, a campfire would be visible enough from the short lip that formed, like a bowl's edge, between us and the trees.

"Your chieftain has successfully established herself in her region, I think," Barim mentioned, looking with me out at the trees. His voice held the subtle strength of a man who thinks more than he speaks.

"Malik has taken cleanly to command," I said. "Once we saw the Rucosti settlements in the Marchland pushing so aggressively into the plains, understanding the Turin perspective on the conflict wasn't difficult."

"It isn't all Turin who see Rucosti expansion as a danger," he corrected. He peered from under his graying hair, breathing slowly. "But Rangrim can tell you more of that when we rendezvous."

I scoffed at our situation. "Though I can't imagine she'll be happy if we don't have Corde in tow."

"No," he said gravely, his voice lowering. "She'd be unhappy, and though I'd follow her to the end of the world, I'd sooner jump off its edge than make her...*unhappy*."

Noted.

Barim turned, regarded me for a moment, and directed his attention outward again. "Malik is rather young to be chieftain," he said.

"Perhaps. But she's no fool; she knew to ask for your help

in repelling the militia. In a situation like this, Kalanosi need to trust each other, to act as one and yield to wisdom and experience. Acting as a series of single clans will shrink each of us in the face of Rucost. We need to work together."

He nodded, grunting. "But here we are," he said, gesturing from himself to the on-watch Callisgrim a dozen feet away, "two Turin. We return to Rangrim, a Turin woman, who has agreed to take you now to her home — the home of the Turin. Who's to say you're helping, and not just along for the ride? Seems to me that Turin are doing the work." He waited a beat. "You speak of trust. Callisgrim and I just spent three weeks with your people, planning, leading them in our fights, sharing meals, and not a single straight answer did I find to a fairly simple question."

My stomach lifted; I swallowed hard.

"Who are you?" he finally asked.

I held his gaze for a long while, failing to feign a confused expression. "We're a coll—"

"—A collective of disparate clans, yes, so I've been told so often these past few weeks. See, when you were off in Periloe hunting down your prize for Rangrim," he said, motioning to the pines, "I asked some of your people who you were. *You.*"

"And what did they tell you?"

"A few changed the subject, which caught my attention. Some merely told me you were a hunter and an advisor. None could tell me which clan you were from. And just this evening you looked into smoke and discerned exactly where this man was. How he was *acting.* And you didn't hide your feelings well enough. I can see your nervousness, Rennik, and it didn't start in this conversation. You didn't read smoke when we were planning an attack on Rucosti farmland. You didn't do it when we needed to find food for Malik's growing clan. For whatever reason, Haston Corde's escape made you nervous, and though you wanted to appear casual in your smoke magic, you lit that fire in desperation."

I knew now that my body betrayed me. My jaw was tense, my breath came quickly, and I could not look him in the eye. I became acutely aware of the descent on the opposite side of the lip. Surely I was faster than Barim, but Callisgrim was young, lithe, and quick to fury.

"Only one reason to hide something like that. You value the journey to our home more than anything else. I didn't think more than twice about why you wanted so badly to earn entry into Ba Turin, but now that you've got these secrets...I'm not sure I trust a man I suddenly don't know—"

"Something's down there," Callisgrim whispered. She was looking down the hill and into the trees. Soft yellow firelight teased at the lowest boughs of the copse. It seemed Haston Corde was at its center, right where I knew he would be. "Now can we get to work, or are you two hens still clucking?"

Ashamed I'd let my focus drift from our goal, I picked up my bow and dropped the conversation. How could I explain to Barim what sounded irrational to myself? "My mentor told me of a woman among your people," I imagined saying, "who *might* know some things about me and the other-worldly creature that grips me."

We'd have time to settle the story after we'd taken Haston Corde.

We descended the hill as shadows.

Callisgrim and I crept around the northern edge of the pines; Barim took a solitary path along the south. I half-expected to receive an interrogation from Callisgrim as we walked and watched, but she was set firmly into focus. Her hunter's eyes were cast in the silver light of the moon and pointed sharply into the trees.

"Cut in here," I whispered after a time. "I'll do the same a bit further west." She nodded before melting into the dark. Fifty strides further, I found my entry point.

There are few floors more accepting of silent steps than a bed of pine needles. The trees near the center had ample protection from the wind, so no dead limbs lay waiting to snap underfoot. As the canopy was greedy for sunlight, few branches reached down to my height; I strode amid the beams of a proper pine ceiling.

I was a minute in when something moved to my right. It was only for a moment, but I trusted my eyes against the tricks of darkness. I didn't expect Barim to have entered so close to me, though any plan that put allies out of earshot was prone to errors.

Perhaps Corde had anticipated our hunt. I reached instinctively for an arrow but thought better of it; my fingers found the handle of my axe.

There was something like a coughing noise near the center of the copse. I continued forward. Firelight bounced from bole to bough as I drew closer, envisioning how to best tackle and tie the man.

Another cough, raspy and further to my right than I expected. Corde may have taken a position to the south to ambush—

But there he was. Haston Corde was standing by his fire, alert and drawn, sword pointed to the source of the noise. The knife he'd used to roast a piece of hare had fallen too close to the fire; a threadbare traveling blanket was spread on the ground behind him.

His face hadn't seen enough sun to crack in his forty-some years. He was still wearing the fine city clothes I'd found him in, though they were road-worn now. The point of his sword betrayed his trembling hands, exaggerating each movement in pitiful parody. Haston Corde donned the mask of a brave man only to find that it didn't quite fit.

His mouth worked in a stutter before speaking. "Get yourself gone," he commanded to the sounds in the dark. A moment passed, and he tried in his coltish Kalanosi: "Leave. Go far."

My instincts told me to wait. In no time at all, the camp was empty save for a few pine needles falling to the ground after Corde took to his heels and ran.

Another cough — raking, wet.

I took a silent step and leaned around the trunk of the nearest tree, searching for the source of the noise at the edge of the firelight. There was only darkness. I continued forward.

I'd taken four long strides before I saw him.

My eyes adjusted to the sight of Barim, his back upon the needles, hands clutching his throat. What little moonlight shone through the canopy made silver pools of the blood pouring from his neck.

I turned and ran, expecting at any moment to swing my axe in stride.

Sree, this far south? Rucosti bandits?

But Marchlanders were too leashed to their farms to come this distance, and no one knew to come for Corde.

There was a small opening in the wall of needled branches that edged the copse; I aimed to reach it quickly and quietly, but I soon stopped dead in my tracks.

The silhouette of a mountain lion moved noiselessly into the trees.

The fire.

The head of the beast snapped toward me as I dug my heels into the ground. I pounded back but knew I couldn't outrun the creature. I had no tall grass, no ripgut to use.

The axe swung through the darkness as I twisted my body. Cold air grazed at my knuckles.

My blade met the beast with the crunching of bone and a sibilant slide through its pelt. The mountain lion had already leapt and came crashing into my body, claws scraping against my neck. We rolled against the bed of needles and clambered for footing.

I turned to where I thought the cat was and cut senselessly through the air, but I soon heard its wounded growl, stone sliding on stone from its throat, and I took toward the still-burning fire.

Corde's camp came close; I barreled in only to meet a rushing figure from the other side.

Callisgrim had been torn across her shoulder. I felt her blood smear across my chest as we collided. We fell to the ground together, scrambling to stand.

"*Nagithanka!*" she said breathlessly, gesturing behind her with a knife.

"There's another behind me," I told her.

And then I froze. The recognition had not come to me for all my panic. I scanned the firelit trees. Muscles clutched at my heart, tightening, wrenching the breath from my lungs.

"*No,*" I managed. My ears filled with the sound of rushing water. I knew before I looked, knew as the horror gripped and turned my head what was beginning, what had already begun.

And there it stood, the empty shape of a man, waiting in the half-light before us, as silent as the night that took Macha.

The Shiver had found me again.

Callisgrim saw my reaction and followed my eyes; she was searching the trees to its left, to its right, almost as if...

As if she couldn't see it.

The mountain lion launched from the darkness. Callisgrim was thrown into the trees behind me. Her arms shot up to guard her face but were cut to pulp in moments.

Something else was now running from behind her, charging my position with the sounds of a lethal determination.

The Shiver was walking steadily toward me, its void figure eclipsing the pines behind it.

The fire grew tall and red.

Callisgrim fell silent.

I couldn't breathe.

The furious pounding behind me came closer, and I remembered being trapped between bison and ripgut, surrounded by death's wish to crush and cut.

In my choking state I fell to the ground. I looked up powerlessly to the coming figure, tried to heft an axe in a hand turned black.

The running creature reached the camp, and it was the dog that leapt from behind me to throw itself at the Shiver. The body of the lightless figure changed — it seemed to expand, to widen, to tense above the dog as though to swallow all the night into its form. A bellowing screech erupted from the pines.

I clawed at my breathless and blood-slicked throat as the black of unconsciousness descended upon me.

2

THE GRASSES BETWEEN

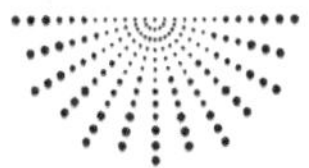

...and though one may steal a sausage, burgle a bungalow, purloin a party or abduct an aunt, the greatest theft of all is treason. Treason is the only crime that steals a people's right to feel pride in their fellow countrymen, and a nation without pride is no less empty than a perfectly pilfered purse.

— EXCERPT FROM REMI GRENFALLOW'S *PHILOSOPHY OF CRIME*

Haston Corde was nervous.

The patina of this feeling was his being bound immobile and prostrate on the back of a blanketed horse, surrounded by miles of hills he didn't know, stones stuck unsympathetically into the earth, hidden animals that were hungry. It was a wilderness that seemed to him the greatest cage of a civilized individual.

But Haston Corde was an intelligent man, and therefore

kept powerless by lack of knowledge — this was the core of his terror. His eyes leapt between gossamer guesses, left, right, and left again, attempting in vain to produce a solution to the initial question, the one he had yet to answer: *why am I here?*

He was tense as he wandered and wallowed within his uncertainty. This was *not* his furrier shop. This was *not* the quaint Marchland city of Periloe. This was, to borrow a Rucosti concept, hell for Haston Corde.

Though I'd spent a considerable amount of time on my journey with Barim and Callisgrim wondering why, indeed, Haston Corde was important, I was now concerned with something greater. After that night full of dark pines and dead companions, I woke to find myself on a bedroll in a camp of Rangrim's making. The silence confirmed my assumption that Barim and Callisgrim hadn't survived the night. Corde was tied to a tree, sour and silent. The Turin woman had said nothing as she helped me to my horse and placed the wounded dog on a drag sled. Her scarred, hatchet-like face was contorted with a thousand questions, but she did all of this without a word. A full day and night passed, and I likewise said nothing — first as a symptom of exhaustion, then as a symptom of vague apprehension. I didn't know how much of myself I could share with strangers, and I wasn't about to make the mistake of trusting someone too much. We rode for the first half of the second day in such a state before the tacit agreement of silence was broken.

The talk was small when we eventually talked at all. I would speak, and she would acknowledge me with a grunt or curt remark. We were a slow-moving beetle on the back of the world, swallowed by its blossoming maw. As I sat behind her on my bay roan, the ebb and flow of attempted conversation kept time with other such rhythms typical of a long journey.

"Sometimes I wonder how far the ripgut has traveled," I mentioned once, staring out at the river-laden plains.

"I wasn't aware it could walk. You northerners are full of fun facts," Rangrim responded.

"I'm talking about the seeds," I continued, despite her tone. "During the rainy season, the seeds at the top of the stalks fall into the water and float to wherever the currents take them. They can end up miles from their parent stalk before the water recedes and they find good, fertile soil."

"That explains the birds," she said, gesturing to the small figures streaking through the air, picking at the little islands of clustered seeds on the water's surface. "But are you ready to tell me what happened?"

"Yellow-headed blackbirds," I said, looking at the larger of the two animals and ignoring her question. "They bully the longspurs. They don't like to share." It hurt to keep my head turned; the mountain lion had cut my neck superficially, but still it burned.

She waited a moment before finally joining in. "Looks like warpaint on their heads. Hard to blend in."

"They don't really need to."

"The longspurs do, clearly." She was studying the mousey color of one such bird that alighted nearby. Her crescent-moon chin and flat, broken nose cut a clean profile against the Kalanosi wilds.

"They've both learned to pluck out the ripgut seeds during the rainy season. Everything in competition..."

We rode for a moment in silence, listening to the light, frenetic chatter of the longspurs. The blackbirds sounded a bit like the metal parts of Tenal's wagons when they squeaked, but mostly they made angry screams at the longspurs plucking away at the seeds left to fate. I could feel the quiet build between us, pregnant with the questions she wanted to push, with the answers I did not want to give.

"The good news is that most ripgut grows at low elevations," I said. "Better to lose their seeds in deep water this time of year. That means I can leave the damn things behind."

"Can't imagine one would miss it."

I flexed the scarred muscle on the back of my arm. I heard the screaming Sree riders of my memory turn to sickening silence, saw the brief, dispassionate shaking of the stalks.

"No," I told her. "I won't."

Foreigners often assume grasslands to be still, bereft of any excitement or motion. The matter, though, is simply one of perspective. We're often too big to notice it.

I could see from my mounted position that the plants were crawling with insects, moving, communicating, congregating; entire clans were living life as normal in the microcosm at our feet. I wondered what a longspur looked like from the eyes of beetle. To see such a massive creature command the skies, giving no heed to the small, must be humbling to say the least. Then, when the terrifying, beastly longspur is shoved aside by a violent blackbird, a flea beetle or cricket must think, "such gods above our heads, wrestling and warring among themselves. I should be glad to be a bug!" and go about their business unfazed and indifferent.

I looked to the sky and saw nothing to note. I suppose this is when our legends would tell me to look for evidence. Perhaps the pooling water filled the great footsteps of the Dalkhur. Perhaps the birds eating seeds are distant great-grandchildren of the Wahkeen. My attention fell back to the ground, where a crew of ants were hauling loads much bigger than themselves.

I was jealous of the small things: they could *choose* indifference. A younger Rennik thought himself to be in a similar position, looking at the yellow-headed blackbirds who called themselves Sree, killing and damning at a safe distance.

What a fool he must have been.

She said we would reach the foot of the mountain by nightfall.

WHEN FIRST I SAW THE SHAPE OF BA TURIN IN THE DISTANCE, its mountains did not render in me the indomitable notions of wonder that seem to obsess poets and storytellers — not at first, anyway. When I saw the sun-tanned slopes and snowy peaks, I thought of Gatsi.

A year had passed since I'd seen him — or rather, since he abandoned the Achare. It'd taken time for me to change that word; at first, he'd *disappeared*; then, he'd *left*; now, I'd sunken reluctantly into what was surely the truth: he'd abandoned us with the same detachment he'd recommended for me before I left with the scouting party. It was clear he knew the pale man was coming for him, clear he'd sought to save his own skin first, but there was still so much I needed answered. Where did he go? Would he ever find us again? And to put the ache in my chest into words: did he know he'd made me a target of the pale man by showing me the power of the Delkhi? Perhaps he somehow knew that I would come out alive, but I doubted it.

It isn't easy to look back at childhood this way, to see crude selfishness in one of the few caring men there were. Chaska said Gatsi wasn't Achare. He left me to die. I worried that the next time I saw him — if ever — the man wouldn't match the memory.

The mountains rose like earthen hackles over the horizon. It was evening as we reached the foothills; Rangrim halted our horses, retrieved Haston Corde, and guided the Rucosti prisoner to the trunk of a cottonwood where he remained bound and out of earshot.

"I have something to show you," she said upon returning to me. I followed her cautiously around a collection of boulders and toward the edge of a wide trail that snaked into the sky.

Before me were three women of stone.

The first took her hue from the mountains. They were great, god-like mountains, sanguine with the presence of iron. Her height, well over fifteen feet, would have dwarfed me were she not flanked by peaks that pierced the sky. Her expression was stern: furrowed brows gathered above severe cheekbones and a farsighted stare. She was vigilant. She was commanding. She was the first of the Turin to call the mountains their home.

The second had no head. Her likeness was defaced, quite literally, after she led the losing side of a small civil war. Water had thus collected in the crags of her jagged neck and dwelt deep in her chest. One exceptionally cold winter was all it took to turn her heart to ice, to expand within the white marble from which she was hewn, to split her bosom like the schism of her people. Her name was Grim, and her history was likewise.

The third woman was grown of flesh and bone, though her voice suggested a stony core. Rangrim stood before me with her slate-like gaze poring over the pumice of my quietude. Around us were the scents of our journey — grass, wildflowers, and earth smells, though I wondered if all Turin smelled of raw iron like her. She bore with her a patient disposition as she studied every inch of me. In the rainy season, there is always a storm coming, either on the horizon or more distant in the plains, and these storms were hers as the patience was hers. Something in her words and movements spoke of a lightning that reveled in the silence just before it struck.

"These women," she gestured to the statues, "have stood in this spot for generations. Senna, daughter of the Mountain Mother, founded both the vale of the Hanallta and the lineage of chieftains that lead our people. The role has passed from mother to daughter since the dawn of our clan, not once interrupted..."

Rangrim paused, looking reverently into the eyes of Senna. "The Turin were as one stone for much of our history until a woman challenged the chieftain and led a failed usurpation. Her true name was stripped from her, and she was renamed Grim. Her new name was meant to be a badge of disgrace, but she wore it proudly. She was exiled into the Shadowlands and never heard from again."

The dog pressed against my leg. A streak of hair was missing from his back, the exposed skin blackened with a strange wound from his battle with the Shiver. I scratched at his cheek, happy as always to have feeling in my fingers.

"Your name," I said to her, noticing a rise in her chest. "And that of your friend. I assume some sort of connection to the usurper?"

Rangrim bristled at the mention of her dead companion. "Any woman deemed to have traitorous intent against the chieftain is likewise stripped of name and exiled."

"But not the men?"

"You'll find that to be more an insult than a privilege. This is a title given to those who become a threat." She sat against a boulder, and I mimicked the gesture a few feet away as she continued. "I managed to escape the Hanallta and establish a home elsewhere in Ba Turin. Over the next few years, many in the vale were accused of being in league with me. I'd become the excuse and scapegoat of their politics. Some were fortunate enough to leave before being forced into the Shadowlands, and inevitably, they found their way to me. Callisgrim was one of them. She'd actually approached chieftain Moddimok with an axe in hand and said aloud what we'd all been thinking. She shouted to everyone in Mother's Hall that Moddimok had secretly allied herself with Rucost to ensure her own survival at the expense of her clan, that she'd given them permission to use Kalanosi lands, that she'd branded any potential opposition a traitor and sent them away. She called her a coward...and she barely made it out of Ba Turin alive."

"Callisgrim was undoubtedly fierce—"

"And yet," she interrupted, silencing me with her tone and standing, "I found you unconscious, fingers black as night and cold as a corpse, with both of my best fighters slain not twenty steps away."

I stood and raised my hands defensively. Rangrim's eyes scraped quickly over the surface of a whetstone, sharpened by the time they'd found their mark. She pierced me with a look and pinned me to the mountain at my back.

"Enough of your avoidance. It wasn't you who killed them, and it sure as hell wasn't that whimpering pantomime of a furrier. You will tell me what happened, and you will tell me now. *Speak.*"

Caught between a rock and the daggers in her eyes, I began to tell her the truth.

3

THE PROFITS OF A KILLER

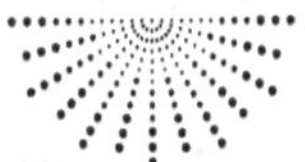

The anxieties of our past must be wrestled and
tamed. What is done is immutable; how we
understand it is not.

— GATSI

There was a one-eyed man who haunted my dreams.

Against his gut was pinned the mangled head of a snake. His silks were bloodied, his blades unbrandished. His right eye, rolling with occasional curiosity, sought mine. His left was obliterated when my arrow broke through the back of his skull.

Yet he watched me with a sickening calm, kneeling in the unburnt grass, waiting only for the world of my guilt to grow heavier upon my shoulders. I could not picture the softness of my old home without the stain of him. The plateau imprinted in my memory was the frame for his always-bleeding body. I wondered if this is what it took to kill, if the sacrifice of joy was the coin with which to buy a man's erasure.

Malik and I had grown closer over the past year. We couldn't help but notice our recreation of Achare leadership: she was the chieftain, and I was the knowledgeable user of secret magics who advised her. But to suggest the guidance didn't go both ways would be a lie. We'd often find ourselves reliving our night under the stars. I would tell her of this guilt, of the blight of Zamri Malnostos, and she would try her best to reorient me.

"This nightmare isn't showing you the whole picture," she told me. "That man was holding Avid an inch away from certain death. You saved your brother's life."

"Then why don't I feel that way? Why can't my memory be a poultice rather than a poison?" I would have been tearing a piece of grass, breaking a stick, something to keep the hands busy. "Sometimes I wonder which is truer: the guilt we're given, or the excuses we make in reply."

"You still haven't changed," she'd responded. "A year ago, you didn't think you'd take action to defend yourself against an enemy, and now you won't defend yourself against your own head. But you did. And you will."

As wrong as it feels to admit, guilt wasn't the only result of that day. Even beyond my brother's life, there was a priceless profit to killing that man.

After Avid had recovered from his fever, he began to see things he wasn't supposed to. As the pale man said in his conversation with the Yohri chieftain, there were "worlds of knowledge" to reap; one simply needed the right sort of sickle. For people like him, the tools by which to harvest this wheat were the people in his path. Avid and I, however, were given a second option: if we were within the reach of the Delkhi, we could see distant things at the cost of reliving our near deaths. For me, a numbing and airless plunge into a river; for Avid, a torrid disuse of the leg and a brief delusion of the mind. From all that I'd divined, the Delkhi drew its power from the space between life and death, and so that space became its proof of presence.

We left the Delkhi's reach to find the surviving Achare, and I'd been more than happy to rid myself of its symptoms. As I tried to explain to my brother, every time I'd experienced the frostbite and drowning, it was as if another bucket of water had been poured over the clay of my mind, taking a little something with it each time. How long until I was washed away completely?

Avid, however, was determined. And so I needed to find this Turin woman Gatsi spoke of. I needed to find a way to protect Avid from all of this.

"How do you read the smoke?" he'd begged. "You can't be the only one to do it. The Delkhi saved me, too — wouldn't it be wise to have *two* of us who can read omens once we leave its reach?"

"I don't know how it works, exactly," I'd lied.

The Delkhi had shown me the words to use.

Vonokto Altro Kolroso...

But the last word couldn't be prescribed. One must earn it for themselves. The last word was a knife in my chest and a corpse in my dreams.

Malnostos.

We were making our way up the mountain trail, side-by-side save for Haston Corde meandering some twenty feet behind. His hands were tied, but there was no need to bind him to us. Unless he somehow sprouted wings, at this point on the trail he had no choice but to follow her up.

"I want to know," said Rangrim from her horse. "Tell me how to read the smoke."

I understood where she and Avid were coming from. From the outside, it certainly seemed a desirable skill to have.

"You can't," I told her. "It isn't just a recipe to follow. From what I've gathered, magics like this come from a near-death experience in childhood."

Rangrim raised her head slowly in realization. "So the Sree. The Wahto. When people say they send their children out to die...they're trying to make people like *you*."

"I don't know," I told her. "Maybe they've got a whole collection of people who can read smoke, but for some reason, that doesn't seem right."

"Explain."

"Because it just doesn't feel like it's that easy. Children die in Kalanos all the time. I don't know why I was saved, but it doesn't feel like there are many others...it's just a sort of intuition, I guess."

She nodded, taking the idea of intuition more seriously than I expected. In fact, she seemed to accept my entire story — the river, the vision, the smoke — surprisingly in stride. I did not tell her explicitly that I was Achare, nor did I mention Avid, Gatsi, or the Delkhi, but at a certain point in my explanation she seemed to be satisfied. She knew only that I should have died, that I had since learned to do incredible things, and that a strange man with mountain lions killed her companions.

"This person," she began, "that accompanied the nagithanka...tell me about him."

"I think it may not be 'man' at all," I said at the risk of

discrediting myself. But she'd believed me about the smoke, so she may take this to be truth as well. "It is a creature of pure night. A man of shadow. It is a malicious and terrible thing."

She looked to me discerningly. I held her gaze and knew my eyes to be sad, perhaps fearful. She returned her focus to the trail ahead.

"But if a clan sent out dozens of children each year..." she wondered. "Surely they'll find some of what they seek."

"Perhaps," I said.

"If I can't read smoke, tell me what supplies you need. You can portend my return to Ba Turin and warn me of what to expect." She always spoke in statement and command, never in a question.

"I've developed a fairly consistent dry mixture to use. If you want me to help you, we'll need to stop every now and then for pine trees. We'll peel away the bark and strip a section of the soft white material underneath — not the sapwood, but the inner bark just before it."

She nodded, listening intently. "Then you burn it."

"We *chew* it," I corrected. "Not to eat, just to soften. Once it becomes a paste, we'll add by hand some shredded bits of sweetgrass, and the rest depends on what you'd like to see. We could add sage, hair...bones, if it's needed."

"This is a fairly simple mixture," she scrutinized. "Too simple for something so incredible, it seems."

"Well, then there's the incantation," I explained. "And of course, the nearly dying as a child..."

She waited a beat, watching the path ahead. "Not so simple, I suppose."

"Not so simple," I echoed. "But you should know that it's never said much for the people around me. Each omen has touched on my outlook only; something unfortunate could happen to just you, and we'd be none the wiser from the smoke. And it only works once in a while."

I could see the question in her face.

"Every few days, give or take," I finished.

Rangrim traced the hard lines of the mountains, assessing the changes in what was once familiar, in what was once her home. I found myself sympathizing; how much of my empty home would I recognize after I'd been gone for years like her?

"Then we'll start gathering the materials. A secondhand portent is better than none," she determined. "You'll find time to make this tonight. We're making camp a few hours early; I've got a mixture of my own to make."

"Really? What kind?"

"It's known as Senna's Ward. Those who aren't Turin don't always fare well higher up in the mountains. My people are blessed by the Mountain Mother. *You'll* get dizzy, out of breath, complain a lot."

I found myself fascinated. "How would you counteract that? It sounds so...powerful."

"Senna's Ward is kept secret from outsiders," she carped back. "Only those we wish to enter Ba Turin receive its gifts."

Suddenly, like Haston Corde, I felt the bars of a cage in an open landscape. The meaning of this mixture was immediately apparent; if I wanted to follow through with my request to enter Ba Turin and find the woman Gatsi spoke of, I would need Senna's Ward. In other words, it was in my interest to keep Rangrim alive, close, and unangered, and I had no doubt she considered this as well. I glanced back to Haston Corde, sitting quiet and dejected on his horse, and felt thankful that I at least knew the purpose of my journey.

Haston Corde was leashed by his lungs to the woman who wouldn't tell him why.

~

RANGRIM TOLD ME THAT THE STORMS OF THE RAINY SEASON would affect us less the further along the trail we'd traveled; but when a resonant rumble of thunder echoed from the walls of neighboring mountains, both she and the dog tensed with apprehension. Unsure of the situation, I adjusted my position on the horse, ready to urge it forward if need be.

The sound drew her attention to the south.

There, on a distant slope, a scud of swarthy dust was thrown skyward. A swarm of man-sized stones poured themselves down, fell upon even greater boulders, shifting entire portions of the mountainside. The very skin of the earth was molting before us.

The three of us sat in the sort of awe that one feels in moments like these, moments in which the cold-blooded earth reminds you of its ability to destroy the soft flesh of the living.

"The ice near the peaks is melting," Rangrim finally said. "Rocks get loose this time of year."

"Outstanding," I said.

Then, another sound from behind us.

"Have you heard of the great explorer, Martinor the Untethered?" asked Haston Corde. It was the first thing he'd said in more than a day.

"No," I told him after a moment. Rangrim simply elected to ignore him, pushing her horse forward to prompt the group's movement.

"No, I suppose not," he said, raising his chin to the peaks above. "He was an immensely talented writer. A Rucosti who would climb the highest heights and walk the greatest distances, all to put the majesty of the unknown into words for his city-bound readers—"

"Unknown to *Rucosti*," interjected Rangrim.

"Yes, exactly. But he was a marvelous expositor of—"

"Have you read Brallic Severin?" I asked.

He looked at me under a dubious knit of the eyebrows. "...Yes. I have. Have *you*?"

"I have." It was a short response, and I could tell it vexed him, but I hid my smile and he persevered.

"*Moving forward.* He would write so many beautiful passages, but the wilds finally decided they'd had enough of him, and he died in a mountain pass, much like those below. A falling rock had crushed his knees, you see."

I grimaced in response.

"Well, it was the inability to hunt that killed him. I believe the passage went as follows." Haston Corde cleared his throat and launched forth. "It is a cruel thing, this starvation. I wither slowly, weakened too much to act upon the animals who wander within eyesight. I have crawled a small distance from my shelter each day to find and eat what I believe are edible roots or other plant material. I have eaten all that grows around me, and now too shall I eat what grows within me; my stomach reaches out with shortened arms; I will eat my heart; I will eat my head; I will eat the muscles in my hands and the innards in my chest; I will curl into myself and return to the womb, acting in the last as I acted in the first; I will be desperate, unthinking; I will leech from the body that holds me."

I thought back and remembered the days in my childhood when we did not have enough to eat. Though I'd never felt the deeper sorts of starvation that took this explorer's life, I knew, in a way, what it was to depend on what I contained rather than that which surrounded me.

"Appropriately gruesome," I said and nodded, speaking in Kalanosi. But Corde continued in Rucosti.

"His mistake was to fear death. He could have spent his daylight trying to survive. He would not have budgeted such a lengthy time to wax poetic if he had not thought he was about to die. That was not just his typical work; that was a man who'd rather write his own epitaph."

I looked disbelievingly at the man. "You're going to tell me you don't fear death?"

"Of course not. While I submit to the importance of planning ahead and working for one's future, concern with one's death only works to worry the thinker. One should elevate oneself and transcend such base impulses as a fear of death."

A moment passed, and he registered my unimpressed reaction.

"It is simply a fact," he continued, imprisoned on his horse. "It is inevitable that one must die. Why should one fear the inevitable? Accept death, accept the guidance of Ityx, accept that pain will likely be the rough-handed and impolite usher into the afterlife. Knowledge and acceptance are functions of the highest order, Rennik. They transcend the fear of death."

"You fear death." I said it with an even conviction that seemed to frustrate him. My eyes sat comfortably on the horizon ahead, but in my peripherals he stared at me incredulously.

"I do *not*, sir!"

"And the Rask don't fear bears."

"What?"

"It's easy to be brave when something seems distant. You *do* fear death," I calmly asserted. "You've just forgotten the feeling." I continued speaking over his scoffs and rejections. Some of the Rucosti words he'd used were new to me, so my pronunciations were measured. "Death is…inevitable, as you say. But so is fear. People die each day believing in something. Fear is a flinch before the pain. Your Ityx cannot stop it."

"With faith I can transcend the fear of death."

"No. Just because you repeat a mantra doesn't mean it's true. You're lying to yourself because it is more comfortable. Feather beds are soft, but they do not touch the ground."

"This conversation is pointless," interrupted Rangrim in Kalanosi. "You want something grounded? Here's a fact for you: When I put a knife to his throat two nights ago, he begged for his life. When I took the knife back, he vomited. He wept and trembled for an hour."

Corde seemed in his speaking to have swelled and risen above his captive situation. He'd grown confident, but Rangrim glanced coolly in his direction and pierced his sail with a few pointed words.

"You fear death, Haston Corde. And so you fear me."

WE'D STOPPED FOR THE NIGHT AT THE THRESHOLD OF A massive stone overhang. There was a long, time-worn cloth flagging from a cairn to mark a common waypoint, and with rain clouds coming and dry mixtures to make, the natural roof was an obvious choice for shelter. Haston Corde and I laid our bedrolls on the hard floor while Rangrim moved to a more secluded section of the overhang. Despite my prodding, she could not be moved to share any details of Senna's Ward with me, though I'd recognized the smell of garlic from my time with Gatsi. The old man would use it for people plagued with headaches and trouble breathing. The other ingredients of Senna's Ward, however, remained a mystery.

Corde and I were eating from a roasted grouse I'd killed just prior to arriving. He was leering at her. She was a good fifty feet away with her back turned toward us, but still he stared as if the details were clear. I wondered at first what he thought he'd find, but in studying him, I could see the calculation, the eyes pawing at the space of something forgotten. I recognized the look because I too was struggling to remember. The more time I spent with Rangrim, the more I felt there was something familiar, felt that her firelit face at the edge of a conversation had evoked some hazy token in my memory. I decided that I simply missed Malik, her stars, her words, and her face in warm light.

"Tell me," said Corde in a conspiratorial hush, "what exactly is it that brings you to these mountains?"

"I've been sent to find someone. I didn't know the way, so when my clan met Rangrim and her fighters, we struck a deal. Bring you to her alive, and she'd take me there."

"Did she tell you what I'd done to deserve my kidnapping?"

"No."

Something seemed to settle in his face, something he'd concluded with my answer.

"But did you tell her who it is *you* seek?" he asked.

"No," I answered, working through the watery Rucosti language. "And she did not ask." The dog's quivering snout floated slowly to the grouse, and I stripped off a generous piece for him.

"Surely that strikes you as odd," he insisted, lowering his head and voice. "I do not think she is a woman of her word, and so I do not find it likely that she brings you with her to fulfill a promise. This is her *home* we're riding into. What if your intentions were violent? What if you sought to help her enemies there? Shouldn't these be concerns of hers?"

I finished eating and moved to pack the paste of bark and sweetgrass into a pouch at my belt. It would burn well once it dried. I took the moment to consider what he said.

"I have been kidnapped from my home," he continued, "tied to a horse, hunted down in the wilds, bound to a tree and forced up a mountain for a purpose I cannot even begin to surmise. But I do not think, Rennik, that I am the only one in danger here. If an innocent furrier can be swept into the incalculable whims of a rebel leader, surely you can, too. You must ask yourself: what purpose of hers do you serve? What is her plan?"

"You're overlooking the simplest answer," I told him.

"And what answer is that?"

"That Rangrim keeps her word, and that you either aren't admitting to or aren't aware of your significance to her. Prisoners aren't entitled to information, Haston Corde."

"No, Rennik," he said with a gleam in his eye. "They're not."

I DREAMT OF A RATTLESNAKE.

It was knotted upon itself.

It did not struggle, nor did it panic, but it waited patiently before sliding its head back and its midsection over, until finally it was free of that which bound it. Its sharp pupils passed over my face and landed on my hip, and it began to move toward me.

Its tongue tasted at the knife on my belt.

Beyond the overhang were silent flashes of lightning, but after each flash was a smattering of luminescent blue stars trailing thinly across the night sky. There was a rumble — not one of thunder, but of a bestial throat against my ear.

It was the dog's growl that plucked me from sleep and back into reality, though so much of what I saw remained the same. Rain poured down at the edges of the overhang; the approaching storm loosed its ire upon the earth.

And it was in a flash of lightning that I saw a man prowling under the stone ceiling.

The bedroll of the Rucosti and the sheath of my knife were both empty; the ropes that had held his hands lay in tatters on the ground. As quietly as I could, I reached for the axe that waited diligently by my hand each night.

It was gone.

And the shadow of Haston Corde stooped to Rangrim's bedroll with my fang-like knife at the end of his coiled arm.

I spun and found my footing quickly, lunging through the air. My shoulder met his chest and we were tumbling over wet earth and jagged stone, thrown into the storm.

As he wiped the rain from his eyes I struck with my fist and felt a dull crunching from his nose. His shout was drowned in thunder, and he fell to the ground. Blind to his new position, I took one moment to find a solid stance.

The rock-slide sounds of the storm echoed in the throat of the mountains. I kept my breath steady against the percussive rain.

Haston Corde hurled himself against me from the cover of darkness and landed on my chest as my back hit the dirt path below. I managed to force my hands against his shoulders and pushed, but the man was more competent than I thought. He struck the inside of my elbow and drove his knee into my chest, throwing a quick punch into my jaw.

The massive figure of the dog met Corde's body with force enough to disrupt his balance, and I shoved him to my right.

I ran to the overhang and fell into my bedroll, searching

for the bow and quiver I kept near me while I slept. They were not there, but instead had been moved several paces away and tucked behind a boulder, surely as a stealthy precaution on Corde's part. Rangrim was nowhere to be seen.

I nocked an arrow and stepped back toward the fight.

The dog had the man's right hand in his teeth, and Corde was leaning toward a dead and barren trunk, pummeling the animal with his left to little effect.

I drew a bead on a moving target that was yet to come.

"Release!" I yelled.

The dog obeyed; Haston Corde's hand flew upward from its jaw.

My arrow met the hand mid-swing and pinned it to the tree.

The man was bleeding, screaming not just in pain but in outrage.

"You dolt!" he yelled, shouting then in the long, inarticulate vowels of fury. He tugged at his hand, and the pain magnified his howling. *"Can't you see what you've done?"*

Rangrim came striding by with my axe in her hand, cold purpose upon her face. She said something impossible to make out above the thrashing storm. Even through the rain, I could see the fear in him, the wide white terror in his eyes, but for all his pulling he could not wrench himself from the tree, could not bear the jagged gash my arrow made between his bones.

Then, like lightning to the tree, Rangrim severed the hand from Haston Corde's body.

4

REMORSE

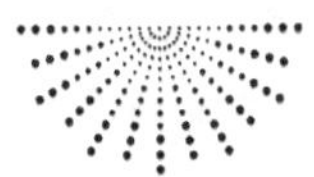

It doesn't matter that they don't help you. It
matters that you help them.

— RAISHA

My mother had been loath to let me leave.

After the burning of the Achare, when she thought she'd lost her children, she was reluctant even to let us out of her sight for weeks — and understandably so. But I'd learned much about myself in the previous month, and to know myself is to know my mother.

She needed to keep her hands busy.

In a matter of weeks we'd gathered wandering Kalanosi, some in natural nomadic paths, some cast from recently ruined clans. With conflicts along the border of Rucost increasing, we were forced to organize, to defend, and eventually to attack.

My mother had made a thorough study of the leather armors taken from Sree, Wahto, and the Marchlanders. She began making light protective garments for our newfound clan, improving the design with each repetition. She designed the circular chest guard that pressed against my heart.

Avid had done wonders for the construction of small things, and I'd provided insight and food. Our family was suddenly respected, or, dare I say...*loved.*

Nineteen years is all it took. Nineteen years for me to find a group of people who expressed appreciation for the others around them. The feeling was alien, like embracing a stranger, but I found myself much more willing to risk my life for this new clan, for what I eventually realized was a true found family.

It made my parting from the clan easier. My mother was hurt at the thought of my leaving, but I knew she had so many to look after and so many to look after her. Never had I felt my family to be so safe, and we were still at war with the Marchland cities.

After leaving my mother, I stopped to see Malik. I told her how difficult it had been.

"In a way, you're lucky," Malik told me.

"How's that?"

"Not everybody has someone to cry for them."

THE BLOOD OF HASTON CORDE FLOCKED DESPERATELY TO THE ceiling of the overhang.

Riders through the village. Red paint on canvas.

I'd ripped off the sleeve of the shirt under his doublet. His scream climbed higher as the motion moved his wounded arm. I did what Gatsi had once told me to do: I placed his arm between my legs, kept it as still as possible, and put pressure on the wound with the fabric. After a while,

I tied the fabric above his elbow. The rivers beneath his skin dammed; the blood became a trickle.

He became sick with the shock of it. The man leaned into me, cradling his arm and whimpering.

"I think she knows," he muttered. "I fear she might know me..."

"What do you mean?" I asked him. His eyes fluttered. Something I'd considered on the surface became deeper with realization. "Who are you, really?"

"We left her people alone..." He became limp, and I let him fall slowly to the floor as he lost consciousness. Save for the pitiful pules that slipped from his mouth, he was silent.

I was effectively trapped beneath this overhang with a man struggling to live and a woman who could dismember someone without so much as a grimace. I could not sleep. I could speak to neither the belligerent Rangrim nor the bloodless Corde.

The storm was intense, but not untraversable. I could risk the sliding mud, the strong winds, the lightning...but it would be dangerous — perhaps more dangerous than a night with Rangrim. And so I decided to wait and see.

She approached me at my fire just as the first hints of sunlight brushed over the horizon.

"Here," she said, handing me a tightly-packed mixture. It looked a bit too much like an owl pellet to qualify as anything appetizing. "Senna's Ward. Chew it before we leave for the day. This one shouldn't have any," she added, pointing at Corde.

"Because it thins the blood?" I asked.

Her eyes narrowed. "Yes."

Thinning the blood makes elevation more tolerable, then.

"I'm not sure he'll be ready to travel — and if you wanted

him to live, perhaps you should've left his hand attached to the rest of him."

"I aimed for his hand, not his head. I allowed you to help him. He tried to cut my throat. You have an odd sense of killing if you think this is my attempt."

"This isn't some wound to be stitched, Rangrim. He would've died without my help — and he still might. You overreacted."

"Well, then," she said, sitting down next to me and placing my axe conspicuously upon her crossed legs. "I'll be sure to have this conversation with a cool head. You will look into the smoke. Now."

PINE LOGS MAKE PLENTY OF SMOKE, AND QUICKLY — LUCKY FOR us, pines were the dominant denizens of the mountain.

"...*Malnostos.*"

Once the smoke had its body, I looked to its heart and pressed a silent question forward.

The specter became a featureless pillar, wanting for purpose and shape. Then, at the shoulders, expansion — walls that fluked inward at my gaze yet did not allow me to see through completely. A tentative warmth.

Defensive, but accepting of me. A cautious welcome.

It did not seem so surprising. A people's distrust of strangers is healthy. I thought it best not to think myself into conjecture and left it at that.

Then, below the answer we sought, something I'd never seen before.

The embers of the fire strung themselves along in tangled constellations and changed — not in shape or pattern, but in *color.*

The stars became a light blue as they took position and halted, floating dutifully within the currents of smoke, skies above rolling storms.

I looked for the Doe's Tail, the Delta, the Archer — and found none. These were not a night sky, or at least not one that I knew.

Something in the wrong place? Something upside-down, something...

The stars did not change, did not move or shift color. I willed for more information, but nothing came.

The specter bowed into itself and became dormant within the rise of mundane smoke.

"Tell me what you saw," Rangrim said, eyeing the situation without comprehension.

"The Hanallta will take us, albeit cautiously. But something strange happened...do blue stars or fictitious constellations mean anything to you?"

Rangrim paused and furrowed her brows. "No," she said. "No, they don't."

5

A REBEL RETURNED

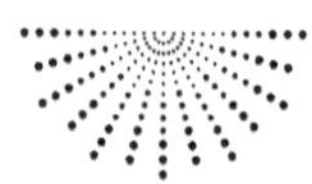

Consider the Turin in a series of nesting dolls:
Kalanos contains Ba Turin; Ba Turin bears the
Hanallta; the Hanallta harbors the People; the
People possess Iron.

— EXCERPT FROM BRALLIC
SEVERIN'S *KALANOS: A STUDY OF*
PLACE AND PEOPLE

The sun rose like a blister over the hand of Haston Corde.

It shone red in the early skies, red on the mountain, red on the raven breaking fast on his flesh.

The trail to the Hanallta was silent. The dog followed my horse closely, eyeing Rangrim at all times.

Ropes kept Corde secure upon his saddle. His mind drifted away from his eyes and back again; his body dipped forward unconsciously and spasmed upright in panic. It was a routine that kept him exhausted. He needed rest to live, and rest was not something we'd find before reaching the Hanallta proper that evening.

I, too, felt the slowness of exhaustion. The combination of the smoke's torpor and my lack of sleep would have been hard to push through had it not been for Rangrim and Corde. I didn't want to let my guard down.

"That was a different man last night," I spoke forward to Rangrim.

"It was," she said. "And don't get too comfortable with your own tongue. Believe it or not, he's fluent in Kalanosi."

I thought back to the night of his recapture, how he'd stuttered through his second language even when in danger.

"You said when you found him, he vomited and cowered. A few hours ago he stole my weapons and tried to murder you. He was more than a capable fighter in that storm. How can a man transform so quickly?"

"Because he isn't one man." Her face twisted spitefully. I looked back to him and let her continue. "The man behind us is a talented actor and a criminal. His real name is Giligas Crattle. He is a calculative, malicious man who made the mistake of betraying his master. He became the furrier in Periloe to hide himself away."

"Who did he betray? What sort of criminal? Why..." I cut myself off before falling into an Avid-like ramble.

"You want to know why I've gone along with the act," she finished, casting a knowing look my way. "Because, as you said, he was a different man. If he had reason to think I knew who he truly was, we would have had the capable and aggressive Giligas Crattle to deal with. But if he thought the façade of Haston Corde held strong, he would not abandon it. It's safer to be a pathetic tradesmen than a dangerous master criminal — and safer for us to keep him that way. People are often what they pretend to be."

"That's a lot of faith to put in a man you don't know too well."

"Oh, I'm never without a plan of contingency," she said frankly. "I had something he didn't have, and it ended up working exactly as I knew it would."

"And that is?" I asked.

"You."

My eyes narrowed. "But you don't know me that well, either. You place a lot of trust in strangers."

"Not in strangers, but in my sagacity," she said. "It's not that I trust you — I trust you to be consistent. You're noble. You spend all your time thinking, and every thought you have is measured against your rigid morality. You protect those who need protecting. And in this case, that's me."

"You're wrong," I said with conviction. "I'm just here to receive my end of the bargain. I get you your quarry, you get me where I need to go. I fought with Corde — Crattle — whoever — because if you died, I'd likely have trouble walking straight into the Hanallta. And you're my only source of Senna's Ward. And I think you're very aware of that."

"You brought me Giligas Crattle without a single scratch on him," she said. "Last night, you shot him through the hand. You could have hit him anywhere else. It would have been easier to wound his foot and immobilize him than to pin him to a tree."

"What's your point?" I didn't like being looked into so deeply. Her assessment made me squirm.

"You're noble," she repeated. "Losing a foot on a mountain is far worse than losing a hand. You're empathetic and feeling, and that's what makes you predictable."

I reached for the nearest defense in my mind.

"I once broke an old man's nose with a skull plate for insulting someone close to me."

Rangrim stared ahead, and a strange transformation

began in her face. Her eyes widened, her jaw tensed, and her lips pursed.

And she broke out in riotous laughter.

"What?" I demanded. "Would you have expected me to attack someone like that? Is that *consistent*?"

Rangrim picked herself up from the rare bout of mirth, turned her head to check that her prisoner was still unconscious, and looked forward again with a sigh.

"Rennik of Kalanos," she said expansively to the path ahead, "protecting those in need since the day he was born."

THERE WAS A RIVER SPOUTING SLOWLY FROM THE SPACE between stones.

It worked in alternating strokes with the wind to carve into the red mass of Ba Turin. This primeval wearing down left what Rangrim wisely referred to as "slickrock."

"One of a thousand reasons to employ good Kalanosi horses in Kalanosi lands," she said. "Those iron-shod louts Rucosti call workhorses would slip straight from this path and into the gulch, rider and all, at the first hint of rain. Best if you can find a mule, really." She assessed the land beneath her. "Our home," she continued, "has a way of chewing up the unwelcome and spitting them straight into the dirt." She glanced back at one of us — it was hard to tell whom.

Our horses, surefooted and Kalanosi, which appeared redundant in Rangrim's mind, soon made use of crude staircases far too convenient to be natural. Below us, the distant expanse of the Kalanosi lowlands exhaled, shrinking in detail and growing in size. Vegetation became exceptional in the unforgiving stone. The final few cottonwoods shed their seeds in ephemeral breezes over sego lily and scrub oak.

Nutcrackers of white and black plumage rambled through their vast repertoire in blissful ignorance of the tension strung between the three of us. The world was a simple palette of green, white, and red — of sego, stone, and maidenhair all painted together by the brush of mountain streams.

Then we came to a place where a long and feathery shadow lay thrown across the mountainside. It was an adobe tower sprouting from the side of the trail. A series of windows pursued its thirty-foot height, and someone had ducked away from the uppermost opening upon seeing our approach.

Rangrim had seen him, too.

"Go ahead, old man. Send your raven," she shouted up to the tower. "Send the blackest of your messengers to the Tempest Throne."

A few of the sooty birds preened upon the loftiest peaks of the tower.

"Tell them I've returned," she continued. "Tell them Rangrim comes with a gift."

～

"What will that letter contain?" I asked her after a few minutes had passed. "Do the Turin have a written form of Kalanosi?"

"In a way," she told me. "Once you've spent some time in the Hanallta, you'll see the nettles of Rucost's influence in everything. The chieftain's mother developed an adulteration of the two languages. Kalanosi glyphs yoked with Rucosti letters."

"I'd love to see it."

Rangrim made an unsurprised sort of scoff. "I can get you

into the library in the palace. You'll need the right escort, or the Red Wardens would toss you in the cells just for trying."

"Red Wardens?"

"The personal guards of Moddimok. Recruited at a young age and fostered to be the most well-trained and fiercely loyal fighters in Ba Turin. A few generations ago, the chieftain might've kept four of them at a time, just enough to keep her safe even in private quarters. Now, though...there were at least two dozen when I was cast out. I can't imagine they haven't grown."

"Seems sour to you," I said, noting the way her face contorted as she spoke.

"Should Moddimok wave her hand a certain way," she said, "they'll be the ones to kill us."

WHEN SHE SAID WE'D KNOW THE CITY BY THE SENTINELS, I thought she'd meant *guards*.

These were five massive statues, each a woman with an animal's face, staves placed firmly into the well-trodden path like stones to break the trail's current. The raven's news must have spread quickly; people began crowding at the feet of their guardians, a hushed sort of clamor building at their presence. They pressed themselves against the mountainous walls that framed the path as though they dared not stand in our way.

"It's true—"

"The traitor is back!"

"Moddimok will have her *killed!*"

We rode past the fixated crowd and under the confident stance of the middle Sentinel. As the curtain of stone was pulled away, the home of the Turin was revealed to me.

A lush vale swept along the heights of the mountain range. It was as if my plateau had been plucked from memory and stretched into miles of soft knolls and adobe homes. Laborers assembled pinewood scaffolds against the ruddy stone that jutted abruptly along the landscape, children ran races between rows in a garden, warped pines dotted each grassy canvas between home and hillside. It was strange to come from a world of tightly winding trails and sheer drop-offs to such a vast and welcoming plain.

"I worried I'd never see the Hanallta again," Rangrim said from her horse, looking out at the view. "Strange how one can miss a home that doesn't miss them."

"I know that all too well."

"You're certain in your reading? They will not try to kill us?"

I gave an honest shrug. "Certain as I can be." I noted her momentary break in composure.

She looked over the heads of the crowd and donned an affected confidence.

"Come, Rennik. Chin up. The evening is young, and we have nations to upset."

DESPITE THE OPEN LAND, IT WAS CLEAR WHERE WE WERE headed.

Almost everyone in sight had lined up from the Sentinels to a sheer rock wall on the opposite side of this thin strip of the Hanallta, anticipating the path we'd be taking.

At its end was the biggest cavern opening I'd ever seen.

The entryway was a forty-foot art piece that made shapes of the empty space it contained. Along its downward-curving edges were voids in the shapes of eddies and wisps, like spray from a waterfall, carved in wandering patterns and mirrored perfectly on either side. Its great contours terminated behind armed guards — Red Wardens, I suspected — and led to what Rangrim referred to as Mother's Hall.

We dismounted and walked, her in front, I behind her supporting Corde.

The inside of the hall consisted of colossal cut pillars that clashed against natural stone walls, purposely kept in their raw form, or at least I imagined. Beneath our feet were polished, glassy pebbles fixed into the stone that traced forward and branched out in secondary paths to whatever rooms lay adjacent to the main walkway.

The last set of pillars ended in massive stone hands that seemed to hold up the irregular ceiling of the cavern. They were incredibly detailed and impossible to miss, and for a moment I was glad that the man whose head rested on my shoulder was not awake to see them.

When at last we stepped into the main chamber, there was no doubt of where one was meant to look first. There were tusk-like arches trailing the walls, beams of twilight sun reaching from the back of the room to our feet through the cavern ceiling, twin waterfalls flowing on each side of the room into pools of colored clay tile, and dozens of people waiting on either side of us.

But all eyes were drawn to Chieftain Moddimok.

She was an imposing tower of skin and sinew with a raven-feather crown at her head. A throne of assembled earthen fragments sat behind her, burned with horse-hair to form a tumult of thunderbolts, rampant and black, a crafted and captured chaos fit to seat the Wahkeen themselves.

"*Killer!*"

The chieftain shouted.

"*Deceiver!*"

Her voice echoed in the silent chamber.

"*Traitor!*"

A seething anger rose from each face in the room, a wicked miasma for which I felt no envy.

"What possibly possessed you to enter this sacred hall? What makes you think you'll be leaving alive?" Moddimok craned above us from her stone dais; an advisor in black haunted her shoulder.

"I've come with recompense," said Rangrim. "A gift that may bolster your influence with Rucost...and serve as an apology." I listened intently, but something distracted me in Moddimok's face — something distantly familiar. It occurred to me that, aside from the nose, she looked quite a bit like Rangrim.

"What gift could possibly be worth sparing a nameless cur like *you*?"

"I suppose the gift of seeing your daughter isn't enough for a mighty chieftain?" She spoke sadly, but I detected a faint spoor of sarcasm in her voice.

"I have no daughter."

"Then it must have been the wind that brought this treasure to you," said Rangrim, gesturing to the bloodied man for whom I was a crutch.

Moddimok did not halt in her fuming, but her curiosity was clearly too much to quell. "A half-dead Rucosti?"

"A wanted criminal. A man the nobility of Rucost would be grateful to receive. This, Chieftain Moddimok, is Giligas Crattle, betrayer of his country, slayer of Kalanos."

There was an immediate murmur throughout the chamber, and I was staring at Rangrim in an instant.

Slayer of Kalanos?

My heart was pounding. What did she mean? This wasn't

the pale man, nor was he a Sree charger. What had he done to earn that title?

What sort of man do I have on my shoulder?

Moddimok raised a slow hand for silence.

"So," she intoned, "the mind behind the Crooked King finds himself captured and — *handless?*" The chieftain chuckled. "How dreadfully embarrassing for one of your reputation, Giligas Crattle. Though I suppose I should wait for your waking hours to bedevil you properly." She turned her eyes once more to her daughter. "And what, girl, do you presume I'll do with such a captive?"

"I presume, in your lofty wisdom, that you would send a raven to Rucost to make it clear to the nobility that you have something they want, and that you're willing to give it to them. You've been ever so desperate to prove yourself an ally. Here's another chance."

The advisor at her side leaned forward to whisper. Moddimok looked now to me.

"And you bring only one other with you? Where are the rest of your nameless kin?"

"I didn't think I'd need an army to come home."

"You would have been wise to expect a fight."

The room tensed. I thought not of my weapons but of the distance to the exit.

"But," continued Moddimok, "now that you've brought this gift of a gutter rat...I will allow you to stay. Tentatively, and under close supervision."

The many onlookers in the chamber began muttering to one another in awe. I couldn't help but notice Rangrim's evasion moments before; her mother wanted to know who I was. Was Rangrim keeping me a secret, or was she simply victim to the opportunity to quip at her mother?

"Take the Rucosti," Moddimok demanded. Two guards

approached and did so. "For the guest," she continued, gesturing at me, "find someone to house him for the time being. The lot of you can leave," she said to the crowd.

"I have some business with the one called Rangrim."

~

IT WAS THREE SMALL ROOMS HALF-CARVED INTO A ROCK WALL, half-built out from it. My escort of two guards informed me that the woman's name was Hegira, and that she'd be busy in her *sacha* until sundown. From what I gathered, it seemed to be their unique word for "farm". They said they'd tell her of my staying, and that I should, in the meantime, take the far room; I would likely be called upon in the morning.

In the corner I placed the saddlebag I'd carried from my horse and left my bow, axe, and quiver next to that. There was a garden adjacent to the house where potatoes and a few types of flowers grew. The flowers were unfamiliar to me; perhaps they only grew at high elevations.

I know of a Turin woman, Gatsi had told me.

But these people were so scattered. There were those who lived in the Hanallta, those who lived elsewhere in the Ba Turin mountain range, Rangrim's outcasts, and, according to some of the talk I'd heard while walking here, some who now lived among the Rucosti. The Achare were simple to understand: we lived next to the ridge by the river — *all* of us.

My best, and perhaps only, means of investigation were to talk with the Turin. But what would I ask?

"Is there a woman here who sees the future?"

"How many of your neighbors talk to smoke?"

"Has a big tree ever wrapped its roots around your grandmother?"

I strode politely into Hegira's central room. There was a

sharp, sweet smell that greeted me, and I found the source to be a bundle of fresh mint hanging from the ceiling. There were recessed shelves cut into the stone, and the stone walls themselves were painted in sky blue along the top. I wondered if they made their pigments the same way at the top of the world.

There were chairs and a table that seemed to be carved like the wood I'd seen in Tenal's wagons. Crouching down, I guessed that the maker had used a tool called a "planer". Avid had been wanting one from the Marchland cities, but upon describing the thing to me, I told him it sounded too much like a simple draw knife to risk stealing one from the Rucosti.

"But you can *adjust* these!" Avid had argued.

I shook my head at the memory, hoping he wasn't sitting in a Rucosti cell for stealing a tool that resembled a bladed shoe.

I was about to walk into the final room when a woman stepped into the home.

"You must be Heg..." I started.

Rangrim stood at the threshold, a distant crowd staring at her back. She looked at me for a moment with a raised eyebrow.

"I am not a hedge, no." She entered the room and invited herself into a chair. "You'll need more of Senna's Ward before the sun sets. Sit."

Nearly a week's worth of travel, and I still wasn't used to the way she spoke to me.

"So, the chieftain is your mother," I stated, propping my elbows up on the table.

"Yes."

"And that means you're meant to succeed her in ruling the Turin." *And why you've returned*, I guessed silently.

"I *was*," she said matter-of-factly. "I lost the title of 'daughter' when I lost my name. And the motherless inherit nothing."

"But this Crattle man seems to be a way back, right? You're going to earn your place again?"

Rangrim turned her head and looked out at the dissipating crowd. She took a long breath. "It's not going to be so simple. Giligas Crattle wasn't the centerpiece — he was just the key to getting into Mother's Hall alive."

"Then what's the rest of your plan?"

"Not my plan, Rennik. *Our* plan."

"You can't be serious. I've done what you've asked of me. Our trade is complete. I need now to focus on finding one of your people—"

"I don't care what you think you're here to do. Those damn...that *plague* of a people found a way to corrupt my mother and have been at it for years."

"The business between your mother and Rucost is no business of mine."

"I don't know what they're doing. I don't know how they've changed her, what magics they've employed, but..."

For a half second, the steel of Rangrim's countenance wilted. Her eyes wetted. Her shoulders dropped in an emotional fatigue rather than grow tense with anger. A word caught in her throat, the first shape of a question, before moving into a stuttered exhalation.

Then, she was back, carved of sharp marble.

"You are a seer, Rennik. You have eyes that know what others cannot. The mother I know would never voluntarily betray her people, and this is the true reason you are here—"

"The true reason I'm here is to find—"

"*I* am the reason you are here!" she shouted, toppling the chair as she stood. She slipped into the well-worn saddle of rage. "I am the reason you are alive after my companions were killed! I am the reason you were welcomed into the Hanallta at all, and so it is I who will determine the purpose for your being here!"

I clenched my jaw.

"You want me to solve a mystery? Fine. Your mother was *bribed*, Rangrim. Your mother was threatened, lied to — your mother fell victim to the whichever plan was your enemy's simplest strategy because they wanted to expand their territory. Does your mother even *use* the land beneath the mountains? What you're seeing is very likely the consequence of a transaction."

"I would break your jaw were there no table between us."

"You can't break through a table, Rangrim. And you can't coerce the facts of the world to your will."

"Let's not think about the world for a moment," she said, holding her hands wide and then bringing them close. "Let's start small and work our way out. Right now, you sit in a small room with me in the way of your only exit. You sit atop a mountain breathing borrowed air — you *need* Senna's Ward to continue that *transaction*." Her last word seethed through palisade teeth. "You are here by my will and continue to exist by my will, but there's something else that needs to be made clear to you, Rennik of the Achare."

I grew cold when she said it. I hadn't told anyone which clan I belonged to. I knew my face betrayed my fear.

"The Crooked King took his hordes through Kalanos two years ago to look for those who could read what he read — he slaughtered thousands looking for people like *you*."

"The pale man," I muttered involuntarily.

"Yes, Rennik, the 'pale man'. I know this because I spent weeks at his side. I was his Turin advisor."

It hit me like a stone.

That feeling I'd had, that moment beneath the overhang when I sensed familiarity with her, it was because I really *had* seen Rangrim before. When I sat beneath the boughs of the Delkhi, when I witnessed distant things, I saw the pale man speaking with the Wahto, with the Sree, and with a woman with purple thread in her hair. He'd been speaking with... *Rangrim.*

She grinned as I came to the realization.

"And Giligas Crattle did not simply break the laws of Rucost. No, Rennik, he betrayed the trust of his pallid king and has been avoiding his lethal justice ever since. The Rucosti may be coming in as soon as two weeks to retrieve Crattle, but the raven I sent mere minutes ago means the Crooked King's men will surely be here sooner. If you do as I demand, if you discover how Rucost has gripped my mother and bent her to their will, his forces will know nothing of your presence here. If you refuse my demands or fail..."

They'll take me, too.

She left the evening's dose of Senna's Ward upon the table.

6

TABLE MANNERS

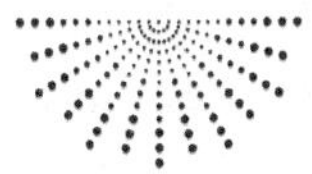

*Children learn to hate the taste of home. They do
their best to leave and let their wanderlust pull
them through life. But they will grow older,
and they will come home.*

— TENAL

A healing wound hurts.

And when the entire body needs to heal from a long journey, the trek from the bed to one's feet requires a colossal effort.

The ceiling of Hegira's home was an upended canyon; lengthy rivulets meandered their way around stone walls that pointed to the floor. I thought again of the blue embers I'd seen two days ago, when a stormy night sky set itself patiently at my feet. Perhaps the sky hadn't been flipped over, but rather I'd been *above* it — though I still didn't know how to interpret such a symbol. And never before had the smoke behaved like that, at least not in the Kalanosi plains. I wondered if something about the mountains of Ba Turin had altered the smoke.

I attempted to sit up and was physically able to do so, but my vision became a tumult of my surroundings.

Damn this elevation.

I was sure — or at least hopeful — that Rangrim had left my morning dose on the table again, though my reluctance to travel to the next room kept me still. I'd grown accustomed to headaches ever since my fight with Ciqala, but I so rarely became sick that I hadn't truly learned how to deal with it. When I heard sounds from elsewhere in the home, I assumed it was my still-unfamiliar host, and finally found the willpower to stand and walk.

She was older than my mother. Her skin was no stranger to the elements, and she moved with confidence as she placed small potatoes and peppers on a wooden plate. The dog was there, staring obsessively at the food. One of the woman's ears was notched in the lobe, and her hair sat heavily over strong shoulders. Two patient eyes met mine as she spoke.

"You look like shit."

I couldn't help but laugh. After a fight with a Shiver, several days up a mountain, and a nearly-lethal skirmish in a storm, I hadn't given a single thought as to the state of my appearance.

"Baggy eyes, bad posture, unfocused vision. You've got it bad," Hegira said. Despite the criticism, she smiled in a way that snuck into the words she spoke. "Some folk from the plains don't find it easy to breathe up here."

"And I'm one of them," I told her. "Did Rangrim leave anything for me?"

"She did." Hegira retrieved the mixture from a nearby

shelf and handed it to me. "It's better if you eat it before the food."

Senna's Ward tasted like I felt, but the vegetables Hegira had placed before me were delicious, seasoned with hunger and stress. I tried not to shovel them down too quickly.

"If you need something a bit more," she said, "I have some salted mutton hanging around."

"I'll try not to eat everything you've got — it's already too kind of you to let me sleep here."

"Nonsense," she asserted. "The Mountain Mother provided us with a home, and I'll do the same for you. Eat what you need."

I was left staring at her for a moment.

"Everything okay?" she asked.

I looked down at what little food was left. "I grew up surrounded by people who didn't care if I starved before their eyes. So few of the Achare would have found me a place to sleep if I needed it. I'm just...I've known you for a matter of minutes, and I guess I'm surprised that someone could be so generous so quickly."

Her brows furrowed. "I'd always heard the Achare were a kind people. Or at least peaceful."

"We were," I told her. "But that's what happens when you know people at a distance. You get an impression of how they treat others, but not how they treat themselves."

"It's my own little sacha," Hegira told me, looking reverently at the garden adjacent to her home. "Seven edible roots, four varieties of peppers, and a few flowers from Rucost's coast — had to trade for those. It's been my private obsession ever since my wife passed away and my daughter left me with an empty house." She smiled, knelt, and ran a hand softly against the soil.

I looked around. There was so much visible from Hegira's home. The Hanallta was certainly too large to observe in its entirety, but from this garden one could see dozens of homes to the east and the heads of the Sentinels to the west. Between their unmoving post and the entrance to Mother's Hall was a natural structure known as the Great Wing. This was a huge mountainous shelf larger than the overhang we'd camped in the night before last. The space was kept clear of buildings; it was reserved for things like gatherings and caravans.

As my eyes wandered, I noticed movement at the back of her large garden. Whatever it was ducked away quickly. It was chestnut-colored and no more than a few feet from the ground. It seemed to have found an escape in the stone behind Hegira's home.

"How do you keep animals from getting into it?" I asked.

Hegira scowled. "I've planted a few things on the edges to keep the bugs away, though we don't get as many as you do down in the lowlands. I keep an eye out for birds, and we all keep our eyes out for marmots — it takes a village to poach a marmot," she finished in a disdainful mutter.

"Might've been one just now." I pointed to the place where I'd seen movement.

"Well," she said, "it's gone now. Conniving, oversized rats...they know when to hide. Do me a favor and shoot the next one you see."

I smiled. "Maybe they'll bother you less if I make you a marmot-skin hat."

She laughed and looked back to me. "Yeah, that'll probably do the trick."

"I keep hearing about these 'sachas'," I said. "I'm not familiar with the word."

"Well, that makes sense. You wouldn't have use for anything like that down in the plains. You've got all the room in the world for sowing seeds."

"What exactly are we talking about?" I asked. I pictured the Hanallta I'd seen thus far and couldn't figure where they'd put the many acres required to sustain the Turin, unless they busied the farthest reaches of the vale with long stretches of crop.

"Maybe it's best if I just show you," she said.

Hegira walked me through the Hanallta, out beyond the living space of her clan, and after a mile at the top of the world, I saw the true power of the people of the mountain.

ON THE NORTHERN MOUNTAINSIDE OF THE VALE SAT A SERIES OF long, stratified ledges, each at least a hundred feet wide. They stair-stepped down for half a mile and continued to the east as far as I could see before a corner of the mountain hid their true reach. Each ledge, or "terrace", as Hegira called them, held enough crops to feed hundreds of people. Looking such a distance brought my newfound vertigo back, and I had to take a moment to steady myself.

The terrace closest to us grew a variation of maize, while the ones below it boasted things like tomatoes, carrots, and potatoes. She explained that the maize wasn't usually this tall before midsummer. The dog, in a sudden spurt of energy, ran wildly into the flourishing maize and flung himself down into the second terrace. Judging by his lolling tongue and wagging tail, it was likely he'd found something to chase.

"Don't worry," she said. "There are stone steps every quarter mile." She gestured to the mountainside. "Each terrace sits about seven feet higher than the one below it, and each terrace is a series of layers in itself. The crops are planted in a few inches of good soil. That soil sits on a few inches of coarse sand and fine gravel. Then, stones no bigger than your palm make up the bottom layer. Water doesn't sit still anywhere near the Hanallta; it's all guided or ported to the top terrace. The water drains into each layer and feeds the terrace below it. None of our crops are taken away in mudslides. None of our water pools, none of it is wasted. The next time rain climbs the mountainside, you'll see just how wonderful Ba Turin is. What look like natural stone formations will feed water toward certain places in the city, like Mother's Hall, and the rest drops on our sachas."

I stood and marveled at the giant staircase.

"It seems I've misunderstood the Turin for my entire life," I said.

"How so?"

"I guess I've imagined a people in the mountains to be close to the sky, but truly, you are a people of the water."

Hegira smiled. "A people are never just one thing, Rennik. But if we had to label the Turin, we would be neither a people of the sky nor the water. We are a people of craft."

"What happens when there isn't enough rain?" I asked.

"When our terraces need more than what is given by the sky or Mother's river, you'll see two things: first, a sort of clay water jug strapped to people's shoulders, making its way from spring to sacha from sunup to sundown."

"And second?"

"A lot of aching backs."

"And full bellies, I assume."

"Always," she answered with a proud smile. "When I realized the Mountain Mother blessed me with a talent for all that grows, the Hanallta became my table, and my clan became a hungry guest."

"That's an incredible burden to have placed on your shoulders," I told her.

"I am not the one with a burden," she said. "Those of us who struggle through a season, whose sachas get less sunlight, less rain. *Those* people have a burden. To me, this is a gift, and it would be insulting for me to think of my talents as a burden. I'm simply living the life the Mother intended for me — intended for all of us."

The dog barked, apparently having found his quarry. "And I suppose I should follow through with my own talent," I said with determination. I nocked an arrow. "I think my friend has found something worth pursuing."

Hegira waved me on and returned to her investigation of the maize.

I crept to the edge of the maize terrace and looked for the dog. I could not see him, but soon enough I heard his barking again. This time it carried a howling sort of melody, a short, playful variation of his voice. The maize made long hallways in four directions.

Spoiled dog, I thought. *Stop toying with your food.*

I dropped to the next terrace and landed carefully among the tall tomato stems. There were no signs of a trail, no prints aside from the dog's, no disturbed or burrowed-in earth. A moment to quell my dizziness, and I strode forward to look down into the third terrace.

I held steady to my bow and made a point to breathe more deeply. I wasn't sure if that was the solution, but it felt like the smart thing to do.

Far to my right and more than my height beneath me, the dog had his prize beneath his massive head. I jumped a final time to the third terrace and walked confidently toward my beast of a traveling companion.

"Alright, boy," I said. "Let's see what you've found."

"Nothing — *I swear!*"

I stopped walking. I blinked hard.

The animal was still hidden beneath the dog's huge frame.

Did that marmot just...speak?

My thoughts caught up to me.

"Release!" I commanded. The dog bounced gleefully away from his prey, and I stood astounded at what he'd found.

The creature was no creature at all, but a boy with a bucket of leaves.

7

A BOY AND HIS BUCKET

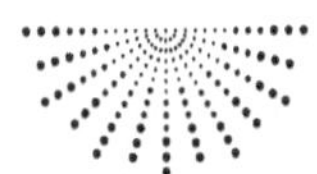

*A shield is many things in peace: a memory, a
table, a seat or a plaything. Only in combat
does a shield protect, and only in combat does
a shield become a treasure.*

— EXCERPT FROM TORKULLUS'
TOME OF WAR

He lay on his back and clutched the bucket as though it kept him afloat. He looked up at me with terrified eyes.

"Please," he whispered. "Don't tell Hegira I'm here!"

Without saying anything, I offered a hand and helped him up.

His face had a subtle edge to it, almost like it'd been pulled forward with a string, and it made his eyes seem horse-like. He was, frankly, an ugly child. On the side of his head, just in front of his ear, hung a series of small turquoise shards on a black string that was tied at one end to his dark hair. I gauged him to be about nine years old, and as I looked into his bucket, the purpose of his presence became clear.

"You're a thief."

"I am not!" he said. "These are the leaves she wouldn't even want! Look — they're bad for the plants!" He held a handful of plant matter toward my face.

"Where are your parents?" I asked, ignoring his hand.

The boy looked to the ground. I waited a moment before continuing.

"I had to find my own food too, when I was your age," I told him. "Hegira doesn't seem like the sort of person to scorn a hungry child, but I imagine you know the people here better than I."

He nodded. "You learn all sorts of things when you're sneaky like me."

"Like what?"

"Well, I know that Hegira thinks you're hunting pests right now."

"And what does that make you?" I asked half-playfully.

"A marmot." He smiled as he said it.

"Alright, Marmot." I looked around to ensure we were still hidden from Hegira. "If you're such a know-it-all...tell me about Moddimok."

Marmot stood and walked east, away from where I'd come. He stopped at each tomato stem and studied its leaves, sometimes reaching well over his head to prune whatever he decided was detrimental to the plant's growth.

"She's dangerous," he said. "People don't like to say things about her that might get them in trouble, so they only say those things when they're sure no one else is listening."

"And what do they say then?"

"That she changed. People are worried that Rucost is going to take our home and use our sachas to feed their armies. They say she must be sick, because a true Turin like Moddimok would never betray their home."

"But what exactly has she done to make her people doubt her?"

"Big groups of Rucosti people come into the Hanallta sometimes. Not everyone here speaks their language, but people say they talk about the iron in our stone, the steel we make, and the crops we grow. Some people think Moddimok is making deals with Rucost to pay them with our resources."

"Pay them for what? And don't other people benefit from the merchants?"

"Well, there are merchant caravans, but there are other groups that visit Moddimok. I think they're more political. And as far as paying them..." Marmot shrugged. "To let us be, is what people guess. I think it's easier to give up what you value when your home is at stake, so I guess I understand what she's doing, but..."

Hegira strode past us on the terrace above. She glanced down to me, smiled, and continued on her way, oblivious to the boy in her tomatoes.

"But?" I asked.

"Well, only a few people talk about this, but...they say there's a reason all these Turin have spoken out against Moddimok. Her daughter was one of them — you know, that lady you came here with. But for so many people to speak like that knowing they would be banished to the Shadowlands means they really believe what they say."

"And what do they say?"

"What everyone else only says when they think no one's listening."

A few moments passed. Marmot's bucket was nearly full.

"Do you think they're right?" I asked.

"About what?"

"Do you think Moddimok is sick? Do you think it's led her to betray the Turin?"

Marmot looked me in the eyes and seemed to think deeply about something. "You've got mountain sickness, and I'm pretty sure you're not going to tell Hegira about me. I don't think sickness breaks people's loyalty like that."

"Maybe Moddimok and I are different people. Maybe we're different kinds of sick."

Marmot shrugged and turned back to the tomatoes. "Maybe she's just spoken to the wrong sort of people."

"Rennik!" Rangrim's commanding voice thrust my name down from the Hanallta above. "We need to speak." I could just see the heads of Rangrim and a few others pressing into view above the highest terrace.

Marmot clutched his bucket and flung himself to the edge of the second terrace, pressing his body against it to hide.

"Don't worry," I whispered. "She's more bark than bite... mostly. Actually, no, she's pretty dangerous. Any more room down there?"

He shook his head.

"Well, then." I looked to the wall of the terrace and pictured the climb. Marmot looked up at me from his hiding place. "Do you like her?"

"No. I don't."

He grinned mischievously. "If you want to fluster her, I've got something *really* good you can say."

RANGRIM STOOD ABOVE THE HIGHEST SACHA WITH A GROUP OF nine attendants. They were dressed impractically and wore black and white paint on their arms — a sign they belonged to Moddimok's court. They studied me silently as I pulled myself to their level.

"I've given you a job to do," Rangrim began. "You've been tasked with your end of the deal, yet you're spending your time in the sachas."

"Well," I started, sensing that I shouldn't go into detail with the attendants present, "it's been less than twelve hours. I figure I should familiarize myself with your clan."

"I don't imagine you've made any progress."

"I've got a promising start." I noticed she had changed from road-worn traveling clothes into courtier's fabrics, bright blue on subdued sienna and black. "Perhaps I could speak to you alone?"

The attendants looked to Rangrim as she feigned a reluctant acquiescence. We walked west along the mountainside until we were out of earshot.

"Your mother seems to have changed her mind about you," I said. "She's given you nearly half of her court."

"They're not here to dote on me, Rennik. This is what it looks like when my mother needs eyes on me, and it's the reason *you* are to do the investigating."

"No Red Wardens?"

"This isn't protection."

I glanced back to the nine attendants, who chatted coolly but kept their eyes on Rangrim. "You're not going to make this easier for me, talking openly about the 'job' I have."

"Don't worry," she said. "I told them that a mutual acquaintance of ours stole something important and is hiding somewhere in the mountains."

I openly rolled my eyes. "Does your mother seem...sick?"

"No."

"Or unwell compared to how she used to be? I've got a source suggesting that people think she's sick."

Rangrim scoffed. "A 'source'. Rennik, you've been here for less than a day, and the only person you've spoken to is a farmer. And trust me when I say she wouldn't know much about my mother."

"It's not Hegira, and if you doubt the veracity of my source..." I looked again at the attendants. The dog was creeping slowly toward them, playfully hunting like he did with Marmot. Not one in the nine of them looked amused. "I've found out plenty."

"Do tell."

"There's a small and well-hidden tunnel in Mother's Hall that leads from your old quarters to your mother's and out to an isolated ridge on the side of the mountain. You used to use it to sneak in and try on the raven crown, and later to sneak out of Mother's Hall entirely."

Rangrim's face was a concoction of pallid shock and torrid offense. Her hand came up a few inches as if she were about to grasp my throat.

"Who...how...*who told you that?*"

She wasn't the only one of us surprised. I thought the information Marmot had given me was either flaccid or fabricated. I certainly hadn't expected it to disarm this one-woman force of nature. She stole a quick look in Hegira's direction.

"I'll be the one to worry about the investigation, Rangrim. You run along in your cozy fabrics and chat with your painted patrons."

She looked as though she wanted to cut me open then and there, but for once I felt like I had the upper hand.

I looked over Rangrim's shoulder at the sound of a panicked man. The dog was making little hops at his feet, clearly interested in something the courtier had. The others took several steps away and let their friend deal with the beast alone. The man tried each weapon in his arsenal: a "no" fell flat, a "down" accomplished nothing, and a "go away" did not move him. I whistled sharply, and the dog turned immediately to me. He came halfway toward us and stopped.

Odd, I thought. *It's not like him to keep distance when I call.*

"We didn't have people like them in the Achare," I said to Rangrim.

"Rucost's influence. They saw what it's like to be pampered," she responded in a low voice. She reached into her pouch and produced not one, but two mixtures. The first was Senna's Ward, but the second was a half-completed recipe for my smoke-reading. "You mentioned the addition of ingredients after it'd been chewed. This should be enough for you to complete and apply before today's end."

"Yes, it will be. But it might not work — we did this yesterday."

"We will try."

"We will try," I repeated.

"Good. There is a question you will be asking."

"Past, present, or future?"

Rangrim hesitated. "Present."

I wanted to remind her that smoke only concerns itself with the reader, that anything I see may have nothing to do with her. But there was something in her eyes that reminded me of Ciqala, something that told me she'd press her will into the world and expect to win every time.

"This evening, then. But only if you do something for me."

"You don't have room to bargain."

"I just want to speak to him," I said.

"He's being held deep underground, Rennik. Even if he's awake, I can't guarantee he won't be delirious from his injury."

"I *will* speak with him."

Rangrim looked back at her attendants, then again to me. "Fine," she said. "I'll let the guards know to let you in and escort you. Tomorrow."

"Tomorrow. Maybe he won't be able to say much, but... you called him 'the slayer of Kalanos.' Why?"

She scoffed. "That's a better question for the man himself."

"Then I must speak to him. He has to know more about what happened to my people. You have your own problems here on the Hanallta, I know, but surely you can understand my need for more information — maybe even closure."

Her face actually achieved a soft expression.

I stepped close to her and brought a hand near her cheek. She froze and looked fearful, clearly under the impression that I was trying to create an intimate moment.

I plucked a hair from her head.

Her eyes went wide in fury, but before she could respond I laughed took a step back.

"Magic has a cost," I told her, brandishing the strand. "If you want the smoke to speak of the present, we'll need your hair."

As she took a deep breath and turned back to her attendants, I knew she didn't suspect the lie.

EVENING FOUND US IN A SECLUDED LITTLE NICHE AMONG THE mountain walls. Roughly forty square feet in each direction, flat earth, and high stone walls meant interruption from neither Turin nor the elements.

I packed her hair into the mixture and looked to her, lowering my voice to a sober pitch and volume. She was reverent in regard to my abilities with smoke, and I sought to entice her with that gravity. I felt a little like the charlatan fortune tellers Tenal said worked in Rucosti cities.

"What is it you'd like to know?"

"It's fairly straightforward, I'd think," she said. "I want to know if my mother currently entertains any Rucosti influences in Mother's Hall."

"You worry she's squirreled away a foreign advisor?"

"Mother's Hall has more hiding places than you'd ever know. Large rooms only reached by undetectable passages. It's rife with the potential for surreptitious activity."

I considered jabbing at her with Marmot's information again, but felt it best not to poke the bison.

"Alright," I said. "It's going to take a moment, as you saw before, but know that smoke can be complex — and it's interpreted from the perspective of the reader, which means it may look wildly different to someone at a different angle."

"I understand," she said.

My breathing became deep. My chest felt heavy as the stone of my power settled downward. I began the incantation.

"...*Malnostos*."

The smoke did not hesitate.

The shoulders erupted into an inky black void, nearly shapeless save for the smallest of movements. My eyes tracked diminutive wisps as they were crushed by the heavy, fist-like plumes that fell upon them over and again, relentless and passionate in their violence. A torrid heat.

I realized that I'd fallen back on my hands and pushed myself away from the fire, and from the other side of the obstruction stepped Rangrim, bewildered and apprehensive.

Then came the embers.

From the ankles came thin blue patterns that floated from the fire in constellation-like lines. They settled much like they did before, the night Giligas Crattle had lost his hand. Never had the smoke given me such a concrete sort of pattern, so to see it twice was nothing short of astonishing. A mollifying chill.

I threw myself over and began drawing in the dirt, trying with little grace to record the patterns in the little constellations.

"The stars," I muttered. "They're back. This is…"

I managed to trace four series of the blue lights before they began to fade.

"You saw those before," Rangrim said, "and you acted like it hadn't happened before. Do you think this means something for me?"

"I don't know."

Rangrim looked again at the shoulders of the smoke.

"I can't imagine that much black to be a good omen," she said.

"No," I told her. "It's not."

She may have been right about general feeling of the smoke, but what she didn't know is that I'd asked my own question. I did not concern the smoke with Rangrim's interest in her mother, with Rucost's interest in the Turin — I didn't even look for answers of the present. Instead, I wanted to know if I should trust Rangrim to hold up her end of the deal, to let me leave when I'd found her answers.

And now, with the dark weight of the blackened shoulders above, I was sure she was going to kill me.

8

CLAN INTO FAMILY, EARTH INTO STEEL

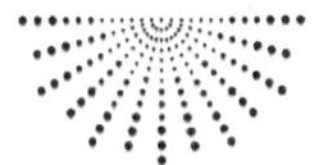

It is often debated whether the object of thievery should affect the punishment. Stealing from the Temple of Ityx is high crime, but can one blame a hungry hand for palming an apple?

— EXCERPT FROM REMI GRENFALLOW'S *PHILOSOPHY OF CRIME*

It is a skill to see a threat and pocket it away.

Haston Corde's warning from two nights ago had been prodding at me all day. Prisoners aren't entitled to information...And to the smoke, I'd asked a very definite question: "what does Rangrim intend for me?" The answer was clear enough.

The secret to this skill is distraction, whether it be forward motion or a moment of calm.

So I decided to whittle away the remaining hours with Hegira.

She had finished in her sacha for the day, and after

cleaning herself up, we took two chairs outside and ate at the wide table of the Hanallta. We were speaking of their neighboring kingdom.

"It surprises me," I said to her, "that the Rucosti people can be so varied. Some hate Kalanosi as a rule, and yet Rucosti merchants are set to arrive sometime this week."

"A people are never just one thing," she replied, repeating her words from that morning. "But what are your experiences with them in the lowlands?"

I shook my head as I chewed on a pepper. "The idea of another place and culture used to excite me. One of my closest friends was a Rucosti merchant. We'd trade stories, explain our people to each other..."

"But now?"

"I don't know," I said. "The past year has found me fighting Rucosti in their Marchland. They've built upon that earth like ants build mounds. They've spent the last few years stabbing northward and claiming land for small farming cities, so there was nothing left for the southern Kalanosi to do but contest them. Some of the people in my new clan told me they'd been defending themselves for years, that they used to settle in those areas to weather the winter months. The rural Rucosti had begun burning huts, stealing horses, chasing Kalanosi people away...it was hard to see anything but a need to strike back."

"And you helped them?"

"Of course. My family and I hadn't personally been attacked, but we were alone...there were only seven of us at the time, counting the dog, and we needed the safety of numbers." I'd stopped hiding the details of my past from Hegira. She was my most trusted ally at this altitude, and she seemed to understand that it wasn't information to share.

"Safety in joining a small war," she responded. "I can't decide if that's wise or decidedly foolish."

I chortled and ate more.

"Well," I continued, "it's certainly put me in some dangerous situations. My chieftain decided we needed to keep the Marchland folk on the defensive and encourage them to stay them in their cities. So we did. We burned barns, loosed livestock, stole wagon wheels, always in the darkness of night."

"Rennik," she began. "There's something I've been wanting to ask you."

"Anything," I told her.

She inhaled, held the breath cautiously, and continued. "The people Rangrim kept near...they're never good people — at least, not *peaceful* people. She brings a fight with her wherever she goes, and when she returned to the Hanallta with only you and her prisoner, I think most people assumed you were some sort of killer."

An arrow through an eye. Ripgut trembling.

"No," I told her. "I try my best not to kill. But I suppose you'd like to know that I've hurt people. Many people, really. I grew up defending myself from my own brutish neighbors, and when I saw how the Rucosti were attacking the Kalanosi, I decided I wouldn't wait for the fight to come to me. It's a lesson I wish I'd never had to learn."

"You do your best not to hurt the people of the Marchland?"

"Well...usually, yes. A few of the older veterans have put on armor from their soldiering days and tried to rally a militia to defend their cities. It's usually my job to 'ring the bell' if I have to."

Hegira looked confused.

"Sorry," I said, "that's what we call a nonlethal arrow to

the helm. If you can give enough of them a headache or dent their armor, they typically get disorganized. A few of us will do that from alleyways and rooftops while others cause a bit of bedlam elsewhere."

"You mean you've actually skirmished with fighters in the streets? This is more than a little chaos, Rennik. You really are in a war."

"I'm in an effort to keep our home *our home*," I offered.

"I hope they don't associate the Turin with your clan," she said. "I like the safety of my mountains."

"And would you protect your home if you had to?" I asked.

"...I don't know."

"The kind of Rucosti that live in the Marchland cities might associate us. They're ignorant, and if they see someone who looks like us," I gestured between the two of us, "they'll just see 'Kalanosi'. And they're not the ones traveling to trade, anyway."

Hegira made a contemplative noise. We ate for a few minutes more, watching the Hanallta grow darker as peaks intercepted the sun, watching children wander, watching the dog as he traced the movements of passing people. Two Turin plucked at stringed instruments, one larger than the other, and let their notes poke around the corners of evening. The Great Wing was cast in deep shadow this late in the day.

"Are your people lacking strength without you there?" she asked. "The way you talk, you're an incredible marksman."

"I am," I admitted, "but I'm not the only one. My chieftain might still be more accurate than me, and us lowlanders have a knack for archery in general."

"You're saying the Turin don't?" She feigned an insulted look.

"Unless you're cutting crops at a hundred paces, I'd venture to say exactly that," I said with a smile.

"Don't you fear some sort of larger response? Rucost is a big place. They could sweep southern Kalanos with an army fairly quickly."

I shook my head. "The elite of Rucost don't seem to consider the Marchlanders a priority. The local lord seems to think we're a passing threat at best. Besides," I explained, "most of their fighting folk have been gathered up for something elsewhere."

Hegira looked concerned. "They're gathering an army?"

"They're not charging Ba Turin," I said, trying to pacify her apparent worry. "I think they're fighting with the nation at their western border. That should make our little war a bit easier, if anything."

"You should hope the merchants haven't seen a wanted poster with your face on it."

I shrugged. "I'll just break my nose another few times. That'll freshen up the look."

She laughed a bit, but I could tell the discussion made her a bit nervous. We had each finished our food, and the dog was chewing at the stems I didn't eat.

"At what point do you think Rucosti merchants won't be allowed to travel into Ba Turin?" I asked.

Hegira scoffed. "I don't see Moddimok blocking their entry anytime soon."

"I meant it the other way around. Do you think Rucosti leaders will cease trade with the Turin?"

"I think," she said, "they like our iron. I think they like our land, and more importantly our *knowledge* of the land. I think they have a whole, tiny economy based just on Kalanosi goods. And I think if their nobility told them not to, the merchants would come anyway."

"It's strange to me to see leaders who attempt to dictate so much of their people's lives. My old chieftain would only interfere if you were doing something truly awful. And when he spoke, we listened."

"They can make as many rules as they want," she said. "But before their culture, their king and their kin, the loyalty of merchants will always land on their gold."

~

THE TURIN TOOK THEIR IRON FROM THE SKY.

"It was a gift of the Wahkeen," they say, "to send us those seeds."

The metal was formed in the great birds' gullets and heaved mightily from above. These stones crashed to the earth and spread their roots, forming the iron veins mined by the Turin.

The story was given credence when it was discovered that those holding iron tools were more likely to be struck by lightning in a storm.

"I saw one, once," an elderly Turin man told me, "when I was about your age. There was a huge streak through the sky, and we found the stone in a crater not far from here. We let the stone sit for two years to let it take root, and sure enough, when we began to mine, there was iron stretching deep into the mountain."

I decided that if I were to find the source of Moddimok's corruption, I should look at the source of her wealth. Some of the process, however, turned out to be a closely-guarded secret.

The closest mine was a deep trench that followed a vein along the earth until it became a cave-like reserve of iron. The Turin had a system of pulleys and ropes that carried bucket after bucket from the deepest parts of the mine to the carts above. As I watched them breach the surface, I saw they were filled with large chunks of red rock.

After this, the foreman told me, the stone was hauled out to be broken up into smaller bits, then washed in one of the rivers nearby. "But some of these ores," he said with pride, "are bigger than your head. The sheer *size* of what we mine has no equal."

I followed the carted chunks. Their journey ended at large beds of charcoal roasting in an open section of the vale, far from the homes of the Turin. I learned that the lowland regions to the northeast of Ba Turin were miles upon miles of pines, grown in rows and harvested yearly. They ported the wood up a slow-rising, curving trail. It was used for nearly everything that could not be made with iron or clay. But the most common usage of pinewood was the making of charcoal. The Turin burned large passels every day, and whenever a scaffold or the like were disused elsewhere in the Hanallta, it was added to the pile. It was hard to fathom that such a large operation was necessary to produce small bits of metal.

When I tried to follow the charcoal, I was stopped.

A few soot-covered individuals told me that outsiders were not allowed to see the rest of the process. I wracked my brain. There was a man of the Achare, Graff, who used to smith simple tools and weapons. He used charcoal to roast the iron. He said it made it stronger, but that seemed like it'd be common knowledge.

As I turned and left, I caught sight of a cart filled to the brim with leaves, stalks, and stems.

Plant matter? Is this what Marmot was collecting it for?

Although I couldn't see what was beyond that step in the process, I'd seen the pieces necessary to understand the whole. It started with huge holes in the ground. It ended with billets of iron and steel.

The Turin were convinced that Moddimok would sell some of their land to Rucost. It seemed to me, however, like they were *all* trying to sell it. So much of the clan's energy was spent packing their land into tight little bars and carting it straight out of their sights in exchange for gold.

Some of the metal, however, stayed in their home.

Turin reaped the fruits of their environment as well as anyone. Steel was shaped into weapons. Iron was shaped into tools.

And it was stretched into the bars of their unbreakable cages.

9

ATONEMENT

I wish you to know that your death has meaning.
Your people are a currency...

— THE PALE MAN

I'd learned of prisons before, of course. I heard that the Rucosti would dedicate entire buildings to keep criminals inside and feed them.

The concept seemed so very backwards.

When the Sree took captives, it was typically for a specific reason — I'd heard they only imprisoned people when they wanted to enslave or kill them. If one were hated enough, they'd find themselves bound to a pole on a bald hill, abandoned to suffer the elements until the sky reclaimed them. When the vultures leave the bones, it's said they've consumed the name of the prisoner, and their crime is consequently absolved. Keeping a prisoner without express purpose was something I found hard to justify. Crattle was kept to trade for political gain, but after seeing so much more of Rangrim's manipulation, I couldn't help but wonder if there was a secondary purpose to his imprisonment.

His cell was carved of deep mountain stone.

The descent was cold and dark. It felt like a different world after I'd spent all day in the sun, speaking to Ba Turin's people. I stumbled several times on the uneven steps, and my eyes, struggling to transition from the twilit vale to the lightless tunnel, focused on the torch of the man leading me down.

The stone of the mountain had its own song at this depth. There was a slight, nearly imperceptible rumble, as if the earth around me were humming to itself.

Then, there was the sound of flesh striking stone. I thought I heard the guard chuckle softly to himself. Slats of angry light swung over a figure hunched beyond iron bars. The guard lit a torch suspended on the wall and walked away into the darkness.

The persistent staccato of the sound revealed itself as I reached the cell. Even in the torchlight I could see the raw skin of his remaining hand. He'd been slapping it against the stone floor, and his face was one of desperation.

He stood halfway up, saw me on the other side of the bars, and fell pitifully against the back wall. His face became softer, something with which to garner sympathy. At least that's what I told myself.

"They don't feed you here, you know," he told me.

"They expect you to starve?"

"They expect me to *scavenge*. To beg the earth for a morsel," he said, opening his palm to me. In his hand were a collection of small, crushed bugs. "They hang honey from the ceiling outside the cell first to tantalize me, then to encourage these *insects* to march from the cracks in the wall past your feet, over your body while you sleep — if I can sleep at all, that is. Hunting for your meals like a sparrow with a manstomach is a chore of endurance."

The man had lost so much blood, and still they were denying him sleep and a proper meal.

There was a whistle as he breathed. I'd nearly forgotten I'd broken his nose.

From the barred darkness and the hum of the mountain came a soft sobbing. The small cracks in the wall behind him found their way into his voice as it faltered, weakened, and lost its shell.

"I've had a little over two years to reflect on my life, sitting in Periloe with nothing to do but watch people walk and talk and drink. I started to truly wonder how I'd ended up hiding in a city like the one in which I'd grown up. If I'd simply stayed the course, I would have turned out more fortunate, I think. I strove for a honeyed future, and found myself crushed in the palm of the world."

"I need you to answer my questions," I told him, ignoring his reverie. "So much has happened to me, and I feel I have too little context to know what to do next."

"What makes you think I know any more than you do about your own life? I'm a poor fool of a furrier," he intoned in melodrama, "who couldn't tell a cwm from a col."

"Because you know the man who led the horde," I said. He shut his eyes slowly and looked to the stone floor in understanding. "The pale man, this 'Crooked King' as Rangrim calls him. She's suggested to me that he isn't acting on behalf of Rucost. Who is he? Why did he slaughter my people?" I did my best to sound assertive rather than heartbroken.

"He said he is from a place called Haeth-wyrael." He pronounced the words carefully and attempted an unfamiliar accent. "I knew nothing of it. I hadn't even *heard* of it.

The name he gave was Eladran Kesevirot. Does any of this mean anything to you?"

I shook my head.

"Truly unknown, then. I did what research I could, and Haeth-wyrael appeared in just one text, referred to as a region in a landmass far east of our own, across the sea."

"The Rucosti came from across the sea a few generations ago."

"Yes, but from the south. It would appear we in Rucost have no cultural knowledge of this man's homeland."

"Then why did you help him? Why would you commit yourself to monstrous acts for a man you could not identify?"

"Desperation, I suppose."

"Desperation? Did he threaten you? Threaten your family? What leverage did he have?"

"He did not threaten, Rennik. He offered."

"Offered what?" I was growing impatient, my voice rising in volume. I exercised some control and wrestled it down.

"He said he knew how to find the answers to anything, the information that each individual following him could use to live a life of affluence and influence."

"What exactly did you do for him?"

The man grimaced. "I was the first he found. Kesevirot, the 'Crooked King', needed a small army. I began by helping him find information on each criminal exiled to Kalanos and their whereabouts. Those would be the first of our forces."

"And then?"

"Well, those were the *first* of our forces...I located an interpreter and we took our small army north, where the plains meet the Inkwood. We recruited some second and third sons from towns along the way, then we...*gathered* some Kalanosi."

"Gathered?" There was venom in my voice.

Crattle held up his hand defensively. "I was the first of us to know, Rennik, that when powerful people stand before you, their offers are difficult to turn down."

"You coerced the small clans to the west into serving you."

"And eventually the Sree, the Wahto...you can gain the confidence of a clan so quickly when they fall into discord just as you arrive. When a people suddenly feel as though a home is no longer theirs, they seek another option..."

"You turned people against each other. You took those who would follow you and burned the rest. Is that right?"

Crattle said nothing.

"Until you had enough of an army to stop offering. Until you came to people like the Achare and needed only to threaten their lives — and then to take them."

"I have never killed anyone!" he shouted, rising unsteadily to his feet. "I helped plan, I organized, I set the foundation for his campaign, but never did I kill a single one of your people, Rennik. You must understand the position I was in!"

"You say you never killed, yet they call you the 'Slayer of Kalanos'. Forgive me if I don't take you at your word."

"I," he punctuated slowly, "have never killed anyone. They simply equate my planning, my giving Kesevirot the information he needed, with a release of the arrow that killed Kalanos."

"The hand of the archer merely obeys. *You* could have left his service. You could have said no."

"It was not so simple. You must understand—"

"I do not understand, Corde, or Crattle, or whatever name falls upon your craven shoulders. Please," I said, dragging my voice away from a shout once again, "explain it to me."

"There's a writer I adore—"

"Martinor the Untethered," I interrupted.

Crattle laughed under his breath. "Oh, how I've underestimated you Kalanosi. I didn't even recognize her face...No, Rennik, a different writer. An anonymous woman writing under the name of The Osprey. She tantalized much of my generation. You see, ours has always been a nation of communal effort, of hundreds of thousands acting in the interest of the kingdom. But it turns out strife gives purpose, and after the migration to this land, after the war ended, my generation grew up to find nothing to fight for, no place to travel, no great cause to unite us...we looked all around us and found only peace. She incensed a restlessness in many people my age. She suggested that the individual is right to break from what is mundane to find a greatness for themselves. It was a surrogate meal for those of us starved for meaning."

He looked deep in thought, as if searching for words.

"I feel like you're about to quote something." I mentally prepared myself.

He nodded. "Her most famous character. Tillinor, or 'Tillie', they'd call him. A character famous for doing nothing."

"That sounds dreadful."

"Well, that was the point. He was supposed to be *us*. There's a passage from a funeral he'd gone to..."

He cleared his throat and recounted the The Osprey's words.

"He looked to the body in its small pine box. He knelt in the pew and laced his fingers together. He mumbled the words to pray for the dead man's peace, to thank Ityx for his own family, for health, and to pray for a good return in his investments. Though deeper, in his heart with neither words nor ear to receive them, he prayed for fulfillment, for he sensed a keyhole but had no key, saw the garden but held no seed, knew there was a space for which he was meant but knew neither what to become nor where to become it, and he carried on through the rote motions of his living, no more meaningful than the man who'd died.

"He'd spent his childhood reading of great men, not average ones. He knew only the will to achieve, and not *how* to achieve. He did not have a model for mediocrity, and so he felt himself to be a great man when he was in fact far from it.

"This foundation of sand was that upon which he built his façade of laughter, passion, and prayer, and the shift of his walls kept him forever anxious that he was not as he should be."

I thought for a while. "So you wanted greatness?"

A short, cynical scoff escaped him. "And here I am, having tried desperately to become something of magnitude, borrowing someone else's words to explain myself. I have failed tenfold by my own standards. I thought joining Kese-virot would bring me to a higher stage from which to start my climb. It was the first chance for power and adventure that had ever been offered to me. I thought, well, opportunity has knocked. Now is the time to become great. I was hungry enough to eat the poison he presented."

"You are astonishing."

He looked at me confusedly, as if having interpreted the comment as a compliment.

"You helped to orchestrate the massacre of Kalanos. Here I stand before you, one of the lone survivors of a clan erased in part by your machinations, and you utter no apology, you beg for no forgiveness, your knees have not buckled for desperate atonement. How was it you criticized that explorer's death? 'He would not have spent such time to wax poetic if he had not thought he was about to die', right? Well, Giligas Crattle, you have not only failed to become a great man in your past, but you fail to do so in your death. A great man would spend his final moments fixing his errors. A great man would have earned the introspect to know to look outward at his effects. But perhaps that is the failure in your tales of great men — they teach you how to live and to conquer, but never how to die."

It was as though I'd struck him in the stomach. He leaned forward, fell onto his side, sobbed, and rolled again to his knees.

"How, then?" he asked through his tears. "How could I possibly atone?"

"I don't think it's possible. I'm not sure I believe that people can truly atone for any wrong they've committed," I told him. "But I know how you can start."

He looked at me with pleading eyes.

"Tell me everything you know about Moddimok's manipulation. You may serve this Kesevirot, but you're also a learned man of Rucost. Surely you know something, anything to do with how they turned the chieftain of the Turin into a Rucosti sympathizer."

"I don't know, but...it isn't natural. Kesevirot spoke of a sort of magic he used, and it was why he...well, it's the same that you use, I suppose. It may be, even though Kesevirot has no ties to Rucost, that his magics have something to do with this corruption you seek. The only reason he left the Turin alone was due to his inclusion of Rangrim in his inner circle. Perhaps without that deal in place, something else was done."

"You traveled with Rangrim for days. Why didn't you recognize her?"

Crattle croaked in sardonic laughter. "Simple ego, I

suppose. The ego of culture acting through me. I did not give her the time of day, did not consider her worthwhile. I hardly knew her face…"

"Tell me where this Kesevirot is, what he's doing next, and why he wanted people like me dead."

"He said, once, that the biggest threat to his power were others like him, other people who could see what he saw. He spoke of finding people like you — seers, he would call them — near specific sorts of places. He would know which clans might have your sorts and which didn't."

Places where something like the Delkhi would take hold, I thought.

"And where is he now?"

"His Kalanosi campaign was to end somewhere east, probably within the Rask territory. By the time I was considering leaving his company, he'd already stopped telling me specifics. It's…difficult to hide things from him."

"Then you don't know where he was going after he was done with Kalanos?"

"No. I don't."

"Do you think he'll find you here?" I asked him.

He gave in to a defeatist's laughter and shook his head. "If the Rucosti receive me here, I'll stand trial for my crimes and find myself either in prison or exiled to Kalanos. The 'Crooked King' will find me here or out in the plains. Regardless of my conclusion, the outlook is bleak, and I won't hope for one over the other. I am simply a man waiting to die, Rennik."

Giligas Crattle brought his hand down with a sudden slap and crushed an insect in his palm.

10

RAVEN & CROW

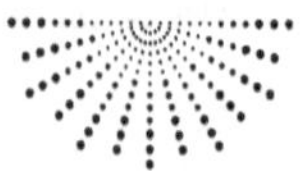

Mother cried
a thousand times
for splinters and for thorns.
But tears are naught
compared to what
made silence of a storm.

— TURIN SONG OF THE
WAHKEEN

"There's no way," I said. "There's no way this man can cook better than Kinran."

"It's true," said Marmot, as if he knew Kinran and could measure the two against each other. "Kheze is the better cook. Makes goat as tender as bison sirloin with a heat like a ricito pepper. And he's probably only a little older than you — people say he's good enough to open a place in Rucost!"

"What does that mean?"

"I don't know, but it sounds nice!"

Marmot had been giving me the details on many of the

Hanallta's inhabitants, but I wasn't sure a list of people's names and the respective trades practiced would do me much good. Jepi wove the nicest-looking baskets, but they didn't hold much before falling apart. Wren got her nickname by attempting to teach the small birds to carry messages, but it didn't work out so well. Larevit learned to make wine from Rucosti traders and has been at it ever since.

None of these people seemed to have any connection with Moddimok. But after he'd told me about the tunnels in Mother's Hall, I thought I might find something worthwhile if I listened closely and waited.

"You know what?" he told me. "You should visit him. Kheze cooks for just about anyone. He and Hegira are alike in that way — he even uses her vegetables for the most part, since hers are the healthiest. Takes whatever people can pay him for the meal. Maybe he can tell you more about what you need to know."

"I'll be sure to do that," I told him, wondering if I truly was wasting my time talking to a child.

"You get a great view of the lower valleys if you look out of his windows just after sunset."

"*After* sunset? Wouldn't I just see darkness?" I asked.

"You'd be surprised what you can see in the dark."

He said it flatly, but there was a subtle gravity that caught my attention. I wished he'd tell me outright if something was important, but he seemed to enjoy pulling at people — not like Rangrim's manipulation, more like it was a game to play.

"Sooner or later Rangrim will insist to know just who it is that keeps telling me these things," I told him.

"Insist?" he asked wisely.

"Well, *demand*, I guess. And I don't think she'll believe that a pest from Hegira's sacha is a know-it-all."

"Hmm. Well, you two will just have to piece it together on your own," he said with a cheeky smile.

It was obvious enough to me: intimate knowledge of the secret tunnels in Mother's Hall, a brazen confidence, doesn't ever seem to be in a hurry to get anywhere, and he threw himself into a hiding spot when the Rangrim's attendants arrived. He was the son of someone in Moddimok's court, feckless and finding entertainment in my company. But if he was happy with the illusion of mystery, I had no purpose in breaking it.

"I'll make sure Kheze knows you're coming for dinner," said Marmot.

I SAT ON THE GRASS OF THE HANALLTA, WATCHING A WRITHING pack of animals with a grin on my face.

The dog had found plenty of its kind here. Those of the Turin were just as large in body and mane, just as eager to wrestle, jowls wide and grasping at the necks of their brethren in the wriggling tides of play. He would run after his quarry, then they would stop; he would drop down low on his legs, then sprint away in his own turn as the lure for the chase.

It'd been too long — since our journey through the grasses, since we'd been split by the blade of thundering bison and failed in finding our companion. Ikoda and her four dogs walked out of the village. Two of the five returned. I was glad, now, that he found his own kind. I imagine it felt like the home we'd built in our new companions, where Avid and my mother were now. I thought warmly of returning.

I saw in the edge of my sight that Rangrim was approaching from the west. She was alone and covered in the mountain's red dust. She stopped a hundred feet away and motioned for me to meet her where she stood.

A private conversation, then.

I began the short walk, and the dog followed me. But as we neared the daughter of Moddimok, the dog suddenly slowed, brought his head low and growled in her direction. I stopped immediately. I'd learned, in the weeks-long walk from the scar of my village to the Rucosti Marchland to read his body language and react with trust. But Rangrim was familiar, and had never hurt the dog. I hadn't seen such a response elicited from him since the night she removed the hand of her prisoner.

I could not deny a change in the air — something precipitating a quiet sort of storm. It was as if the trail to The Hanallta, ruddy with the anger of our travels, had slid sickly into the valley. The change it brought was ethereal, insidious as it alighted with its bloody talons on the heart of Rangrim.

Her leer did not break from me. She stood in the expectation that all things would bend under her muscle, that I would join her there and that the dog's behavior meant nothing.

"Stay," I told the dog. I walked begrudgingly to her, telling myself she wouldn't dare attack me with so many of her people nearby. "You've been on the trail today?" I asked her innocently. "Seems you brought some back with you."

She said nothing. I followed her toward the sachas which ran along the extremities of the Hanallta's broad plain. Perhaps all powerful people assume their silences to be weighty, that their unspoken expectations bludgeon others into obedience, and I decided not to show her complete success. I relaxed my shoulders and walked coolly. Confidence kills coercion — at least that's what I told myself.

We reached a point that jutted proudly out above the

grassland void below, that cut a sheer wall through the sachas and came to a sharp awn of stone beyond. She looked uncomfortable. Before, in the foothills, when she brought me to speak before the statues of Grim and Senna, there was little warning before she became angry. Seeing such obvious emotion and discomfort on her face put me on an edge that felt just as dangerous as the one at my feet.

"Do you have my next dose?" I asked, walking confidently up to the edge. She'd never know I'd spent years with my toes over the precipice of a great drop.

"I grow impatient, Rennik," she responded. "My mother has been warped, and you, for all your magic, cannot tell me why." Her feet were planted firmly. She stood between me and the Hanallta. I stood with my back to the drop.

"I'm trying to—"

"You're playing with animals."

"And which hand of mine will you take because of it?" I managed to get in, raising my voice. Her eyes narrowed. "I am learning your people. I cannot put the pieces together unless I find them first, and they seem to be scattered among the entire Hanallta. Perhaps access to the books you mentioned would give me what I need."

"I cannot give you access yet."

"Then you must accept my reading of potters and ironsmiths."

"And what secret wisdoms did they hold? What did they have to say about my mother, about me and my past? Did you manage to solve the mystery with a lesson in charcoals?"

"What I managed to do," I said, achieving a level tone, "was determine how much of their trade has changed lately. Did you know an entire mine your people work in the southern foothills has been quietly taken over by a Rucosti guild? They think Moddimok let it happen."

"And I'm telling you she wouldn't. She *couldn't* do something like that so simply."

There was something new in her face. The coiled-snake patience she had was now the agitation of biting midges, quick, imprecise, and unpredictable. I sought for the source of this change and saw nothing.

"Rangrim," I said softly, my hands pacifying before me. "I'm willing to bet that practicing patience was easier before you returned. Even when you knew your mother was changed, it felt different with a great distance between you and your home. And now that it's put in your face every day—"

"Your magics told you of the hidden passage in my quarters," she interjected. "I was wrong before to assume someone had told you. There is no one who would know."

"Rangrim—" I tried.

"—So it appears that you *choose* to divine such secrets in the smoke while leaving others untouched. You need Senna's Ward. I'm the only one permitted to give it to you. You're stringing me along, Rennik, as you search for your fictional sorceress."

"That's not true—"

"There's a story we Turin have," she continued, "that I don't believe the Achare would tell."

"And what story is that, Rangrim?" I asked, incredulous as I walked from the edge of the drop to her left side. The air was tempestuous here, whipping one way, then the other, once warm, then cool, then still and quiet. She was historically impatient and borderline explosive, but my instincts told me something was different now. Sometimes the best way to weather a storm is to let it speak.

"The story of Raven," she said. "She was not as she currently is. Raven was Dremma's most prized creation, and in her love gave her deceit enough to escape hungry Drakka. So Raven came to the earth wearing *every* color; not as a spectacle, but sewn to the very seeming of creation. Raven wore the precious white petals of the sego lily, dressed in snows and starlight; she donned the deep emerald of pines and pastures, became viridian vale and crimson stone. None could see her, for she was the world."

As Rangrim spoke, I noticed a twitch in the veins of her neck. Her eyes became wide, surely in the unbridled anger she held within her.

"But Drakka's hungry flock would find her in time," she continued. "There came one night a murderous storm upon the mountain, and Raven kept tight to her home in the high karsts of Ba Turin. Approaching her threshold came Crow, son of Drakka, eater of the dead. Hungry for her trust, Crow begged for shelter from the tempest. Kind Raven gladly made room in her karst den and was sure to offer a dinner of fresh vegetables and fruit with Crow.

"Crow took none of the fresh harvest and instead dropped deeply into feigned slumber. Raven left food for his breakfast, and she slept honestly.

"But Crow kept one eye open, waiting for lightning to strike down to the prairielands. Soon enough the Wahkeen sent a deadly bolt into the grasses below, and Crow wasted no time pushing Dremma's daughter, colorful Raven, into the pits of Kalanos."

She spoke now in a tight hiss, her throat squeezing the words violently from her. A tear began to form in her eye.

She brought me here, yet I was a parasitic guest. She held the axe of altitude above my head, yet I was the threat. I thought back to that morning on the trail to the Hanallta. "How can a man transform so quickly?" I'd asked her then.

But Rangrim wasn't hiding her identity. I felt myself leaning away, like a child with a dog who'd suddenly grown tense.

"The tongues of immolation could not stretch to Raven before she spread her wings to save herself, but here her most treasured powers of survival conspired against her. Her feathers, changing in their cleverness to match their surroundings, found nothing but the black smoke of burning prairies, of dismay and deception. She flew for days trying to find her way back home. And so black smoke she forever became.

"Crow left the karst, feeling his job well done, turning Dremma's precious work into fair game for his wicked father. No longer would the wonderous colors of the world roll in wisps upon her feathers. No longer would creatures of the mountain fail to spot her. She hungered now not for green growth and fruit, but for the red flesh of Drakka's design, the inevitable color of the living."

Rangrim stepped toward me. The toe of her boot dug into the earth. Her eyes shook, unblinking as the words left her.

"Crow cackled as he descended into the home he'd burned."

I felt the wicked winds of the drop at my back.

"Rangrim," I started, kneading my fingers into their palms and trying to stay collected. "If I didn't know any better, I'd think you were going to push me."

And I walked right up to the edge, I thought, seeing the idiocy of my actions.

"I simply don't understand, Rennik, why Crow would betray she who fed him. Why he would take for granted the open doors of her home and the trust she gave."

"I'm going to help your mother," I told her. "I swear to

you, Rangrim, I want to help, but magic and investigation take time."

She took a step toward me.

"If not me, who?" I asked with a stone in my throat. "Who else brought you Crattle, helped *you* into the Hanallta? Who else has been worthy of your trust if not me?"

She hesitated, eyes wide and wet. Her hands shook at her sides. She opened her mouth and forced the words from her chest, croaking as they came, wrestling with a strong opposition. I was reminded of a starry night one year past, stood between two pyres with the wind in my throat.

She managed a single sentence.

"Perhaps I can give you more time."

She turned and walked away.

She had pivoted completely in a moment's passing. I stood still, too startled by the notes of something unusual in her voice and body to do anything but stare.

And I realized then that her eyes were not the eyes of fury.

Something had changed.

She was afraid.

11

SHAPES OF EARTH & SKY

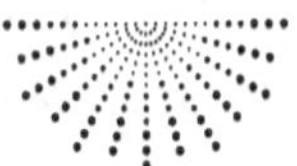

I don't like the dark. You can't build anything
without at least a little light.

— AVID

Kheze's home was covered in color.

The walls were a collection of marigold, turquoise, and soft strawberry reds that seemed to suggest a hazy sunset. The colors traveled to the ends of the outside wall and became varied in their imagery, now a river, now a mountain, now a sacha with enormous white flowers.

"Rennik," said a deep voice from the door. I nearly jumped out of my shoes, still on edge from my encounter with Rangrim earlier that day. In truth, it was a relief that his house wasn't built near the vale's edge; I felt at any time that Rangrim might charge forth and throw me to my death. Having followed the images to the back of his home, I stepped around to the front to find the speaker.

He stood a little taller than me, and his forearms seemed to be as thick as my neck. I wondered if this man painted these pictures — strange how a set of arms so huge could make such delicate movements. His hair was shaved to stubble. He wore a simple shirt, no shoes, and a smile that seemed fixed in place.

Why do good cooks always seem so happy?

"You must be Kheze," I said. "I appreciate the welcome."

"And I appreciate getting to meet someone who isn't Turin. Please, come in." He gestured through the door, and I entered.

While the outside of his home boasted sights to behold, the inside was filled with the greatest smells I couldn't entirely identify. There was something savory floating about, salt, something with a bit of bite that seemed vaguely familiar, and a woody, autumnal scent that crooned around corners and set itself warmly on my shoulders. I sat at the table at his invitation.

"I was admiring the painting outside," I told him as he leaned over a small wooden countertop. "Is that your work?"

"No," he said, laughing above the food he prepared. "My daughter. She's an insatiable artist."

"She must keep you busy appraising her work," I said.

He shook his head. "She's never asked for my feedback, and a good thing, too. I couldn't draw a snake in the dirt. She was actually the one to tell me about you — she mentioned you're from the plains?"

"I am," I told him. "I'm actually here to look for a certain — ginger!"

"...What?"

"I've been trying to identify that smell. Is that ginger you're frying?"

"Yes," he chuckled out, "this is ginger. But the rest is nearly done." He stepped over to some sort of oven built into his wall. It was sealed with a clay panel on iron hinges, about three feet tall. Inside was a modest fire, above which sat two pieces of goat on a small wooden scaffold. Kheze took the meat and placed each piece on a clay plate. "I prefer sometimes to cook Rucosti-style. It's a bit more fun to produce a few big meals rather than many small morsels throughout the day."

He placed the plate before me. On it was a pile of small orange beads drizzled with a red sauce — the source of the woody smell, I realized — all atop a few dark green leaves. Next to that was the goat rubbed with a collection of spices.

"Salmon eggs on dried seaweed with rose haw sauce," he said, pointing to the orange beads. He gestured to the meat. "Goat loin with salt, black pepper, and ginger."

"This..." I started. "...This is incredible. I've never seen food that looked too nice to touch."

Kheze laughed and dipped a wide wooden spoon into the salmon eggs. "It's meant to be disturbed, don't worry. Have you ever seen Kazel sand art?"

"No," I said, surprised he might have.

"They call them 'nohu'. They have these huge, flat slabs of stone they dedicate for the practice. They dye their sands — not sure how — and then make complex circular patterns on the stone. Some of them take days to finish."

The goat was so tender and smoky I nearly forgot to listen. The ginger and black pepper would bite subtly at the inside of my mouth, and though it wasn't exactly the same, I was reminded of takar from home.

"And then," he continued, "when they finish it, and a few people have looked at it for a few moments, they remove these little cloth walls on the edge of the stone slab and let the wind destroy it."

"Sounds like a lot of work for no payoff." I imagined

living a life that didn't require constant movement, constant finding-of-food, constant fearing-for-life.

"They see something sacred in it. But it's not far off from cooking like this, I think. It's a lot of work and a lot of learning over the years, but the result is something beautiful and short-lived that makes people happy."

"This makes me *very* happy," I told him. "But you can't eat sand. This, at least, has a purpose."

"Does everything need a purpose? Can't something just be beautiful? You said yourself you were afraid to touch the food. You clearly valued it for its beauty before its purpose."

"True," I said. "But I also wouldn't let the wind take it." It was strange, I realized, to be speaking this way with a man close to my age — to share words and ideas without sharing enmity, or tension at the very least. Kheze seemed to be as warm as Hegira, and far less crass.

A girl no older than Avid stepped into the house.

"Is there any goat left?" she asked.

"I wrapped a bit of mine in seaweed for you, just over there," Kheze told her. The girl walked out of view for a moment and returned with her food in hand. "This is my daughter, Owasa. Owasa, this is Rennik. He's a northerner."

She was big for her age, taller than Avid and broad-shouldered. She clearly inherited her father's predilection for strength and size. "Mother's welcome," she said, so quietly I almost didn't hear her. She turned back to her father. "Can I go to the cave?" she asked him.

"It's going to be dark soon, Owasa."

"That's kind of the point," she said.

"Alright, well...just be careful."

Owasa jumped excitedly out the door and took off.

"She's only eleven," said Kheze, "but she's a talented painter. She has a secret recipe she mixes, won't tell anyone how to do it. Whatever it is, it makes the paint light up at night. Only lasts for a little while, but it's certainly something."

"That's incredible. I wonder if you could make a sort of torch out of it."

"It's not a strong light. Probably just good for things *without* purpose," he said with a grin.

"Seems like she takes after you quite a bit."

"No," he said, "at least not yet. That painting business is all her mother coming out in her...She'd have loved to see how much they're alike."

I nodded in polite understanding, and he continued.

"She was caught in a cold wind higher up in the peaks," he said. "Sometimes Owasa will go speak to her in the mountain, but...it certainly isn't the same as having a mother. The dead might hear us in our caves, but it's not like having them here...the mountains just seem to..."

"Swallow people whole?" I spoke from memory.

"Yes," he said. "They do."

I'D ASKED HIM WHAT HE'D LIKE IN RETURN FOR THE MEAL. "IT'S hard to find people who can hold a deep conversation. There was value enough in meeting you, Rennik. Come back sometime."

I reminded myself never to eat a Rucosti-sized meal before doing physical labor. My entire body was slow with the fullness of it, and the rose haw on my breath made me want to sit and lounge, not explore the darkening Hanallta. I was battling lethargy outside of Kheze's home when something in the lengthening fingers of sunset caught my eye.

And I wondered if Marmot knew I would see the woman.

She wore a dark cloak and insinuated herself into twilight shadows a quarter-mile behind the house, skimming along the surface of the short vale grass.

You'd be surprised what you can see in the dark.

I headed in her direction, keeping my distance and keeping her in sight. Walking around in a dark cloak at night clearly meant she was avoiding attention, but where would she look to be sure she was alone? Behind her? Toward the homes of the Hanallta to her left? I decided to stay back in her path — that way she wouldn't turn and find me silhouetted by light from people's late cooking fires.

I kept my distance for a half mile before doubts slowed me down. How was I going to follow her when the sun completely set? What if she's simply leaving the Hanallta to speak to the dead in the mountain, like Kheze said Owasa would do?

But Marmot had been strangely keen with his previous information. I had to put a little faith in him.

Soon, when we were out of sight of the Hanallta, the woman stepped around a large wall of stone and vanished. I quickened my pace and peered carefully around the corner. The slate-gray colors of coming night washed over the stone. She was gone, it seemed, without a trace.

I was about to turn away when I noticed something else.

A small shape crept slowly from the stone wall, made its way soundlessly toward me, and as I tucked myself away, I could just make out Owasa sneaking back toward the Hanallta with a pack at her side.

Where did you come from?

I took a few steps along her path until I saw it: the mouth of a cave, no more than four feet high, hidden cleverly by the natural shape of the wall. There was the sound of running water echoing distantly within it, so I assumed it was big enough not to find me bumping straight into my quarry in the dark. I took a deep breath and ducked into the cave.

The floor was mostly flat, though I detected a slight rise as I walked. There was room enough to stand — I kept a hand a few inches in front of my face regardless, as I had no idea what was in front of me.

I turned back to look for the entrance and saw nothing.

My heart raced. There was no indication of the size of this cave, whether it was a single vast room, a series of tunnels waiting to trap me, a natural hall that led to a deep pit. My chest shook as anxiety set in place, my eyes darting for sight by which to anchor myself. I knelt slowly and set my hands flat against the ground, taking an innate comfort in knowing I was, in fact, standing on solid stone. I felt a vertigo like that of my visions from the Delkhi, a spinning void that beat me into submission. I cursed myself for the foolhardy mistake of wandering in the dark.

Then, there was fire.

The torch seemed overly bright in the inky space it occupied, but now the shape of the cave was revealed. The ceiling appeared to be a dozen feet above me, at least where the light could touch. The walls of the cave were inconsistent, hugging the path where I knelt, widening a bit past that, and coming to a sort of close beyond the torch-bearer.

The woman pulled back her hood, and the face of Moddimok's advisor appeared above the cloak.

She stood at the edge of running water, deep enough to look black even though I knew it was entirely clear. Only someone with a stern familiarity of this cave could have walked through the dark and stopped impossibly at the edge of a river.

You walked here in the dark, I thought to myself. *So why the torch?*

I'd brought neither my axe nor my bow, but I'd kept a knife on my person at all times since arriving with Rangrim. I checked that it was there, and I waited to see what this woman would do.

"It's been so long," she said into the water. She sat, set the torch next to her and balanced it on the end of its handle, which seemed to be broad, flat, and carved for the exact purpose of standing on its own. "I spent so long learning her logic, divining what reason she would apply to each problem set before her. And when she denounced you as a traitor, I...I did my best to believe her...to convince myself that her reason was sharper than my years with you. I justified the exiling of my own sister, and that is the knife I must sleep with at night, the decision that cuts at my thoughts and keeps me awake.

"But now..." the woman was sobbing. "Now she's become much more undone. I don't know what it is, but something found a loose thread in her and pulled, began her unravelling until she was awful to her own people, to her own home. I worry what she'll become when she is entirely disentangled from herself. I worry what power does in the hands of the paranoid. I worry that the first break in her sanity was your banishment, that I should have known you and her well enough to see what should not be...I worry I could have saved you from the Shadowlands."

She sat in silence for a moment. Her arm found a pack under her cloak and brought it out.

"Forgive me. I know this bloody stone cares not for my confession. But I have been a coward in the midst of your killers. You are the ruins of mutiny, but now I see your cause was right. Over the waters of your wound I promise...the house of Ba Turin will falter under its own weight. Familiar will be the hand to hold the dagger. The hillock will see the mountain fall, and those who acted for their purposes will groan for the burial they deserve.

"I know you can't hear me from here, but...I hope what they say about this river is true. I hope what they say about the Shadowlands isn't...I hope you've found what I've left for you, and...I hope you know that I still love you."

She held the pack lightly above the river, its dangling strap darkening upon the water's surface.

"I'm sorry."

She dropped the pack into the water and watched it disappear.

I did my best to trace its path and saw it taken beneath a stony lip that swallowed the water into the mountain. I realized this river, nearly fifteen feet across in this cave, came from and returned to somewhere beneath our feet. I remembered the springs Hegira mentioned and wondered just how extensive this river was.

She picked up her torch and turned in my direction. I pressed myself into an alcove in the wall. I could speak to her, ask her about Moddimok and what she's witnessed. But there was simply no way to justify scaring her.

Hearing what she had to say was inarguably beneficial, and finding this cave certainly piqued my interest, but I couldn't help feeling the shame Avid hopefully felt when he used to spy on Gatsi.

The woman passed by. As she did, I made note of the path to the outside world.

I let a few minutes pass, and I exited the cave.

THE VALE WAS A CHAR-BLACK PLANE MADE BLACKER BY THE lacking moon. A few stars managed to poke momentarily from beyond the thin sheet of clouds, but I was left to navigate back on my own.

I had so many questions. I decided to split up my thinking and consider one thing at a time.

Moddimok's advisor wanted her chieftain dead. At least thats what it seemed. She said something pulled a loose thread...and I couldn't help but think of Rangrim, too. I needed to find a way to speak to the advisor. I needed to know which hand was unravelling Moddimok.

Owasa was in the cave and either didn't want to be seen or didn't want to disturb the advisor. There must be something in the cave she uses for paint. I shook this thought away; there were much more useful things to go over.

Marmot knew about Rangrim's childhood, which I attributed to his probable status as a courtier's child. Then he'd pointed me to the advisor, and for some reason I trusted his insight. But there was something strange about his ability to give me the words to say and put me in the right place at the right time that I couldn't let go of. Gatsi had once cautioned me, though, that three is a pattern and two is a superstition. Perhaps the boy was lucky, or clever enough to be vague, half-right, and interpreted conveniently.

The advisor — I really needed to learn her name — said she hoped her sister had found what she'd left. I wondered if there were tunnels beyond what I'd seen in that cave, something else to explore. I needed to find someone who knew anything about the secrets of this mountain. I decided my first course of action in the morning would be to investigate through Rangrim how best to approach the advisor.

Finally, as I was starting to worry I'd never see proof of my heading in the right direction, I saw the impression of a house in the darkness.

But something was wrong.

Some of the stars on the horizon were now uncovered by cloud and quite clear to me, but they behaved strangely. Instead of tucking behind the building, they seemed to trace its shape in three dimensions. As I came closer, my perspective on the stars changed, and they seemed to move as I walked. One swung slowly right, another stayed put, and the entire lot of them seemed to be spacing themselves out right before my eyes. And then my thoughts caught up with reality.

Those aren't stars. It's paint.

I approached Kheze's home to find it dappled in the portents of yesterday. Could the smoke have been leading me here?

The echoes in the deepest wells of my understanding told me that this wasn't it, that it wasn't this simple.

But as the constellations I'd seen in the smoke played out patiently before me, I knew that Owasa had seen them too.

12

NAME & NATURE

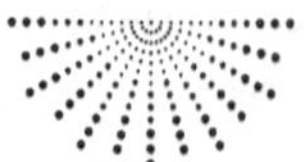

Some scholars go so far as to question the validity of country. What truly makes one individual different from another? Their place of birth? The color of their skin? Their language, their gods, their art?

— EXCERPT FROM REMI GRENFALLOW'S *PHILOSOPHY OF CRIME*

Owasa was a difficult person to find.

"Try the Sentinels," Kheze told me the next morning. "There are Rucosti traders coming up the trail today, and she probably went to see them arrive."

But it seemed the *only* child missing from the feet of the Sentinels was Owasa. Even Marmot waved at me from the gaggle of children, who were watching a few stubborn mules plod into the Hanallta carrying basic goods and apathy from Dellimair.

"She might be out west a little. The flowers there are

good for red paint!" suggested a parent overseeing the children. I made a note to visit the traders when I could, and made my way west.

There were indeed flowers — there was no Owasa.

"I wonder if she went to the springs on the other side of the Hogback!" suggested an old man with a basket of red petals.

There was indeed a spring; there were no hogs — and there was no Owasa.

"Maybe she dug a hole and fell in! I bet your dog could find her!" suggested a young girl that reminded me that not *every* child was full of useful secrets — though the dog did enjoy the fruit she offered.

I was circling back to Hegira's home, hoping she could grant some insight as to the whereabouts of Kheze's daughter, but I stopped short when I realized she was not alone. I turned to leave, wanting in no way to interrupt her.

But as I walked away, I heard the man speak through a window. "He certainly looks like Rangrim's typical mercenary fellow. I'm sorry you have to house him."

I felt an urge that became familiar in the days of my home village. When you can't have full conversations with many people, you tend to listen whenever you can. I stepped along the rocky wall that ran toward her house and perked an ear toward the window.

"...actually a very appreciative young man...unlike your sister." Hegira finished the sentence with a quiet and judgmental tone. I could practically hear her raise an eyebrow. "Rennik doesn't seem like a killer. And really, it doesn't seem like he likes her too much."

"How could you?" asked the man with a scoff.

"I get the impression he's some sort of hostage, or that they have some sort of deal. Either way, she seems to only drop off Senna's Ward when he's not around, and when she did come to find him, the tension was obvious. Anyone could've picked up on it — even your emotionally stunted si—"

"—Yes, yes, my emotionally stunted sister," the man finished.

"How is old Rissa these days?"

"Sedentary and available."

"Figures."

"What does it seem like he wants, this man from the plains?" he continued, pointedly moving the conversation back to true north.

"He mentioned something about looking for someone. Doesn't look like he'd have family here."

"Doesn't look Turin at all," the man agreed.

"I think he'll tell me in time," she told him. "He's sweet, but he looks like he's seen a few ghosts already. He gets so quiet — which I don't mind at all — but..."

"...but?" the man prompted.

"Well, he has this strange habit. I've noticed it both times he's helped me in the sacha, or when he's out looking over at my garden...he just...talks."

"You just said he was quiet."

"He is, really, but there have been a few moments where I'll think he's talking to his dog, or talking to himself, but he seems to have entire conversations on his own."

"Well," the man said, "everyone talks to themselves sometimes. He's just thinking aloud."

"No, that's not quite..." Hegira hesitated. "I was curious about it, once. I don't think he knew I was in the maize, nearby enough to listen, but I heard him speak, then start to say something and stop like he was interrupted, then... *respond.*"

"...that is strange, I suppose."

"But when I looked down at him, from where I stood in the maize, it was just him standing there. The dog was running around elsewhere, and he was just looking around with an arrow nocked, searching for vermin to kill, holding one half of a conversation entirely on his own."

I felt my stomach tighten.

Marmot so often knelt down in the crops, perhaps she just hadn't seen his small figure against the plants. No. She looked down from the sacha above us. She would have seen him. Why was she speaking like this? It was almost as if...

My mind raced with sharp memories of claw and fang, of a void figure that swallowed the night, of the cold waters that followed me from the heart of Kalanos to the Rucosti Marchland, of a fire fading fast in my blurred and dying eyes. I saw Callisgrim, just before her death, searching for the Shiver in the pines.

As if she couldn't see him...

IT TOOK A FEW MINUTES TO WRESTLE MYSELF FROM PANIC. These moments came often enough after leaving my home. My lungs would shake, become shallow and choke as if I were a crying child. My hands would turn to trembling animals, and I would weep for a thousand unnamed sorrows brought forth by an inescapable feeling of helplessness. I let myself fall slowly against the stone, stuck my hands in my hair, and made myself small.

Luckily, I managed to stay quiet and let Hegira and the man finish their conversation.

My panic turned to a resolute sort of anger, a determination tinged with the betrayal of a trusted friend.

I struck out to find Marmot.

The children were still grouped near the Sentinels. The younger ones were making noises borrowed from the mules they'd seen and were encumbering each other with bags and pouches. The older children were betting on the goods the traders had brought back to the Hanallta. Marmot was there, laughing at the children playing "mule". He stood directly in the middle of a conversation two children were having.

They looked through him as though he were not there.

Then came Owasa, giggling with dried paint on her hands, finally out of whatever inadvertent hiding place she'd been in. As an older child, she was headed past the game and toward the children her age, but she stopped, looked at Marmot, and exchanged a few words with him. None of the other children joined in on the conversation.

The flock was eventually broken by the winds of shallow attention and were sent in the wild trajectories of childhood to every home, corner, and field of the Hanallta, each one running, skipping, or rolling after their own fashion. As parents swooped down to collect their errant offspring, one man stopped directly next to Marmot, nearly smacking the boy's head as he lifted his hands to shield his eyes from the sun.

Marmot saw me, smiled, and began walking my way.

I focused on breathing. I focused on what I knew and did not know. I focused on the fact that this child, if I could call him that, had yet to show me any ill-intent.

He came within five feet of me and stopped.

"You look funny," he said.

"We should talk," I managed to say with only a slight waver.

"Okay! But I've got some things to do. Want to walk with me?"

I agreed, and in the middle of a perfectly unassuming day, I followed an invisible child through his daily routine.

BEHIND A HOME THAT WAS STRANGE TO ME, HE FOUND A LARGE waxed basket and strapped it to his back. There was no one around to witness the act, but I wondered if the basket would have seemingly levitated of its own volition, or simply vanished from sight.

The next destination was a cold mountain spring, sheltered above by a rocky overhang that almost qualified as a cave. He stopped at the water, filled his basket, and shouldered a burden that seemed too great for a child.

He was a Shiver. The only other one I'd seen had slain Macha and stalked me in the night. In our legends they were the ruin of heroes, the quiet killers of innocence, love, and life. If all things existed in duality, Shivers were the total atrophy of good.

But Marmot wasn't like that. He wasn't a malicious predator of pitch and suffocation. He was a boy who hauled water to gardens, pruned leaves, and found happiness in the people to whom he was a phantom.

He knew something was different as I followed him quietly. After only a moment in Hegira's first terrace he stopped, shed his smile, and let the basket land softly on the grass with both of his tiny hands on its sides. A hard silence tensed, the kind indigenous to the space between people at this sort of precipice.

"What are you?" I asked him.

"What do you think I am?" A grin teased at one corner of his mouth. His eyes remained intent on mine.

"I don't have a name for your kind," I lied. "There's something similar, something that's followed me through the grasses for over a year — something only I can see. It travels with mountain lions. It *killed* Rangrim's allies and nearly killed the dog. It is a dark and evil thing, so forgive me if I don't find pleasure in your game." I asked again, this time giving each word its proper weight. "What are you?"

"Let's begin with what I am not." He hefted the basket, waddled awkwardly with its bulk in front of him, and resumed his tending to the terrace. "I am not a dark and evil thing. I'm just...Marmot. I tend to the crops and watch the funny people of the Hanallta."

"The Kalanosi would call you a Shiver."

"Strange. I'd call myself Kalanosi."

"Surely you understand the difference."

"What good is a name from people who can't organize what they see?" he asked, ignoring my comment. "For all you know, this 'something' that's followed you is entirely different than me. It and I could be as different as a blowfish and a turkey. You can't just decide that everything that isn't you belongs to a single name."

"What is your true name?" I asked.

"Marmot."

"That's just what I've called you," I said. "What did you call yourself before we met?"

Marmot smiled and shook his head. "A name is a difficult thing, Rennik. There are true names that exist in each living being, but they are rarely used. You do not have my name — you may not even know your own. But you say 'Marmot', and I listen. You say 'dog', and the dog comes, never mind the fact that his name is Karay."

As he finished his sentence, the dog promptly sat and cocked his head, one ear perked up halfway at attention.

"Karay?" I asked. The dog turned his attention to me.

"Rennik," said Marmot. I looked back to him. "See? You can call people anything if they respond to it. Most names are nothing more than smoke and spiderweb, but the webs will pull you all the same."

I shrugged off his philosophizing and pressed at a different angle. "How old are you? Really?"

"I don't know," said Marmot, this time without his cheeky tone. "I remember most of the people who've been here."

"Here? On the Hanallta? Most of the people...*ever*?" I asked.

He nodded after a moment. "Yes, I think so. It's why I like Hegira so much. Her parents were...awful. The fact that she turned out so incredibly kind is a miracle on par with bristlecones and sunrises."

"And the success of her sacha..." I started, looking to his hands as they groomed the stalks of maize before us.

"Don't blame me," he said. "My help would be irrelevant if not for her hard work."

I remembered a day long ago, when Gatsi revealed to me the secrets of the Delkhi, drew back a curtain and exposed the roots puppeteering my home. Even then I had been stupefied only momentarily before I'd started in on my questions. Here, too, with Marmot bowing stalks as if to pull back the veil of mortal perception, I descended into the comfort of inquiry.

"The Rucosti worship a figure named Ityx—"

"Well, they *decided* to name it Ityx," he interrupted. "Imagine the audacity it takes to lasso all the positive feelings of the world, shape its clay to look like you, and give it a name."

"Okay, yes, fine, but this is exactly what I'm asking. Are you..." I wrestled with the question. It felt clumsy on my tongue, too elementary to ask, but no other words stood at the ready. "Are you a god?"

"Another name, another label, another attempt to simplify and organize. I've known the lives of thousands, Rennik, and you're one of the more clever ones. But even you are fixed in the crooked groove of language."

"I don't know how else to understand you," I told him. "I only have the words I know, Marmot — you must understand that."

He sighed. "Are you a bean stalk?"

"What?"

"Just answer the question."

"No," I said. "I'm not a bean stalk."

"Are you a person?"

"Yes."

"How do you know?"

I recognized the feeling of my old mentor's lessons and took a moment to think. "I know I'm not a bean stalk because I don't share any of those qualities. I've experienced both bean stalks and people. I can perceive the differences."

"Are you a mule?"

"No."

"Are you more like a mule than a bean stalk?"

"Yes," I said, growing impatient. "We are animals."

"Are you Rucosti?" he asked.

"No."

"In a short span, you've given me a sweeping organization. People make piles of information to form their understanding of the world and themselves. There is a group you call 'animals'; the bean stalk is excluded. There is a group you call 'people'; the mule is excluded. Mules are not 'people', Rucosti are not 'Kalanosi', and so on and so forth until you find yourself, the smallest unit of knowing. You are able to know yourself because you've met many, many people, many mules, many bean stalks and languages and birds and days and nights and loves and pains."

He stood with his fingers laced around a stalk, staring inertly at the infinitely small patterns of its grain. The mountain winds ran their hands politely over the terraces, pushing visibly across thousands of stalks, thousands of leaves, green and gold and indulgently beautiful in the sun of midday.

"But you haven't," I said, finishing his thought.

"No," he said. "Never have I had the luxury of meeting one of my kind. I cannot tell you what I am or where I belong because I have precious little context for my own existence. I have been watching over the Hanallta for as long as I remember, and that is what I know."

"Why can I see you?" I asked. "Owasa and I both."

"Because the Mountain Mother wills it," he said, cautiously dropping to the next terrace. "And no, Rennik, she isn't a god. I couldn't tell you what a god is, but I imagine she's quite a bit like something you've experienced before."

"There was a tree," I told him, "in my home."

"Doubtful it was simply a tree."

"It was...I don't know, exactly, but I've come to consider it a sort of heart."

"Of what body?"

"Of the plains, maybe. A sort of center for the great movements of the entire region. A herd of bison, a herd of oryx from far away, and my own people...we gathered there like blood to the heart, involuntarily, naturally..."

"And now it's pumped you away," he said quietly. "You know, you remind me of an oryx."

"Why? I'm tall, and my bow looks like their horns?"

"I suppose that as well. But it's your movements that borrow from the oryx — not the small movements of walking, eating, and holding yourself high — I mean the greater movements. The trajectory you were given when cast away from your home. You are, like so many animals, drawn by the magnetism in the greater beings of our world."

"Greater beings?"

"I think the Mountain Mother is quite a bit like this tree of yours."

"So these Turin who worship the mountain — their god is *real?*"

"The Mountain Mother is very real. What they call her, what traits they create for their fiction, is all in their own collective head. But there is a will to the mountain, and that will comes from her."

"Then why reject the word 'god'? If this is a real thing with a will—"

"Weren't you listening? Because anything with a name is a fictional version of its true self. Names are dragged through the minds of people and pick up all sorts of assumptions that are difficult to shake. The longer a word or name exists, the less it represents the truth."

"So Ityx..."

Marmot shrugged. "It's just a name for an idea someone had once, or maybe something real that's been forgotten."

"Marmot," I began after I digested the conversation. "I may have been tasked to help Rangrim in her goals here, but the true purpose for my arrival is to find a woman I was told of, a woman who is...like me."

"Like you how?"

"I think it has everything to do with my experience with the Delkhi — the tree — and the fact that I can see Shiv... that I can see things like you."

He nodded his boyish head wisely. "I know who it is you seek. But first, you need to know...you aren't the only one to see me. You already know of Owasa, of course, but there are a few here who were plucked from the realm of death and returned to this world with its gifts. Most don't know this of themselves, and any who do have the tact to hide these qualities in order to keep their lives."

"But one of them must be the woman I seek!"

Marmot shook his head. "No. No, the one you seek has hidden herself away entirely. Hidden from your kind, hidden from the sun, from winds and want, from rains and reason. She is the only one who communes with the Mountain Mother herself, and she is rarely seen in the Hanallta."

"Please, Marmot," I said. "Ba Turin is immense. Tell me where to find her."

The ancient boy looked to the top of the terrace and scanned the close horizon with a quiet sadness. "I think I need a favor first," he said. "I think I need your help, Rennik." His face fell, like he already regretted what had to be said.

"You're an invisible person, Marmot. You know this place better than anyone. What could I possibly do that you could not?"

"You've come here to find someone like you, and truly there is one. But you are not the only one with a match in the Hanallta."

"You aren't the only one like *you* here?" I asked. "You said you had no context for your own kind."

"There is one other here," he said in a low voice. I thought I detected a tremble, a note of fear running cold under his words. "It used to follow in Moddimok's close shadow and whisper horrible things in her ear."

The chill in his voice found its way into me. Could this Shiver be the cause of her behavior?

"And now?" I asked.

"And now it follows Rangrim."

Realization fell steadily upon my shoulders.

"I'm surprised you didn't see it," Marmot continued, "in Mother's Hall. Or when Rangrim came to speak to you above the sacha."

"Above the sacha? Two days ago?"

Marmot nodded. "It was standing right next to her, wearing a white tunic with green on the sleeves."

I thought back to Rangrim's attendants. They were dressed finely, painted in black and white, they watched us from a distance...and not one of them was the person Marmot described. I remembered Marmot throwing himself against the wall of the terrace to hide. I remembered the dog's strange behavior that day and his recent distrust of Rangrim.

I thought back to the strange moment when Rangrim threatened me at the edge of a lethal drop, when her throat seized and her message twisted over itself. And a single, horrible understanding came to me.

Marmot wanted me to find a Shiver I couldn't see.

"And I think the only way to do get rid of it is, well...*I think you have to kill Rangrim.*"

13
LEFT TO DIE

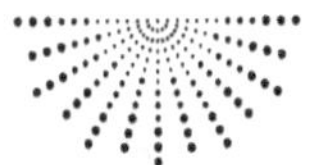

An ear should give no credence to the hasty words
of man; harken to the patience in the voices of
the trees.

— DRUIDIC PROVERB

Ciqala's failure was born of rigidity.

Had he been flexible, his decisions would have been adaptations to new problems rather than an affirmation of his status. He, and many others, would still be alive.

I had to be flexible. I had to accept the uprooting of my comfort and make a move in order to live. Achare are nomadic upon the earth; so too must I be nomadic in my understanding.

Marmot is a Shiver. He is a creature who exists among us and considers himself Kalanosi, but is visible, it seems, only to those who've come close to death. He is the stuff of fiction, but he spoke to me. He felt fear and worry, had habits and favorite people. I couldn't help but wonder, though, of his connection to the Delkhi. It saved me from death, but left one of my feet in an exclusive world of shadow men and immortal children.

Ba Turin was calm. I had discovered in my wandering a singular glassy tarn whose sheer banks were like the edges of my plateau. I was comfortable in the nostalgia of a place resurrected. It was a moment in which I could lie to myself, could believe in the selfish fiction in which there was no horde, no pale man, no magic, no blackened bone of home in the land of the Achare. The mountain water held an untouched fathom against which to measure myself.

I felt depth. I felt calm. I felt, for the first time in too long, truly and beautifully alone.

Karay lay near in gentle repose but made no blemish upon the quiet. His was a companionable solitude. The vale here was coated in short grass and scattered with bristlecone pines. The winds were slow, the plovers were quiet, and the sky had no clouds to carry.

As I stared, I imagined the tarn as a sort of mirror. It reflected not myself, but what I needed to see. And in it was a man scarred with the flames of obstinacy.

I will not become him.

Above me sat a raven at rest, its feathers shaggy and windblown. I wondered if it were not the same bird from before, consumer of Corde, dyed red in torrid alpenglow. If the value of a man were determined by the work he did with his hands, Corde was half-dead, tipping beyond the grasses like I had as a child.

I will not become him.

I just wish I knew who my enemy was. Marmot told me what it looked like, but what was its goal? What does it want with Rangrim and her mother? And most importantly — how do I stop it? There had to be alternatives to killing Rangrim, but Marmot told me Shivers like that attach to people, that they might be hurt if their host is killed. Regardless of her intentions with my life, I couldn't help but remember my own words from the past.

I'm not a killer.

Having no grasses in which to sink, I let myself go to the mountains. My breath journeyed over peaks, dipped into dizzying voids and returned to the unburdened prairies of my heart. It was an hour before that peace was invaded.

They came over the hills with weapons and white paint. Moddimok pierced the horizon, commanding a train of a dozen painted guards with the silent leash of authority. Dark sheaths held swords, saddles held bows, fists held reins in the skein of her power. Unseen but felt upon the air was the tumult of her throne, rippling always from the char-black feathers of her crown. She saw me at the water and directed her dark horse there.

I stood and bowed.

"Rennik," she began with an off-putting grin. "I would ask what interest a lowland mercenary has this far into the vale, but something tells me I'll be seeing you out here again."

"The interest of quiet, Chieftain. I find it easier to think when I am alone." She seemed to enjoy whatever mystery she alluded to, but I tried to show her only calm.

"Solitude," she replied, looking out into the empty skies. "A gift belonging to those without power. I envy you for your possession of quiet."

"If not for peace, Chieftain, what brings you here?"

"Peace indeed," she nodded, teasing at a laugh. "Peace in removal, but not of myself from people. I am here to remove someone *from* my people."

She laughed once, dark and low, upon seeing me tense. "Not you, Crow. Today is not your day to fear me."

"I find it wise to fear any who travel with bladed soldiers."

Moddimok nodded her pitiless face. "Wise indeed. That is the understanding of a survivor." She surveyed the area from which she'd come. "My greatest fight was just over that rise, you know. That was the night the Mountain Mother chose me as chieftain."

She looked at me so as to prompt the question.

"What fight was that, Chieftain?" I offered.

"Leaders of the Turin are not inheritors. We are champions, sojourners of the heights and winnowers of the weakness in ourselves. I was sent deep into Ba Turin to be hunted, as all chieftains were before me. Tradition dictates she who seeks to be chieftain must travel until Ba Turin attempts to consume them, whether maw of rock or tooth or talon they find. My journey was weeks long. Far too long. The mountains provided for me. Each turn I took was filled with food, each night found me in perfect shelter. Ba Turin favored me, but it was not spoiling I was after. I was angry with the Mother. I cursed and spat at her as many daughters do. Then, at night and upon my return, I found my challenge much closer to home.

"A *tankimatí*, mightiest of the mountain bears, stood resolute in my path. It did not sit, it did not stir, it did naught but stare as I came to the rise. I thanked the Mother for her fury and that day sat upon the Tempest Throne with blood on my hands and its head at my feet.

"So know, Rennik...whatever it is you contrive to do here in the home of the Turin, whatever work you weave without fear of justice...I've been killing in the dark since you were an inkling of Dremma's design."

She gazed smugly upon me from her horse. The dog had deigned to pick up its head but had not stood for the chieftain. It was hard to imagine the willow-thin frame of this woman killing something so fierce, but there was a fire in Moddimok that I dared not underestimate.

"Tell me of your accomplishments, lowlander," she commanded. "Where is your bear story?"

It was as if she were dueling with me. I felt myself rising to the challenge. "I once outran a bison mother in the grasses, hid from its heightened smell and left with my bones intact. I once led a friend and myself through a stampede while my enemies were consumed in its thunder. We left with our lives that day. I once saved my brother from a charging Kalanosi horde and came out on the other side."

"You ran, you left, you came out on the other side...Tell me — is the summation of your life found in fleeing?"

"You asked for accomplishments, Chieftain. I consider saving lives exactly that."

"Glory is grown in the fight, Crow. Not in the running."

"Then you'll find no glory in me."

"Pity," she said. "Though I expected none to begin with."

Chieftain Moddimok waved her fighters onward and trod toward her home. As soon as they were gone, I realized what she had said.

"She was out here to remove someone from her people..." I said out loud. Karay nudged my hand.

I traced the tracks of the horses and made my way deeper into the wild vale of Ba Turin.

I'D HEARD OF MOMENTS, EXPERIENCED IN THE EXTREME HEAT of the Kazel deserts, where the senses betray the mind. One can see water where there is none, feel hope when there is none, hear rain when the world is an angry clay oven.

I wonder if Marmot knew I would see the woman.

Moddimok's advisor, the woman who spoke to the lost in a secret cave, was bound and unmoving in the vicious sun of midday. The shadows over her face were cast not by cloud but by the ravenous vultures that circled above. They were black in wing and red upon the chest, stained by the generosity of their prey.

Moddimok left her advisor to die. I had taken two steps forward upon seeing her, but now I wrestled with the unknown.

What had she done? Was she dangerous? Would freeing her render a death sentence upon myself?

There was a one-eyed Kazel man in my dreams, a burned Achare man in the tarn, and a dying Rucosti under the mountain.

There had been enough death.

I strode a bit further, cautiously surveying the close horizon of the hilly land. A darkness had grown in the west — a thunderhead native to the rainy season. I produced my knife and felt glad that traveling with my bow was a habit.

Her face was pointed at the ground. There were quiet sobs coming from her, the kind that come when the lungs are tired of shouting and tears run dry. It occurred to me that I didn't know how long she'd been here. Perhaps the chieftain had stayed to savor her suffering and left only when she'd been sated.

"Mountain Mother," she was saying, "send me to the land of shadow. Bring me to her so I may atone for the worst of my crimes. Let me die for treason uncommitted; let me walk in darkness for my true betrayal. Mountain Mother, send me to the land of Shadow..."

"What is this treason you haven't committed?" I asked,

startling her out of her invocation. She looked me up and down as if trying to determine if I were real.

"She left a Red Warden behind," she said. "She's nearby — if she sees you, she'll kill you."

"What," I repeated, ignoring the guilt in my chest, "have you done to deserve this?"

She looked me in the eye and steeled herself with the conviction of one who means what they say. "My name is Noskre din Costa." She adopted a Rucosti accent when she said her name. "Until today I was Moddimok's advisor for five years. I have done nothing to deserve this death."

Suddenly, there was a figure on the hilltop. The woman Noskre promised, lance lain across her lap, kicked her feet against her horse and plunged furiously down the slope. The blade of her weapon pushed forward between gnarled pines and sent the plovers roiling above.

"Cut the ropes —" Noskre shouted. "Do it now!"

The red cedar bindings fell loose at her feet. She sprang up, skillfully wrestled my knife from my hand and darted away. The dog bounded after her. Having no time to stop her myself, I pulled the bow from my back.

I stood tall.

I squared my feet.

My exhale found the arrow pushed against the bow.

My inhale found its fletching against my cheek.

And upon finding my anchor, the arrow whistled for an instant under the horse's heaving head and tore into its chest. The rider launched forth from her collapsing mount, landing on her hip in the dirt.

I drew again but found her spear hurtling toward me.

My arrow flew wide as I stumbled to escape her weapon.

Then she was upon me, soldier's arms wrenching my bow left and right. Failing to strip me of my only weapon, she darted for the arrows at my hip. I grasped her wrist; she let go of the bow and struck me in the jaw with her right.

I floundered back. She thrust forward in an attempt to tackle, but I changed my footing and spun, sending her behind me.

I nocked an arrow, but too quickly she had recovered and came within arm's reach. She struck me once before stepping wildly to the side.

Noskre lunged forth with the rider's spear, cut her palm in the initial swipe and lacerated the side of her head with the next.

The rider was barely conscious when Noskre pushed the blade through her throat.

Noskre din Costa turned to me with the spear held aloft.

She was a desperate animal, thrown into a death sentence, saved by a stranger she didn't trust. Her jaw was tense. Her hands were bleeding. She did not blink.

"You're the mercenary who came with Rangrim," she said. "From the lowlands."

"I came to Ba Turin with Rangrim, but I am no mercenary."

"How did you know to come for me? And why did you?" she asked.

"I sought solitude at a tarn not far from here. Moddimok found me, spoke briefly with me, and said enough to make me worry for whomever she'd left."

She turned her face to the side in doubt. Her eyes were allowed to travel, to size me up more patiently. I could see her armor softening and was glad of it. "You came here to save a stranger? Even if it meant betraying the most powerful woman in Ba Turin?"

The dead warden's lance drifted uncertainly.

I think I'd been quashing that realization. With a single act of good, I may have condemned myself. But I couldn't let this Noskre din Costa see my impulsivity.

"I don't stomach death well," is all I said, trying not to look at the corpse at our feet.

"Thank you for my life," she said. "But you must realize that you severed your return to the Hanallta along with my binds. When their rider doesn't return in a day or two, they'll send someone to check. Moddimok knows you were out here. You'll be hunted down and killed. Death sentences are contagious to the savior, Lowlander. I suggest you leave Ba Turin."

Noskre pushed past me and strode purposefully, spear in hand, toward the Hanallta.

"What are you doing?" I shouted after her.

"Returning the favor," she said over her shoulder.

I was stupefied for a moment.

"You can't just walk into Mother's Hall and kill the most powerful woman in the mountains!"

"Either I try to kill her now," she said, her voice growing distant, "or I die later."

"Noskre, wait." I ran after her. The mountains had given me an opportunity; I'd be a fool to ignore it. "Wait!"

"What?" she turned and spoke with a bit of venom.

"I think we can help each other," I told her. "But I need you to be patient, at least for tonight."

She eyed me suspiciously, then slowly strode back to the rider she'd slain.

I needed movement to think. I overcame mortal discomfort and suggested we move the dead woman. Noskre led me with the body held between us. It's strange how accustomed one can become, by meager degrees, to the presence of the dead.

"What crime did you commit?" I asked again over the lurching rhythm of the body. She nearly slipped out of her shoes, and I adjusted my hands. I learned in that moment that the carrying of a body between two people is easier if it's facing the earth.

"Against my chieftain? None, save for an unspoken doubt in her sanity."

And she must have discovered those doubts. But how?

"But there's something else," I said. "What is there between you and your lost sister?"

I finished the question as we hefted the body over the edge of a sheer drop. I kept my eyes on Noskre to avoid the view below. She was taken aback. She plucked my dagger from her waistband.

"How do you know about that? What kind of man are you?"

I spoke calmly with my palms facing out. "My name is Rennik. I've been trained in the seeing of secret things — a sort of magic, you may call it. I see in you the loss of your sister and a crushing guilt." Of course of lied. I couldn't tell her I'd followed her through the dark. "I apologize that this is jarring, but our time is short, and I truly believe we can help each other in the days to come."

The dagger was an apt replacement for the spear she'd pointed at me minutes before. In her face was anger, confusion, horror at the hidden needles of her past turned to substance before her.

And then she leapt upon me, landing with her knees in my chest and my own knife against my throat. "This was your doing!" she shouted.

"What are you talking about?" I wrestled against her briefly before the threat of a cut throat kept me still.

"Rangrim came to Moddimok two days ago and told her I couldn't be trusted! She said a secret seer told her I was a threat to the crown!"

"*I am no friend of Rangrim's!*" I shouted as the blade bit tentatively at my skin. I felt a thin stream of blood plunge to the dirt as I realized that Rangrim interpreted the smoke as her own warning. She must have jumped to the conclusion that this woman was the traitor in their court. I sprang into a lie. "There are others like me — others who are Turin and faithful to their chieftain! Think, Noskre, why would I save you if I intended for your death?"

Noskre brought her face close to mine. She smelled of sweat, earth, and iron. "I have lived in Mother's Hall for fifteen years. I was Moddimok's most trusted advisor for five of them. And never have I heard of such seers among our people."

"She's paranoid — Moddimok has many secret limbs, each designed to check the fidelity of the other."

"A true spider," she said, spitting into the dirt. "Then who was it? You seem to know everything I do not. Who is the one who betrayed me?"

"I don't know," I said, wincing at the knife as I swallowed. "Please. Let us find somewhere to hide and talk. I saved you for a reason," I repeated. "We have a common enemy."

Her eyes were calculating, and at the end of it all seemed to be the summation that I was unarmed and knowledgeable. She stood from over me and watched me with caution.

"I don't suppose you can lift a horse," she said, looking toward the dead mass in the open vale.

"Afraid not."

"The bristlecones," she said, gesturing with my knife. "Walk."

I stepped away first, and her footsteps followed.

I braced for the knife in my back. It did not come.

The ground beneath the trees was shaded and cool. She stood at first, the bole of tension unyielding in her back, then sat against a trunk and rubbed her wrists where they'd been bound. Her short hair, dark and rather unruly, pressed against the craggy bark. She wiped the sweat from her eyes and took a deep breath. The knife waited in her hand. I wondered if all of Moddimok's people were infected with anger and distrust.

"The Turin have a tendency to take my things." And by way of speaking I understood, for the first time, that it was Rangrim who took my axe while I slept upon the mountain trail. I pushed this realization elsewhere and focused on Noskre.

"This has happened before?"

"Yes, unfortunately. On our way to the Hanallta, a companion took my axe in the night."

"I'm not Turin. And I'd expect a man who magically sees secret things to have seen that coming," she said.

"If only it were so straightforward. Such sight is narrow, and my control of it is not so consistent as one might imagine."

"Then it seems as though the only consistent factor is you. You shouldn't be so careless with your weapons, Lowlander. If you expect me to fear you, you've failed."

"Noskre," I said. "I just saved you from your death. I told you of my hope that we might work together. Why do you think I want to be feared?" She thought on this for a moment, and I continued, wiping the latest drop of blood from my neck. "I imagine living at Moddimok's side has trained you to distrust. I understand you've just met me, but you'll be interested in what I have to say. Please," I told her, "keep the knife if it means you'll listen."

It's strange to sit in the quiet of dead violence. My heart had yet to slow after our fight with the Turin woman, but the birds were returning to the boughs, and the breeze swept gently through the fingers of ancient trees above us. The world lent me its calm.

"My sister was unstoppable," she started, finally addressing my question. "She had a different mother — a Turin mother, so she was born stubborn and favored."

"But your mother —"

"Earned me nothing." She said. "A Rucosti woman. Died just after I was old enough to remember. My father eventually took me here, to his home, and my sister was born shortly after. She was a natural fighter. Younger than me, but stepped to my defense when the other children would pick on the Rucosti girl."

"You said you betrayed her."

She inhaled as if to answer, held it a moment, let it go, and tried again.

"Moddimok saw me as a useful tool," she said. "Rucost was encroaching on Turin land with increasing persistence, and she thought I could grant her insight into their culture, their way of thinking. It ruffled a few feathers, my being Rucosti-born."

"But your father was Turin."

"That doesn't matter to them. It's the mother's blood they want to see. But Moddimok trusted me as an advisor, and it paid off in some ways. Ironhead Fastness was established, an iron mine near the border — where *we* drew the border, anyway — that was shared between the Turin and Rucosti. It granted them access to the iron, and we learned to use and produce some of their technology...but some Turin saw it as a weakness, even if the compromise worked to secure our relationship rather than keep us threatened. They were convinced Moddimok was giving in to Rucosti desires...and for a while, I thought they were wrong."

"What changed?" I asked.

"Little things. Inviting more merchants into the Hanallta, entertaining diplomats...but time passed, and I could see the wood in her heart warping their way – saw it too late."

She stopped for a while. Her hands were attentive to her chafed wrists. Her eyes lingered on the dead woman's spear. Something rumbled in the distance, born of mountain or storm.

"Have you ever had to choose between duty and family?" she asked, her voice wavering under the tension of things unsaid. "Have you ever seen a sibling throw themselves into certain death?"

"Actually," I started, "...I have. I tried to choose my people over my family when the pale man, Kesevirot, threatened our village." I made sure to watch her reaction as I said it, but she was simply listening intently. Perhaps Haston Corde was telling the truth, and the pale man was not Rucosti — at least not one she knew. "I let my brother run into the village just before the horde arrived. He nearly died, and I don't think I'll ever forgive myself for it."

"How could you?" she asked. It was not a question in scorn, but one of empathy. "How can I? My sister stormed into Mother's Hall one day, her axe lofted as she shouted at Moddimok herself, claimed to the crowd that our chieftain was selling Ba Turin to the Rucosti inch by inch, that she was undone by age and sworn to greed. I'd seen it coming, seen my sister fill herself with hatred and impatience, but I did nothing. I did not speak on her behalf, neither warned her nor stopped Moddimok when she turned to me. That was the last day I saw my sister, and since that day I've realized, too slowly, that Moddimok is not loyal to her people. And so my loyalty has been broken."

There was something in her story, a hook that caught the lip of memory. I felt it tugging as I responded.

"Do you seek revenge on your chieftain?"

"No," she said. I was surprised for a moment before she continued. "Because as of today I have no chieftain. There is only one tunnel before me, and it leads to a knife in Moddimok's chest."

"Then perhaps we can help each other," I said. Her eyes narrowed as if to size me up in a new light. "I traveled to Ba Turin and likewise to the Hanallta with Rangrim, and I'd hoped to find an ally in her. But it's clear my usefulness to her is coming to an end, and I'd rather not be the dead one at its conclusion. She's living in Mother's Hall again, dining with her mother, drinking the same strange poison, and she'll swiftly find herself as lost as Moddimok."

"You intend to kill Rangrim?" Noskre asked. "You, who claim an aversion to killing?"

"I..." it was difficult to produce the sentence. "I think I do, yes. Change isn't easy, and I worry what sort of person I'll become when killing becomes my nature, but it must be done if I am to live...You seem comfortable enough with killing," I said, gesturing to the empty space that once contained a Red Warden.

"I know how to defend myself," she said. She watched me for a moment. "From mercenary to merciful. I think I've misjudged you, Rennik."

I gave a morbid laugh. "And I've misjudged you in turn."

"So how will the killing be done, man of mercy?"

I thought for a moment. "Rangrim comes each morning

and night to deliver Senna's Ward to me in Hegira's home. Perhaps there."

Noskre shook her head. "Too many potential witnesses. And that's only one of our targets."

"Spilling blood near that home seems wrong, anyway. But even without witnesses, won't we be suspected of killing her anyway? Her nearly-executed advisor and a lowlander?"

"Well, if we do this quickly, they may not find out I survived. As for you...the lowlands hold no hatred for the Turin. Moddimok and Rangrim both have enemies in Rucost and her own home. The assumption would sooner land there, I think. Why don't we try Mother's Hall?" she continued. "I've been led to believe there are secret ways in and out, though the details were always closely guarded secrets, I'm afraid."

"I can find out," I told her. "I can search the smoke for answers."

She looked skeptical, but seemed to remember my "divining" her history with her sister. "Well, this is enough of a plan to get us killed tomorrow. But..."

"But what?"

"I understand our interests align, and I may be foolish for placing doubt in my only chance at returning Moddimok's favor, but why don't you just leave Ba Turin? Rangrim can't kill you at a distance."

"There's a greater purpose for my being here," I said. "I seek something hard to find — a pebble in a mountainside, I fear. If I'm to stay and find such a pebble, I need to be...alive."

"It won't be easy," she said. "I can't just stay in the Hanallta overnight while we come up with a plan for murder."

"There's a cave not far from there. It's hard to spot and has clean water inside."

She shook her head. "No good. I know the cave, and too many people visit it. Not frequently, but enough that it's a liability."

"In that case, I've got a few other things I can try," I said. "For now, you'll have to stay here. I think I can get you safely into the Hanallta by nightfall."

She looked doubtful, but said she had little choice but to trust me. We sat a few moments more, silent, thinking upon the task we'd set for ourselves, the lives we intended to take.

"What was her name?" I asked. "Your sister."

"Callyona," she said, smiling a little at the sound of it. Then her face grew dark again. "But when they threw her into the water of the Shadowlands, she became someone else, renamed for her blackened loyalty."

It dawned on me before I heard her say it. I felt her blood upon my chest, saw the tattered muscles of her arms, heard her screams echo from memory.

"Her traitor's name was Callisgrim."

14

FRIEND, FOE, STEW

People aught to be careful. Pray for sun too much,
and you might get a draught.

— TENAL

Hegira was right about the rain.

As it poured upon the mountains, the water was guided through a complex series of canals carved into the stone. Water spread over every sacha, fell into the pools in Mother's Hall, filled freshwater reservoirs in each of the homes.

And it fell like gravel on the Rucosti tent.

The Rucosti traders had clearly been here before. Their tents were designed to prop up against the teeth of the Hanallta, a series of rust-colored karsts that sprang up from the soil near the Sentinels. From the looks of it, they'd used this exact spot before. Each canvas tent was at least twenty feet across, and they encircled the teeth to share an internal back wall. Some of the outside flaps were kept open to form temporary storefronts, and some were well-enclosed to make a private quarters for each trader. I gathered that the leaders of this caravan were camped under the Great Wing.

I hoped with all my heart I'd find Tenal among them, but as I walked toward the canvassed teeth lit with lamplight and laughter, there was no red-bearded tower of a man to be seen, and so the happiness from within was dulled.

In the threshold of one tent was a man, who looked to be thirty, admiring a series of iron nails. He picked one up, tested its point upon his finger, and nodded in satisfaction. His eyes looked through a curtain of blonde hair. He greeted me with the slow smile of a long day's trading as I came into his view, and he ushered me out of the storm.

Within the tent were crates, bags, and barrels, some full with wares to sell, some empty and wanting for Turin craft. A bedroll was lain against the wall, and a modest hearth had been made against the stone wall at the back of the tent. A cooking fire, the small shelf of an iron grill waiting for meat, a hole in the roof to usher out the smoke. He was staying here alone.

"You look like you've had a rough day," he started in Kalanosi, gesturing to my cheek with a nail. I hadn't stopped to think of my appearance after the fight with Noskre's guard. He invited me to sit.

"You could say that," I said. I turned to make sure the flap had closed behind me. The fewer witnesses, the better. "I'm looking for a commodity you don't typically sell."

His eyebrow raised, and his hand hesitated over the nails.

"How much do you charge for a night in this tent?" I asked. "Away from prying eyes?"

The man cleared his throat. "What do you have to offer?"

"Silver."

He thought for a moment as the rain pounded down.

"Two pieces for the night. Three if you'd like me to forget about it, too."

"And if I want you to stay elsewhere?"

His reaction was dubious at best.

"You clearly intend for something clandestine," he said, "and you want me to trust you among my things?"

"I'm no thief. I simply have a deal to strike with an important figure, and if we were witnessed together, it may ruin our maneuver. Surely a trader such as yourself can appreciate the subtle workings of business."

I picked a few silver coins from the collection Tenal had paid me over a year ago. Like I'd predicted back then, I hadn't found any use for the money in Kalanos, but it seemed foolish not to hang on to them. "To prove I have it," I told him, brandishing the silver discs. "I'll pay you when it's said and done." I'd never been sure how much a silver coin was actually worth, so he may have been ripping me off. Also, having never met the man — or many Rucosti for that matter — I was taking a huge leap of faith in trusting him. Hopefully the delay of payment would keep him true to his word.

"Six silver," he determined. "And two of them up front."

"Alright."

"And I want an explanation of this deal you're striking. Perhaps it's something I can get in on. I'll even throw in dinner."

"Perhaps," I said doubtfully. "I'll mention this interest to my acquaintance and see what we can manage."

He seemed pleased with the deal.

"How long are you and your group—"

"Guild," he interrupted. "We're a *guild*."

"Guild," I corrected, forcing a smile. "How long do you and your guild plan to stay here?"

"Well, Tamovier's the one in charge. They like to stay

here quite a while — a fortnight, at least. Gives the smiths time to make a few custom pieces before we leave."

"Good," I said. "I'll be returning tonight with my companion. If you truly tell no one of our staying here, you'll be paid, and the opportunity of profiting further can be discussed. Do I have your word?"

"Depends," he answered. "Do I have your coin?"

I journeyed through the downpour, wishing I'd made more otter skin clothing on my journey. It was harebrained of me to venture into the rainy season with a proper cloak and not the proper boots. I stopped at Hegira's home and found the night's dose of Senna's Ward on the table. She was appalled at the thought of my leaving in a storm.

"I'll be alright," I told her, warming in the hearth of her concern. "It's not a long walk, and the storm's not so bad." It was a futile attempt in persuasion; the water was gushing by the windows so heavily you couldn't see the garden beyond it. "Stay here," I told Karay. He curled himself by the doorway, grumbled, and watched the rain.

"You should take one of my shirts," she told me. "You need to stay warm or you'll catch something wicked."

I took the shirt, waved her concern away, and missed my family steadily as I trod through the deluge. After making a quick stop to speak to a child in the rain, I journeyed to find the sodden Noskre.

She was at first opposed to the idea of both returning to the Hanallta and trusting a stranger with our lives. But I suppose the idea of roof and risk was preferable to exposure and isolation. She was anxious, and as we came through the tent's entrance and out of the rain, she wasted no time in starting small talk. "I'm actually half-Rucosti," she said to the man at one point.

Gone was the angry advisor; here was a smiling diplomat.

"What a coincidence," he said while handing a bowl to each of us. "I'm full Rucosti."

I was too busy thinking to join the small talk, and the conversation quickly became a back-and-forth between he and Noskre, spoken in Rucosti. I found it fitting that her native language was colored with a Kalanosi intonation. As they spoke, her political tact was made clear to me; she seemed intent on endearing herself to him. Noskre mentioned me a few times as if I couldn't understand them, and it occurred to me that she wasn't aware I knew Rucosti. I decided to keep that to myself.

His name was Vivonno, and his food was welcomed. The stew was bland, but the mutton, carrots, and potato that he'd traded for today were filling enough. I wondered if Kheze's meal had spoiled food for me. Perhaps I'd dined too close to the sun.

Tonight, for some reason, I missed chicory root — though I suppose what I really missed was lowland Kalanos. I was tired of surviving this height, where I felt as though I could fall to my death at any moment.

We weren't entirely drenched. I'd given Hegira's shirt to Noskre. It did well enough against the mountain rain, but I busied myself with wringing the wetter parts of my clothes onto the grassy floor against the wall. Vivonno's tent was warm, heated by the small fire made against the stone. A layered series of open slopes where the tent leaned against the structure let the smoke out without inviting too much rain, and it seemed the teeth kept running water from flooding the tents. With the three of us in attendance, the tent felt small, but I imagined the two of us could sleep comfortably.

"Can't say I've run a tavern before," he said, switching to Kalanosi, "but I've got food and an extra bedroll — just the one, sorry. I'm taking mine with me."

"I'm fine on the grass," I mentioned quickly.

"You said you were half-Rucosti?" he asked Noskre.

"My mother was Rucosti," she answered. "From Sess."

"Sess?" Vivonno replied with a grin. "That's quite a place. Beautiful coast down there. Port city, but nothing so big you find a lot of theft. You don't have any Sessian wine, do you?" He looked hopeful.

"No, no, I left before I could remember any of it. My father was Turin. My mother died when I was young, and my father brought me here." Noskre looked to me meaningfully. "She was sentenced to death." Then she looked to Vivonno. "For theft."

He swallowed his food forcefully. "They killed her just for stealing something?"

"It was more than just *something*. She stole a carriage, horses and all, from a nobleman who was passing through. There were valuable family heirlooms of his inside...and a baby she hadn't noticed. She didn't get far once the baby started wailing. The nobleman had some political sway, and he got her killed off."

"Trust the alleys, fear the nobility," said Vivonno. I hadn't heard the idiom before.

It was at this point that the tent flap opened.

"Ah, damn wind!" Vivonno exclaimed. I reached over to seal the entrance, looping string around stick until it was closed. While doing so, I sent a meaningful look into the rainy night and hoped it was unnoticed by the two in the tent. "I suppose that's enough of a sign for me to take my leave," he continued, lowering his voice. "And I assume you've told her about the deal."

"Of course," I said — and it was true. I'd kept her privy to the deception.

But Vivonno made no move to leave.

"What is it, exactly? What sort of arrangement are you two coming to?"

My mind reeled for a lie, but my reserve of mercantile discourse had run dry. Thankfully, Noskre jumped to the task.

"What do you know of Ironhead Fastness?" she asked him in Rucosti. Familiar territory for her, no doubt. I turned my attention to the dinner in my hands as if I couldn't track the conversation.

His eyebrows leapt to attention. "The mine shared by Rucost and the Turin. Makes a hell of a profit on Rucost's end, and I assume something similar for the mountain folk here...why?"

"You're aware, then, that the owners of Migli and Sooths, the ones who staked that claim, will never have to work again?"

"Acutely," he said, eyes fixed as if her words were a priceless gem.

"My partner and I will be in need of a Rucosti associate in the coming year."

"Another mine..." he wondered aloud. "You're Rucosti enough, aren't you?" he asked.

Noskre shook her head. "The Hanallta is my home. I am Turin." There was a sadness sunk in the recesses of her lie. In truth, her home was doing its best to spit her out.

"I've been considering starting my own guild, you know. It's good you came to me and not Tamovier. They can be a true swindler — not me, though, I'm as honest as they come."

"I find faith often precedes success," said Noskre. "People trust you like you trust them. And to initiate the partnership more generously, I'll have something for you tomorrow. A gift that must be kept secret, but one that will fund the starting of your own guild."

Vivonno was visibly excited. "I've got your word, then? We know where the river goes?" He said the last bit in Kalanosi.

"We do." The two seemed to have committed to the change in language. I raised my head.

"And don't go making this deal with the Rucosti coming here after us. I have your word." He punctuated each syllable as if it were physically binding.

"There are more coming?" I asked.

Vivonno nodded. "Scary-looking group. Shared an inn with a few of them near Periloe. One of the soldiers I drank with said they're making a few stops, 'meeting the others', and then heading to Ba Turin to pick up a prisoner."

"Soldiers?" The future seemed fraught with foe.

Vivonno shrugged. "I suppose so. They were all gambeson-and-sword. I figure most people wouldn't wear the armor when they didn't have to — do a bit of doff-and-quaff, you know — but these were some pretty intense people. It takes a mean captain to keep men uncomfortable in repose."

I heard Rangrim's words from days before.

...the Crooked King's men will surely be here sooner.

As we finished the conversation, Vivonno thanked us for the opportunity, shook our hands as all Rucosti do, and made to leave the tent.

"Are you sure you can cover for us if you stay with someone else?" Noskre asked.

Vivonno smiled wide. "If you can't sell yourself, you can't sell anything."

And as the tent opened for the third time that night, my own associate stepped into the firelight.

~

OF COURSE SHE DIDN'T SEE THE CHILD, BUT I ALSO KNEW little of her life and little of the rules.

Perhaps Noskre din Costa had been nearly crushed by a wagon wheel, landed haphazardly on a stony beach, or been bludgeoned by a frothing cobbler. Surely a child could find danger enough in the cities of Rucost.

Marmot found a place near the fire and started to dry himself off.

"You," she said to me, "are very clever." She was more impressed than she should have been. She'd begun rummaging through a few of Vivonno's things.

"I just had the idea," I told her. "You're the one who made it work...I assume."

"Right," she said, coming into the falsehood that was my lack of language. She explained what she'd said to Vivonno, what she promised, and that he wouldn't tell a soul for fear of losing the opportunity. She finally emerged from the Rucosti trader's inventory with a glass bottle. It was a bit bulbous, like an onion. The glass was green, was covered in a lattice of twine to keep it from breaking, and sloshed as Noskre brought it to her mouth.

"And you think *I'm* clever...but you said you'd give him something tomorrow? Like what?"

"Well..." She looked a bit tentative. "When I helped to establish Ironhead Fastness, Migli and Sooths sent a token of appreciation to Moddimok. They were the guild who had happened to stake the closest bit of Rucosti land years before, and therefore were granted the right to operate the mine. They grew wildly rich within months, even after paying the absurdly heavy taxes the local lord and lady had written into the contract. Migli and Sooths sent Moddimok a masterfully crafted pendant that housed the first sapphire found in Ironhead Fastness, and it's...not small."

"Noskre..." I said slowly. "You seem to be implying that you'll give Vivonno that pendant."

The bottle found itself upended, pouring for a moment too long, I thought, past Noskre's lips.

"*We'll* be giving Vivonno that pendant," she corrected when she'd finished. "It's hardly anything to add to the list. If we succeed, if we kill Moddimok and her devil of a daughter, we may as well grab something to sweeten our deal." She raised the wine, invoked the Rucosti saying, *"To hell with it,"* and took another drink.

"But this deal, this secret iron vein of yours...it isn't *real,* Noskre."

"Actually," she said, "it is. And even if Vivonno isn't our man, we can at least keep an ally in the Hanallta for the time being."

"Does Moddimok know about the vein?"

"When you're thrust into the game of politics, Rennik, you must learn the rules quickly. You must gather resources in the form of people and their secrets. And if you can keep a hidden ember hot in your forge...you do it."

She took another swig from the onion-bottle and handed it to me.

"I've never had wine before," I told her. "Any alcohol, for that matter."

Her hand shot forward and stayed the bottle. "Then

perhaps this isn't the night to try it out. Wouldn't want you hurting tomorrow."

"Shouldn't you stop, then?" I asked as she drank again. She rested on her elbow.

"I'll be okay. I've got years of practice, Rennik."

Marmot shifted a bit next to the fire, casting a shadow only I could see. I found a kind of lantern next to a crate and toyed with it for a moment. The glass was very thick, and the whole thing was a bit heavier than typical.

"They carry those during the rainy season," she said casually.

"We should discuss the plan," I said, putting the lantern down.

She was sprawled over the bedroll, wine bottle laid against her hip, her hand resting on its neck. "You're the one with the sorcerer's eyes." Her voice had become quiet, reverent, even.

"I'll try to find the way in." I looked toward the fire.

Marmot spoke in a voice meant only for me.

"One of the canals drains into a pool in the private baths."

"You're joking," I muttered.

"What do you see?" Noskre asked.

"Water. Baths. One of the canals..."

"They always bathe at night, though," said Marmot, "so it should be empty in the morning, and the closest living quarters are Noskre's, so...that's empty."

"The baths near your quarters," I said to Noskre with my eyes toward the fire. "They're fed by a canal big enough for us to fit through."

"The big room with six baths in it," thought Noskre aloud.

"She's testing you," said Marmot. "There are ten baths."

I shook my head, corrected her, and enjoyed the look on her face.

"It seems as though they aren't used in the mornings," I continued.

"Depends," said Noskre. "Sometimes they'll bathe before receiving important guests, and there *are* Rucosti about." She lifted a finger from the neck of the bottle to gesture all around us. "Can you tell if she considers these traders, this 'Tamovier' person, to be important?"

Marmot took a moment to think and gave an uncertain "no."

"They've already seen each other this morning," I relayed, "so probably not."

"I've gleaned over the years," explained Noskre, "that there is more than one way into Mother's Hall. The baths can't be it. Isn't there something else?"

"Let me see what I can see. I thought for a moment I would find something leading to Rangrim's quarters," I said.

I looked at Marmot pointedly.

"Oh, right!" he said. "There's a really difficult path to take to that tunnel. It's well-hidden since...you know, it leads to Moddimok as well. There's also a big rock in the way. There are two passages on the inside that connect to the baths as well."

Noskre sat up when she saw my face become incredulous for a moment.

"Something large...a stone...I think there is a stone shielding that passage from entry."

"Could we move it?" Noskre asked, enthralled with the process she was witnessing.

"It may be possible," I said after Marmot shrugged. "At least from the inside."

"What about getting there?" she asked. "What's the trail to the canal like?"

I repeated Marmot's words: the trail was not to be entirely walked. There are sections of cliff to climb across, some rises to scramble, and altogether a lot of dangerous maneuvering on rocky faces.

"Then we can't do this at night," said Noskre. "We'd fall to our deaths in minutes. What about the space *by* the tunnels? Could we stay there until dark?"

"No," I told her. "Even that is just a thin lip. It's a wonder these are considered escape routes for...well, for anyone."

"The Turin are born climbers," she said, shrugging slowly. "Can you see if there are guards in the way? When they'll be inattentive, if any of them harbor grudges against Moddimok, if they know of anything we can use against her?"

Marmot looked at her with his hands in the air as if to ask if she was serious.

"Like I said," stifling a smile, "such sight can be narrow."

"So we're going to wake up in a borrowed tent, hike and climb up a perilous trail, crawl through a wet tunnel, and kill the two most powerful women in a palace full of guards."

"...Yeah."

Noskre drank.

"I wonder if we can get the attention of their guards somewhere," I said.

"A distraction," she mused.

"A distraction. Vivonno said there are other Rucosti coming soon. If their approach seemed imminent, the guards would be busied, and Moddimok would probably—"

"Busy herself in her quarters," Noskre finished. "Maybe even sit defenseless in the baths."

We looked at each other for a moment as the idea formed.

"We'd need a raven," said Noskre. "The old man in the lookout tower would send one when they were close."

"Think you can take care of that?" I asked, knowing nothing about ravens or Turin warning systems.

"I think I can. I'll wake up before sunrise and handle that. Maybe I can convince Vivonno to talk about the coming soldiers in the hearing of the guards. Get people nervous."

We spent the next half hour finding answers for Noskre's questions, collecting what information Marmot had, and tightening the plan. In the end, he said he'd travel with us in the morning and ensure we didn't fall to our deaths before we reached the tunnels. When it was time for him to leave, he smacked the flap of the tent, wriggled it violently, and had altogether too much creative liberty with the entire ordeal. Finally, "the wind" blew the flap open, and Marmot stepped into the storm.

A thousand years old and somehow still a child.

"Move," Noskre told me as she stepped to the opening. She began looping strings around sticks and made sure it was as tight as possible. "Damn lowlanders, can't even close a tent right..."

When she was done, she stayed kneeling next to me, hands hanging gingerly from one of the loops. Her eyes found mine. They trembled, and I'm sure mine did as well.

"Do you really think we can do this?" she asked. Her breath was sweet with the smell of wine. "I've blamed myself for my sister's exile for years. I want to see my knife in the crone's throat. I want to know her last words and hear her last breath. I want to feel her blood run its last race through the body that took her from me."

"But?"

"But what if we can't?"

"I think it will take an immense amount of control and luck."

"My sister was unstoppable," she said, glancing to the ground, "...but she wasn't patient. When we find ourselves in her palace, in her baths, in whichever room becomes her grave, we need to set everything aside but patience. My anger —"

"— My fear."

She nodded in agreement.

"We can't feel any of it," she said. "Anger or fear. I am so damn scared. One part of me is screaming at the stupidity of it all. To crawl into a canal and find two dozen armed guards who'd kill me just for being there, to become trapped in tight tunnels and never return...but the other option is to wait. Wait until they find my guard missing, wait until Rangrim decides to have you killed. Another part of me knows that... ready or not, this is the best chance we have."

"It's strange to wait in this liminal space, on the blade's breadth between our patience and haste." I was quoting something Gatsi said to me once.

"To think that we found each other...the two people willing and stupid enough to kill Moddimok. The Mountain Mother brought us together, Rennik. I think I have more purpose in tomorrow than I've ever had before."

"Yes, Noskre," I said, finally answering her question. "I think we can do this."

We had not moved away from each other. Our faces were close, and her eyes fell to my lips, flicked up again, sought for something further. The fire made a mosaic of her face, light touching angles then leaving in shadow, like the art of Mother's Hall, graceful in the chaos of it all. I found myself staring.

I broke the moment and looked at the ground to my right.

"We should sleep," I managed to say through the tense night air.

I found my way to the ground, and she to her bedroll. I lay facing the wall and heard the sloshing of the onion-bottle behind me.

Again the memory of Callisgrim rose like a ghost in my mind, but I couldn't bring myself to tell her. It would, at best, stoke her anger, and she was about as patient as her sister when she was angry. I wondered what their father must have been like, what childhood had produced the living flame that was their family fury.

I wondered at the ways my own childhood may have molded me, and what I would have been without its misfortunes.

Rain beat against canvas.

I felt sick. Dizzy.

How calm can one feel before invading a killer's palace?

15

MOTHER'S HALL

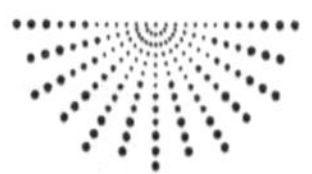

There are no crickets this high in the mountains.

I grew up with their choirs, grew accustomed to the clamor of cicadas and sparrows.

This morning in the Hanallta was silent and dark. The quiet slowed my pace, made me conscious of every step, every swish of my clothes, each breath I took. I felt as though I could press my ear to the earth and hear the muffled sobs of Haston Corde, collecting his breakfast from the one sort of insect that seemed to live at this altitude.

Hegira's home was unmoving. She must have been

sleeping still. As there had yet to be Senna's Ward on the table, I decided to wait.

I crept into my borrowed bed and closed my eyes, hoping I hadn't woken my patron, and let my hand fall upon the wide shoulders of a napping Karay.

The sensation of spinning began as soon as I stopped moving. Having felt better on the walk here, I decided to at least pace the room.

But standing found me falling into the bed again — everything in Ba Turin felt like falling — and I swam in the dark eddies above, before, and beneath me. Time was passing, I was sure, but the chaos in this movement stole its measurements from me. It seemed sudden that the sunrise shone shyly through the window. Hegira's face appeared above me and became the only solid thing I could make out. Karay was standing next to the bed with his head resting on my leg.

"I think..." I couldn't get the words out as she propped me up and walked me to the other room. "This is, uh...what happens when..." She sat me in a chair. There were sounds of vegetables being gathered. "...when lowlanders come to the Hanallta..."

I turned and vomited on the ground.

"Here," Hegira was saying, lifting a cup to my mouth. "Rennik, you need to drink. Try to take slower breaths."

The water hit my lips. They were dry, craggy like parched earth.

"Good Mother, your eyes," said Hegira. "You look like death, Rennik."

"Those were your first words to me," I told her with an attempt to smile.

"No, Rennik. I said you looked like shit. Now is worse."

A few minutes passed, and I was able to drink more, to

eat some half-cooked potato and some sort of meat. The ground stopped moving. My stomach allowed me to stand up straight.

"You're not leaving." Hegira spoke in disbelief, not in command.

"I have to meet someone," I said. "There's a chance I'll have to leave swiftly today. Tell no one I said that, but...if I do, I wanted to thank you for being so kind to me. For food, for laughter...for being a mother when I needed one."

I took the packed mixture of Senna's Ward from the table and pocketed it.

"Rennik, please," Hegira said, catching my arm. She looked as though she were about to say something else, but decided only to tell me to be careful.

As I walked away from Hegira's home, I was sure it would be for the last time.

"She left," said Vivonno. "Said to meet her at 'the liability', whatever that means."

"Thank you," I told him with a pain in my stomach. "We'll find you later to discuss some iron."

Vivonno nodded confidently, and I left.

Walking to the cave meant travelling the length of the Hanallta, past every waking home. Farmers were making their way to sachas, children were running, potters were gathering near manmade pools filled with the night's freshwater.

I brought the mixture from my pocket to my mouth, but no sooner had I done so when the smell made me stop and vomit again. A moment, a deep breath, and I continued on. I told myself that the sickness would get worse without the medicine and forced a small portion down my throat. I managed to hold it in, and decided I would distribute small bites throughout the day rather than attempting it all at once.

"You don't seem okay," said a voice behind me.

"I feel like hell, Marmot."

He looked concerned and placed a hand on my arm. "Are you sure you can do this today?"

"There's no other option. It's happening."

"I suppose so," he said cautiously. I heard him sniffle.

"Are you sick? Can you *get* sick?" I asked him.

"Of course. Why wouldn't I? I walked through a storm last night."

It took a lifetime to leave the Hanallta behind, but I felt stronger by the time we'd reached the cave entrance.

Noskre was waiting in the dark, made visible and wraith-like by the angle of the rising sun. She wore a knife at her hip and a short sword, no more than two feet long, across her back. She looked mournfully from the water to me. I remembered the tension from the previous night and tried to put away my embarrassment.

"I thought I was the only one drinking wine last night," she said upon seeing me. "You better pull it together. Drink some of this water, take a minute...we can't afford this right now."

"Believe me, I know," I said, cupping my hands beneath the frigid water. I drank, splashed some on my face, and stood. "I was bedridden an hour ago, so the progress is actually monumental. At this rate I'll have bison strength by noon."

"Funny."

"I'm going to be fine," I told her. "It's just altitude. We have no choice but to do this now."

"I know," she said worriedly.

"How'd the raven go?"

"Stole one, wrote a convincing note, finagled a fake seal, and sent it off."

I was focusing on standing and taking deep breaths. I thought of Marmot's description last night, of "sections of cliff" we'd have to climb across, and tried to ignore the fact that I was *already* dizzy.

"We need to get moving," said Noskre. "How do we get to this hidden trail?"

"Follow me," said Marmot.

"Follow me," I told her.

$\sim$

THE TRAIL WAS NOT A TRAIL AT ALL. AT LEAST, NOT BY MY lowland standards.

Even the portion we were walking was precarious: a few feet of somewhat flat earth propped up by scree. A tumble down this slope meant lacerated skin, broken bones, bruised ribs, a cracked skull, and, unless my luck was merciful, a slow descent into madness as dehydration and bleeding fought for the right to kill.

Marmot was walking carelessly before us, watching large birds soar overhead, glancing at interesting stones, *smiling*.

In a moment he's going to remember he can fly, I thought.

We came to a place where the trail could no longer be walked. It turned from a thin path into a lip, from a lip to a handhold, and from a handhold to — as far as I could tell — a thousand-foot drop.

"You're sure this is the best way in?" Noskre asked behind me. "It's a little perilous, even for someone who grew up here."

I watched Marmot stretch out his arm and bring himself dangling over the void. He brought his right hand over to share the divot with his left, then stretched his left again, and continued the routine until he was ten feet across the mountainside.

"I'm unfortunately confident," I told her, and made to match his journey.

I had climbed the trail to my plateau for most of my life, over and again until I thought I must be the best Achare climber. Granted, that's not a very impressive claim when the Achare were a people of flat land.

This was leagues beyond my experience.

"Don't look down," advised Marmot from the safe perch he'd reached. "Especially since you've already been dizzy."

I extended my left hand and leaned over the drop. My bodily instincts forbade my foot from leaving solid ground, and I thought it was the best advice I'd ever heard. "I suggest," said my nerves, "that you not hang in the sky by your fingertips while you're sick."

Noskre exhaled nervously behind me, and I realized she'd been holding her breath for my sake.

I slid my right hand across the stone until it joined my left. I was leaning. That's a start. My foot, now the weight of a ship's anchor, was coerced to lift and step into the air.

And then I was swinging, flexing every muscle in my body to stay rigid against the mountain. From my mouth came sounds of someone waking from a nightmare, confused, fearful. I couldn't decide whether to hold my breath or breathe steadily. My stomach lifted and I fought the urge to retch.

Marmot and Noskre started speaking at the same time.

"Left hand," said Marmot to my left. "Just focus on one hand at a time."

"Rennik," said Noskre to my right, "let your legs do some of the work, like your arms when you run. You need to keep moving."

"Don't wait there," continued Marmot. "You're going to get tired."

"Okay," I said, and repeated the word several times.

I lifted with the entirety of my right side, fingers, arm, shoulder and back doing the work of my whole body. I concentrated on the location of the next handhold and grasped it with my left hand.

I found a rhythm, lurching as it was, and managed to reach the final portion of sheer stone. The last handhold Marmot had found was fairly rounded. I pictured where my fingers would grip, where I'd set my palm in order to lift myself.

My fingers held for a moment before they slipped.

The momentum of my swing was enough to bring me to the lip, and I caught its edge with my hands. A flood of Rucosti curses came from the direction of Noskre.

"Don't worry," I said as I pulled myself slowly up to the ledge. "You're next."

Surprisingly enough, the world only spun enough to set me against the wall.

"WE SHOULD HAVE WAITED LONGER," NOSKRE SAID AS WE rested. "You could have rested another hour or two, surely."

We'd reached the final point of our path on the mountain's edge. Just as Marmot had informed me, there was only a small ledge here, just large enough to rest momentarily, but too small to stay for hours. Some grass had managed to grow here on an island of horizontal stone. There was, in fact, a large and inconspicuous boulder here that allegedly sealed a tunnel into Mother's Hall, but I saw no other path by which to enter.

I shook my head. "It was worth trying. They would have known something was wrong by tonight when that rider ends up missing. I took my dose of Senna's Ward this morning, so Rangrim doesn't have reason to suspect something unless my nightly dose isn't taken."

"Strange that you have such trouble with the altitude," she said. "Lowlanders typically acclimate within a few days."

"Guess I'm unique," I said. It wasn't worth the worry when we were in this deep.

It had been about an hour of travel, and though I felt physically exhausted, my body had clearly worked much of my sickness out of my system. Odd, I suppose, that dizzying heights cured my spinning head.

I suppose that someone who'd grown up among the peaks of Ba Turin might find the boulder's presence to be more unordinary. To me, a stone was a stone, but Noskre pointed out to me the striations, the unnatural angle of its edges, and how each of these things did not fit in with the stone of the wall upon which it rested.

"Leave it to Kalanos' greatest craftspeople to haul a boulder from one part of the mountain to the other, and all for the sake of their chieftain," I said.

"I don't think it was quite hauled," she told me, looking upward. "Nor did it fall. I think it was likely carved from the same section of mountain and moved a small distance."

"A small distance? What, from the edge of this lip to the wall? An entire two feet?"

"Leave it to Kalanos' most *paranoid* people to collapse a path once they've used it," she responded, gesturing to the treacherous terrain we'd just conquered.

It was then I saw the handholds not as chance pockets, but of marks left by tool and sundering stone. The ledges we'd walked were the vestigial pieces of a much broader trail.

"There's something I still don't understand," I told her. "Why make an escape route for the chieftain if it leads to a treacherous climb? Did the Turin of the past assume each future leader would be so able?"

"If they can't climb stone," she said with a shrug, "they don't deserve the title."

Or apparently their life, I thought.

Noskre saw my expression and shook her head. "I wouldn't go looking for logic in ancient expectations."

The exertion of the journey and the passing time had granted me a semblance of good health. I took deep breaths that were thinner here than in lowland Kalanos and relished in the ability to just *breathe*. I produced Senna's Ward and ate half of what remained, feeling, for the first time that day, able to swallow something and keep it down.

"I think this will put me back in good standing with my body," I said to Noskre. I looked from her to the boulder.

"You said there was a second tunnel," she reminded me. "Where is it?"

Marmot perked up as if he'd been pulled from deep thought. "Oh, it's higher up. We have to climb some more."

I let my head hit the stone beside me and did my best to curse in Rucosti.

THE CANAL CONTAINED AN INCH OF WATER, WHICH TURNED IT to ice under our feet. I remembered the slickrock Rangrim pointed out on the journey up the mountain trail. Not exactly the ideal terrain when you're thousands of feet in the air.

Its walls were high enough to allow my hands to walk along the edges, which came up to my hips, and the shadowed tunnel ahead seemed large enough to fit through comfortably — if you were child-sized, anyway.

"I would stop talking at this point," said Marmot. "Your voice might echo down the tunnel."

I relayed the information to Noskre behind me. She marveled for a moment, seeing proof, she thought, that my powers of divination were real.

We ducked into the darkened skull of Ba Turin. The wind passing over the opening behind us played the palace like a flute. Deep, groaning chords breathed in dissonance with the mountain's hum.

Marmot stood as he walked. His hair brushed the uneven tops of the tunnel. I crawled forward on my hands and knees, and the curtain of shadow swept into place as soon as Noskre joined in behind me.

What if the tunnel gets too small? I thought. *What if one of us gets stuck and we can't get out? What if they hear us coming? What if this tunnel isn't the right one, and we fall into the pools of the throne room?*

I did my best to focus on feeling the stone beneath my hands and crawling forward a bit at a time. I'd never been in such a small space in my life; up until now, everything had been framed by a ceaseless grassland or the open skies of mountaintops. The last time I'd felt like this was in the old chieftain's home, swallowed whole in the throat of dead beasts.

Stone scraped against my arms, back, and knees. The sounds of shuffling melded into one waterfall of constant noise.

We crept forward and down for ten minutes, but it felt like a thousand.

Then Marmot suddenly dropped out of view, and the room beyond shone dimly into the tunnel.

The baths were enormous. The chamber itself was a monument to open space. Its wide-tiled floor was skirted by ten natural pools; its ceiling gathered steam like a cloud-scape. The walls were carved masterfully, smooth as sanded oak and emblazoned with a colorful history. Heat swept my face as I entered the room, and I wondered at the use of natural hot springs. I'd never come across them before. But why did they shepherd in cold rainwater when they had a natural source of water inside? I would remember to ask one of the Turin later, if I managed to survive the day.

My feet hit the bath below briefly before I fell face-first.

"Again?" hissed Noskre as she pulled me from the water.

"I'm fine." I steadied my swimming vision and stepped with soaked feet from pool to dry floor. I would not let the altitude conquer me on the day I would strike at a Shiver.

"I think she's already been here," said Marmot from the other side of the room, his voice echoing carelessly from wall to wall.

"Moddimok has been here already," I whispered to Noskre.

"She'll either be in her quarters or in the war room," she responded. "She'll have appointed a new advisor by now, and the coming Rucosti soldiers will force them into serious discussion."

"So we'll have company?" I asked.

"Let's worry more about the guards along the way," she said with a groan. "An advisor is hardly a threat. I certainly can't fight the Red Wardens on my own."

Marmot pressed his ear to the wide wooden door that

led, presumably, into a hall. Upon his assurance that it was silent, I walked to the door, found the ringed handle and pulled it ajar. He disappeared into the hall, and in a moment his face reappeared in the sliver between the doors.

"Wait here," he said. "I'll let you know where she's at and when to go."

"Aren't you worried about the other Shiver?" I whispered, covering my face with the door.

Marmot gave me an apprehensive look before he walked out of view. I closed the door and turned back into the room.

"What's going on?" Noskre asked.

"Give me a moment. I'm going to search for the best course of action."

She looked around, bewildered. "In the steam?"

I tried to answer but retched again.

"Rennik," she responded, placing a hand between my shoulders. "...this isn't mountain sickness."

The floor had suddenly found a collection of blisters.

"...you're coughing up blood."

Noskre left without me. I could not speak, could not stand or stop her. I felt that at any minute one of Moddimok's royal guards would find me, and I would be killed in moments.

Think.

I tried to focus on small things one at a time. The lip of the nearest bath. The stream trickling in from the canal. I pulled myself toward it and drank rainwater until the copper taste of blood had been washed from my mouth. Awful, I thought, that if I were to find myself dying of sudden illness, that my last action in life might be murder. I always pictured my death to be waiting outside, under a wide sky with the soil and grasses of home beneath me. But I suppose it'd be worse if my last action were a failure.

I will not die in this room.

A few moments of stillness, and my eyes could focus enough to scan the area. Marmot had said there were two tunnels connected to the baths. If the other were the right one to take, he would have taken us through it right away, but I couldn't walk through the palace proper in this state. Each bath was built against its closest wall, and I couldn't picture any of them hiding a tunnel.

If only Avid were here, I thought. *He'd spot secrets in a building faster than anyone.*

I decided to look at the room like my brother would. He'd focus on things that were constructed, things that were altered, things that could swing and shut. I noticed a door built into a protruding bit of wall that presumably to lead to a small storage space.

Surely it isn't that easy.

And upon opening the door, there were only stacks of soft cloths and jars of oil. I stepped around the protrusion to hold myself against the wall, and I thought my vertigo was worsening when I felt a slight shift in my balance. But a sound accompanied the shift, and I looked downward.

The tile below my foot was as inconspicuous as the rest, but I knew I'd found something. The blade of my knife slipped easily into the floor. I used it as a lever and brought the tile up. With the scrape of stone and a small plume of dust, I had uncovered a hole big enough to slip into.

I silently thanked the absent Avid for his insight, and wondered if I should wait for my companions or move forward on my own.

The voices approaching from the hall made my decision

an easy one, and in a moment I was gone. After a short stay in the warm and colorful baths, the tunnel was decidedly its opposite. It was lightless, cold, and cramped.

"...but at least it's a comfortable room," said a muffled voice from the baths above.

"And you don't know why we're being sequestered like this? It's just that it reminds me..."

"...of what?"

"Of years ago, when the occasional rebel would charge into the palace and they'd clear us from the hallways!"

"Vu," said the first voice, "I don't think there are any threats *left* in Ba Turin. Who would they be searching for now?"

The tunnel became colder. If they were attempting to place important people out of harm's way...

I felt my way forward, hoping the blood I'd left behind would go unnoticed.

I LISTENED FOR A LONG WHILE BEFORE I PUSHED AT THE ceiling. I could imagine a tile rising from the floor in a crowded but quiet room, the dirtied face of a lowlander peering up, the rush of justice for the intrusion.

Instead, there was a face.

One of Marmot's eyes stared back into the tunnel as he laid sideways on the room's floor.

"You have a good memory," he whispered. "I saw other people in the baths, and I figured you'd found the other tunnel!"

I swallowed the thought that I'd known this child for less than a week, that I was now trusting him to lead me as I attempted to kill the leader of the Turin.

"Where are we?" I asked.

"This is Noskre's room. *Was* her room, I guess. I think she's nearby, but we should hurry to help her."

"Help her do what, exactly?" I asked as I pulled myself into the room proper. "Where has she gone?"

Marmot looked at me with concern as he ran to the door. "To kill Moddimok," he said. "She was headed to the chieftain's chambers. Come on, the guards were all called into the throne room!"

"But Marmot, they said they were searching for—"

But he had opened the door and was running down the hall. I drew my knife and followed. The hallway was at least twenty feet wide, vested in torchlight and painted stone. The ceilings wore fine silks that festooned their arching heights. I fought the taste of bile in my throat.

"Wait!" I whispered. "Marmot, they might know we're here!"

"We've already jumped in the water, Rennik! We need to do this now if you're going to stop the person attached to Rangrim." He spoke loudly, unburdened by the threat of being overheard.

And then we heard them fighting.

Noskre was thrown from a door on the right side of the great hallway, her face contorted with rage and pain. Something that looked like a vase shattered next to her head, and she leapt into the room to the left as glass shards settled on the ground.

Moddimok dashed toward her, an ornate axe in her hand, glass crunching under her sandaled feet. Her face grinned the wicked grin of a fighter who relished in their violence. She disappeared confidently into the next room without noticing us.

Upon reaching the door I saw another object below me

— not crudely shattered glass, but a perfectly faceted blue gemstone.

I knew it immediately to be the sapphire Noskre had promised Vivonno. She must have had it in-hand when the struggle began. I swiped it from the floor, tucked it deftly into the internal pocket at my waistline, and stepped toward the fight.

I stooped to pick up a shard of glass. Moddimok was framed in the doorway as she caught Noskre's hand and wrenched it in unnatural angles. The short sword clattered to the floor. Noskre fell back against a table as I sped into the room.

Moddimok raised her axe.

I plunged my knife into her shoulder.

She screamed as her hand dropped the weapon, spasmed, and flexed angrily.

"Guards!" she shouted as she turned to me. There was a desperation in her voice; this wasn't the first time she'd called for them.

Her elbow thrust quickly into my throat as I swiped at her face with the glass shard. She shoved me. I stumbled back into the hall, gasping for breath as my stomach lifted again. The room spun briefly.

"*Where are my guards?!*" Moddimok screamed again, launching herself in barbaric swings at the defenseless Noskre.

If she didn't send them away...

I looked down the hall for Marmot and found him wide-eyed, attention fixed in the direction we'd come from. His head shook back and forth, and he began to cry. A whimper escaped his mouth. His fingers began to knead themselves at his chest.

And then his hands shot up to his throat. His feet left the

ground. An invisible force was pressing him against the wall, choking the breath from the eternal child of Ba Turin. The veins in his arms and neck became engorged, and he flailed at something out of his reach.

I picked up my knife and lunged into the space before him only to find that it was empty. My body sprawled forward. Leaping to my feet, I grabbed Marmot's leg and tried to pull him away, but it was no use. I fought both my spinning vision and a Shiver I could not touch. Marmot's eyes flicked from the face of his attacker to mine, then over my shoulder.

Something wrenched me back and against the opposite wall. Stone bludgeoned my shoulder blades as the light of the room circled again, and Rangrim stepped into the vortex. She pulled me close, fist clutching my shirt, and studied my eyes.

"I didn't think you'd be so bold," she said, "as to attempt murder in the palace. But it appears my informant was correct. And I must admit: this is a better outcome than I originally had planned."

I thrust my knife into the visage of Rangrim and found it as empty as the Shiver. After all this movement, there was no up or down, no solid object in sight. She stepped on my hand and forced the weapon away.

"You told me these people of shadow were malicious," she said. "Something to be avoided. But I've discovered, Rennik, that when you listen to their whispers...the path becomes clear."

"Noskre," I croaked. "Noskre, she's here."

But the eyes in the whorl of Rangrim simply watched the battle ensue, as if an attempt on her mother's life were a passing curiosity.

"Help me, Rangrim!"

"For a day or so," she continued confidently, eyes fixed still, "on the trail, I thought you might be clever. You used learned words, spoke two languages, philosophized with Crattle...but a clever person would recognize when a poultice becomes a poison."

Senna's Ward, I thought with effort. *She poisoned my medicine.*

"Chieftain Moddimok earned the throne with the blood of a bear," she continued. "My throne will be won with the blood of assassins."

I fell fully to the floor and vomited. Blood had found its way into my stomach again, and it dripped now from my mouth and nose. I saw in the eddies of my vision that Noskre was slowly overpowering the chieftain. Her knife, like the bobber of a fishing line, allowed me to trace the movement, and the movement was steady.

"Rangrim!"

The chieftain shouted.

"Rangrim?!"

Her voice echoed in the empty halls.

"Daughter!"

The blade pushed closer to Moddimok, her hands gripping Noskre's arms, slowly giving way, forcing her into the tableside behind her.

"You made it very clear, *chieftain*..." said Rangrim.

Her legs kicked, but Noskre leaned forward and bit the chieftain's arm until she relented.

"...You have no daughter."

And then the knife in her attacker's hand punched heavily through her ribs, and the great and towering Moddimok, keeper of the Tempest Throne, mother to the once-named Rangrim, fell to the ground and died on the stone of her home.

"Mighty Moddimok!" Noskre crowed, punctuating each statement with another stab of the knife. "How low you've fallen! What a small measure for a Turin woman. All of your conquests, your glories, your triumphs and spoils, will come to nothing more than these few pitiful inches. Farewell, you carrion traitor. Wither and rot."

And now it was Rangrim who wore her wicked grin.

"You've lost," I told her through my bloody retching. "You couldn't save your mother, and now you're outnumbered." But as I said it, I saw the unmoving heap of a child in the hall. I saw Noskre speaking victoriously, not to Rangrim, but to the dead woman on the ground, too deep in the nets of her pride to notice the killer in the doorway.

Rangrim stood, pulled an arrow to her cheek, and sent Noskre din Costa down to die upon the body of her mother.

16

MOUNTAIN SICKNESS

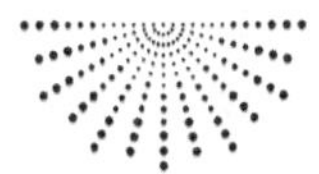

It is inarguable that the best reflection grows from consequence.

— EXCERPT FROM REMI GRENFALLOW'S *PHILOSOPHY OF CRIME*

I could not recount what happened in the moments after we'd failed. I woke with my face in blood. It hurt to breathe. My eyes fell upon a single, small pock in the stone wall before me, and the realization woke me up entirely.

My vision is back.

There was a sweetness in the air, something in the room that was familiar to me but had not been there before. It had grown darker.

I pushed myself to my knees. My entire body hurt, but I could see. I could *move*.

But where is Rangrim? I thought. I looked up.

And through the bars of a deep mountain cell came the laughing face of a Rucosti criminal.

"If I knew I'd be having company," said the flickering visage of Haston Corde, "I would've prepared a meal."

"What..." I began, feeling the whirl of confusion, not vertigo. My hip was sore from laying on stone. My eyes were pounding. I realized the sweet smell came from the honey suspended from the hallway's ceiling.

A single hand, dark with grime and insect pulp, wrapped around a bar of his cell. His face was maniacal, sweat-soaked and streaked with filthy hair.

"Oh, my dear friend. The philosophizing philistine. The brilliant barbarian. What a fitting fate you've come to! You could have killed me under the overhang. You could have killed me when you discovered who I truly was. You could have shot through the bars of my crude cage. It is Kalanosi custom to kill a wounded creature if it will only suffer, but you chose each time to *lengthen* my suffering. And now you must sit and see what you have done. You must *feel* what you have done."

I lifted a trembling hand to the blood and bile on my face. There was a throbbing pain in my head that told me I'd been hit. They must have moved me into this cell immediately after I'd lost consciousness.

My hand felt for my knife and found nothing. Of course they wouldn't leave me my weapon, but reason had yet to join me in captivity.

"You have mountain sickness," he said gleefully. "Though perhaps, Rennik, the true disease of the mountain is the loss of the mind in isolation, or the pressure one feels when surrounded by the weight of the world's stone. Perhaps the mountain turns fear into anger as well as iron to sapphire, and it is that anger that led you here."

Iron to sapphire...

I felt at my hip and realized why it was so sore. It was not simply stone floor that brought on this pain, but the object *between* the floor and my leg. In a single red and brilliant ribbon of torchlight, I produced the treasure we'd been after.

There was a winter storm I'd witnessed in my childhood that trapped the world in thick scabbards of ice. I remember marveling at a blue spruce nearby, and how each of its countless needles were preserved like flies in colorless amber, a matte surface blessed with dimension and shine.

The sapphire was a glassy blue spruce, profound in dimension and large enough to conquer the palm of my hand. It sat in a throne of roughly-hewn iron, a simple saddle for an extraordinary token. There was a unique charm that came from the combination of the two, and I would've admired it further if I'd been anywhere but here.

"I may be dying soon," he continued. "I am a gallows bird with clipped wings, but now I can watch my clipper sink. I do hope it is a slow descent, Rennik, for this may truly be the last thing I relish. A final meal. The natural rhyme and reason of life can outshine the brightest of epitaphs, don't you think?"

"Eat your insects, Corde," I said in a painful rasp. "I was raised on hunger and wait."

I sat against the wall, deep in the dark reaches of my cell, and tried to breathe slowly. Time passed, and eventually I lost the sense of seconds and minutes and hours.

Foremost on my mind was the dual image of Marmot's body and Noskre's death. Rangrim had instructed the guards to fill the throne room, away from the cries of her renounced mother. She hid her favored courtiers in scattered rooms — or, I realized, it was more likely that she intended to use them as a sort of alarm. She knew I would not harm them, knew they would shout and alert her to my presence. I wondered if Noskre would have shown the same restraint, or if, to her, the courtiers of Mother's Hall were collateral in the killing of Moddimok.

Haston Corde attempted twice to goad me further. He told me the Achare were cursed to die and that I would soon follow suit. He told me I would never find what it is I sought. But I gave him no heed, and he soon retreated into general silence, muttering the occasional literary passage he'd committed to memory.

I focused on what would come next.

Rangrim will find me here, I thought. *And then what?*

I felt as though I'd lost much of the poison along with my blood, but my weakness would surely last a while longer. If she came into my prison, I could not hope to fight a strong opponent like her. And I found it much more likely that she'd either have me slain through the bars of the cell or allow me to starve to death.

I was comfortable in quiet, in hunger and patience, and so, fighting off my discomfort of small spaces, I allowed myself to wait.

GATSI ONCE TOLD ME THAT SOME INSECTS WAIT IN THE DIRT for days, weeks, or years before they taste fresh air. They crawl through soil, dung, root, and rock to fly effortlessly into the sky and leave the earth behind.

I would never grow wings. I had no claws with which to tunnel through a mountain. I had only a dwindling poison and a priceless gemstone, which was as useful here as silver in the grasses. And I worried that I would never transcend the guilt I felt when I considered the actions of my past.

I let myself be convinced to shoulder the burden of leadership, and half the Achare died below the ridge. I thought I could outfox the horde and hide the others atop my plateau, and they fell from that height in smoke and char. I thought I could use Noskre din Costa to my advantage and kill Moddimok and Rangrim, and now the only survivor was my only true enemy. I thought I could slither through the palace undetected despite my sickness, and now Marmot was gone and I was locked away.

Moddimok asked me before if the summation of my life was found in the fleeing, and I know now that she was wrong — but so was I. The summation of my life seemed to be a series of failures.

This was the soil from which I must crawl, but I was firmly weighed down by the dead in my wake.

"Crattle," I said. "You said the clans would be put in disarray when you arrived...did the pale man speak of using anything invisible?"

"Shh," he said. "You'll scare the insects." He seemed to be losing his mind.

"Is there any reason he would do that here?"

He did not answer, but looked at me confusedly.

Footsteps echoed down the dark stairs.

Corde seemed caught between suspicion and excitement.

"She's coming for you," he whispered to me. "A shame that you won't suffer longer, but the greatest justice is swift."

I considered the sapphire in my hand as if it were a weapon. Perhaps I could strike her with it like a stone, or use its chain to choke her. My body was still fatigued, however, and I knew this fight may be my last.

But Haston Corde's face suddenly changed, and he looked down the hall in disbelief.

"Is this...is this real?" he asked jubilantly to the space I could not see. "A Rucosti savior! You've come to free me from this savage prison! Oh, blessed Ityx has delivered me again!"

There was a pause.

"I'm not here for you."

A hulking, hairy figure loped into my view and set his ears back upon seeing me. Karay whined, stood on his hind legs, and pushed against the bars of my cell with his paws.

Vivonno took the torch from the wall and maneuvered it to see me better.

"There you are!" he said with a grin. "The dog caught your scent as soon as we came from outside. He practically ran me here!" The Rucosti merchant replaced the torch in its sconce and produced a ring of keys. The fourth attempt turned a mechanism in the iron door, and he swung it outwards.

I stood in disbelief. Karay launched forth and pressed me against the wall in a colossal onslaught of affection.

"I can explain on the way up," he said. "Where's that Sessian business partner of ours? Where's my ironhound?"

"...dead," I told him. "She's dead."

Vivonno's face became gloomy. "I don't suppose you can withhold her end of the deal on your own?" he asked.

I brought the sapphire up to show him, and his eyes widened.

"You got the Ironhead Gem," he said. "And kept it *in here?*"

"Vivonno, what's going on? Why are you here?" My voice was a stone scraping stone after all the vomiting I'd done.

"Well," he said, "I saw them carry you into the prisons —

they made a bit of a show of it, you must not remember — and since there aren't any Red Wardens on this end of the Hanallta anymore, I figured it was profitable to spring you loose!"

"What do you mean there aren't any wardens?"

"Things have, uh...become a bit interesting since this morning. Come on, it's almost sunset, and we need to get you out of here."

He stepped forward, took a second to locate the cleanest part of me, and directed me out of the cell.

"Brother!" pleaded Haston Corde. "My friend, we are cut of the same cloth! We cherish our country! I beg you, please, let me look upon my home instead of these bloody walls! Please! You like precious stone? I'll give you tenfold what that brute can offer! I'll give you anything!"

Vivonno looked to me. "Well?" he asked. "He seems like a pompous ass to me, but you probably know better. You want to spring him too?"

"Rennik," Corde continued. "Please. I can help you find him! I can help you get revenge for your people!"

I looked to Haston Corde and knew the lies for what they were.

"Maybe I should release you now," I said into the iron cage. He looked hopeful for a moment. "I could cut the tendons in your knees and shoulders, throw you into a shallow pit and let the mountain devour you. I could watch as the insects crawl upon your face, watch as you'd try desperately to eat, to wish with all your heart that you were back here, safe from me behind your bars and equipped with a hand that obeys you. Perhaps it will be your name — your *true* name — on my lips when I speak to the smoke and invoke the dead." But I knew as I said it that I would not curse myself that way. Already each question I asked was laden with the name of Zamri Malnostos and the guilt that came with killing.

"No," I concluded. "I think it is the waiting that wounds you. I think the pale man's coming is a pain to you, and whatever death he brings upon you will be justice enough."

17

FARMERS & FIGHTERS

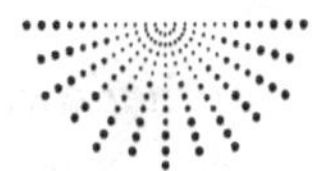

*Do you think the goldfinch chooses to change color,
or do you think it has to?*

— AVID

"It started just after you were taken to the cells," said Vivonno as we emerged from the mountain. "Rangrim announced that her mother was dead, that she killed one assassin and had the other in captivity. But then she went... wild. She pointed an axe at her own people and cursed them for harboring her would-be killers. She said their conspiring would end today. Everybody got a bit worked up and wouldn't move for her. She told her guards to make a path. They got physical, then the crowd got physical, then...well, now she's off east somewhere with her guards."

"Was anyone hurt? Where's Hegira?"

"I think some people were mildly hurt, yes, but—"

"*Where's Hegira?*"

"She's alright!" he said, putting his hands up defensively as I turned on him. "She's with the rest of us!"

"The rest of you?"

"Almost every one of the Turin are holding out with our guild on this half of the Hanallta. Rangrim and her guards have dug in on the other side."

"Wait, what — dug in? What has this turned into?"

"There was only that one little fight, but...more seems inevitable."

"Surely she wouldn't hurt her own people."

"A few days ago, maybe. But she's different, Rennik. Something's changed."

The Shiver, I thought. It was becoming more evident that if Moddimok had changed, had exchanged loyalty for Rucosti favor, it was the Shiver whispering in her ear, manipulating her decisions. But did this Shiver decide to inflict itself upon both mother and child, or did it leave one for the other?

"Do we have access to the trail?" I asked.

"We do. Rangrim has access to neither the main trail nor Mother's Hall." He took a good look at me. "You look like absolute hell."

"Rangrim poisoned me, beat me, and left me in a cell."

"That'll do it."

We walked around the corner of a home and stopped. Carts, pieces of scaffolding, and other assorted objects were leaning against each other, forming an improvised palisade. A shield against their own leader. I shook my head in disbelief, and we continued toward a mass of people near the teeth.

"Why don't you leave?" I asked.

"Why would I?" he responded with a knowing grin.

"Not you. Your entire guild. This conflict doesn't involve you."

"A good trader isn't just a silver tongue and a good eye,

Rennik. It's necessary to have allies, people who think of you first and foster a profitable relationship."

"And?"

"With every conflict, there is a winner. And I think it's clear who'll come out on top of this one." He gestured to the gap-toothed bulwark. "We lease our carts and crates to the Turin for the price of eternal gratitude. People forget a salesman…"

He guided me through the Turin crowd and toward a collection of bedrolls tucked under the Great Wing. Several were occupied by wounded people. Vivonno helped me down to one, smiled again, and finished his thought.

"They never forget an ally."

THERE'S AN OLD STORY GATSI WOULD TELL THAT ORIGINATED with the Rask. In it, a sailor's catamaran capsizes, and she finds herself marooned in a coastal cave, trapped by high tide and lightless stone. When she eventually leaves and returns to her home, she discovers her children are grandparents, the structures have doubled in number, and even the way they'd built their boats had changed. It was apparently some magical effect of the sea salts in the cave that stupefied and preserved her, without her knowledge, for two generations. It was intended to be a warning not to wander too far from home.

It was as if the walls of my cell were constructed of such salts, as if I'd emerged from the mountain a decade later to an alien place and people. Potters toted axes, smiths held swords, farmers carried what varied implements of their trade could best be swung at neighbors rather than soil.

I did manage to sleep, but it was fitful at best. Karay stood vigil against the rest of the world. He became overly protective and rumbled at any who came too close to my sleeping place.

"Good boy," I told him, and fell back to sleep.

~

"I DON'T KNOW WHAT TO DO," I SAID. "MARMOT IS...I DON'T know. I suppose if he can catch a cold, he can die...Noskre is dead. Moddimok is dead. Rangrim wanted me dead — maybe she still does — but she's sequestered to the other side of the Hanallta. Marmot was going to tell me about the woman I was meant to find...maybe it was foolish to come all this way for a single thing Gatsi said."

Karay stared at me. He wasn't exactly a good conversationalist.

"You always feel guilty about others' suffering," I imagined him saying. His voice was something between Kheze and Ko. "Consider the current situation without emotion. You can explore this side of the Hanallta now. You have allies here. You survived being poisoned. And Owasa is probably around here somewhere."

I looked discerningly at the dog.

"That's a good point."

A Turin man stopped, looked confusedly from Karay to me, and continued on. Perhaps he'd tell his companions that the lowlander can speak to beasts. Passing two nights alone made me crave some company.

I found her with her father and a few other men. After sleeping for a day and a half, walking, talking, and thinking were much easier.

So was eating.

Kheze, true to his nature, was cooking right here in the

open air of the Great Wing. A man I didn't know saw me coming and handed me some meat and vegetables.

"They want us to be ready to fight, Kheze. I thought it would just be a show of force, a way to put Rangrim in line," said a woman named Azmi.

"She swung at a *child*," added a man with a black eye. There'd been two small altercations since Rangrim's outburst. Both were merely threats and aggressive gestures, but the tension in the Hanallta had only increased.

"Who's 'they', and how do you know they're in charge?" asked Kheze with a placating gesture.

"It was Pal—"

"Palka's always ang—"

"—and Finch, and Pin Oak, and Marl."

Kheze worried over the cooking meat for a moment. "Alright," he conceded, "that may be true, then."

"She swung at a *child*," repeated Black Eye.

"I've known you too long, Kheze," said Azmi.

"Why's that?" asked Kheze with a grin.

"Because I know what you're thinking. You consider everything with a cook's mind. 'If only they sat down together', you're thinking, 'with some goat and smoked salmon'."

Kheze was quiet while the others chuckled for a moment.

"You're wrong," he finally said.

The group became sober. "How's that?" asked Azmi.

"I was considering pork."

This time, they all laughed together.

Owasa patted her father's arm. "That lowlander is here," she said.

Kheze turned to me. "Rennik! Word is you were poisoned. Hope that didn't turn you off of food for good."

"I'd hardly call Senna's Ward 'food'," I said. The group

smiled genially in response. "So this conflict between you and Rangrim is that dire?" I asked.

"That's the feeling around here. She really poisoned you?"

"She told me herself. Boasted about it."

"She spent too long beneath Ba Turin," said Azmi. "Got high off all the air, maybe. Forgot who she was."

"She swung at a *child*."

"What exactly are you going to do?" I asked. "March into their slice of the Hanallta and lean on your numbers? How many Red Wardens are there, anyway?"

"Probably three dozen. Iron armor, swords, spears, and formal training."

"Does the average Turin know how to fight?"

"In their imaginations, I bet. But the violence below has left us alone. Guess we got complacent. Never thought the attack would come from one of our own, not since Rangrim was exiled, anyway."

"Do you aim to kill her?"

I didn't mean to silence them. Azmi's mouth worked with an automatic response that never came.

"Right. Well, I was actually hoping I could speak to you, Owasa."

The girl looked at me doubtfully, then to her father. In times of conflict, children tend to stick close to the familiar.

"Concerning what?" asked Kheze curiously.

"Your paint," I told her. "I think it's incredible that you have talent like that at a young age. Do you always paint things you've seen?"

She nodded her head.

"Was the sunset on the western wall an important one?"

Kheze cleared his throat. "I think it was the last one with her mother," he said quietly.

The others wandered away after that comment. Kheze looked exactly like a concerned parent should — clearly, I was dredging up uncomfortable memories.

"Well, you've captured the colors and beauty of Ba Turin perfectly."

"Thanks," she said with a sheepish grin. "I never grow tired of them."

"And what about the stars?"

She looked puzzled.

"I saw them once, the other night. They were glowing — it was unforgettable, Owasa," I told her with a smile.

Her face lit up. "Oh! Those aren't stars, they're..." And then she darkened, looked downward, and grew a little red.

"Owasa," Kheze said. "You can tell him. He's a good man. He's a friend."

"It's a secret." It was quiet, hardly a mumble.

"Sorry, Rennik," said Kheze. "Can't blame her. Sometimes children need a bit of the world to themselves."

"Of course they do," I said. "Really, Owasa, you're a wonderful painter."

She thanked me quietly and left. I wonder if Kheze knew how much she'd actually told me. From years spent with Avid, I recognized evasion when I saw it. She wasn't keeping a secret from me; she was keeping a secret from her father.

She'd been somewhere she wasn't supposed to be.

18

THE DARK HEART OF BA TURIN

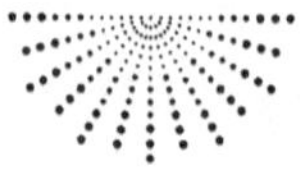

A coat should be worth its weight.

— KALANOSI PROVERB

The winter after I'd nearly died, my parents became determined. Their hearts were in the right place, of course, but this wasn't the same as gutting your first deer, when your hands are forced into a first gruesome act to make the rest of them easier.

This felt different.

My mother had dug a tunnel in the snow for me. She told me that the cold and the dark couldn't hurt me if I stayed calm and made smart decisions. But each time I descended, I withdrew as if it were the river. I don't blame myself — it's normal to avoid certain death, and my mind couldn't help but see the water that nearly killed me the year before.

My father watched from the hilltop, cradling a tiny, wriggling bundle and smiling warmly down at it. The first winter for his newborn, the last of his own.

My mother coaxed me into the tunnel again. She told

me that the world would never take it easy on me, that sometimes we must grow our own thick skin. She didn't push me.

Eventually, I learned to let myself drop.

~

ROPE IS ALWAYS HEAVIER THAN I EXPECT IT TO BE.

Normally, I'd feel bad about stealing something, but most of the houses and tents were empty, and I wanted to quit the sheer edges of Ba Turin as soon as possible. When I pictured it, I'd be walking down the trail, or riding a mule, or perhaps careening violently to my death.

I didn't expect to swim.

The sort of torch Noskre used, the kind with a flat end, was easy enough to find in Mother's Hall. I was surprised to be the only person in the palace. The Turin seemed to revere the place as much as the Mountain Mother herself. In the safety of solitude, I'd also located a journal in Noskre's room and pilfered several books from the library. I left those in a hiding place near Hegira's home.

I'd taken the heavy lantern from Vivonno's tent, but I intended to return it as soon as I was finished. Currently, the torch was standing next to me. It was surprising, I thought, that I had made my way into this cave unnoticed. I'd had to travel through the section of the Hanallta that Rangrim and her guards claimed.

The knot seemed sturdy enough, but I wasn't exactly confident in my knowledge as a plains-dweller. One end of the rope was gripped tightly to a piton, a sort of iron implement that stuck into stone.

I looked into the moving water. Surely, if Owasa could manage the feat, so could I. If the journey was too long, I could pull myself back with the rope. The current didn't seem immensely strong.

I hung my toes over the edge.

They were safe in my moccasins, and though I'd considered going in with minimal equipment and clothing, I feared the jagged stone that might lurk beneath the surface.

I tested the rope at my waist. It was secure. I palmed the handle of a long knife at my hip. My hands instinctively sought the bow at my back and found nothing. No use bringing arrows into a cave — at least that's what I told myself. For all I knew, the caverns beyond were filled with ill-tempered turkey.

If there were caverns at all. I was sure, though, that Owasa had either seen the glowing stars or was getting glowing material from somewhere in this cave. She was far too suspicious that night I followed Noskre. And the smoke suggested finding those stars...

"You're stalling," said my mother. There was snow in her hair.

"I don't know what's on the other side," I said both then and now. "It feels foolish."

"And if you continue to sit here, you'll never know. You're Achare, Rennik. It's time to wander."

I filled my chest.

"How fortuitous," said a voice from the dark. "You belong in the Shadowlands anyway."

Three figures entered the torchlight.

I exhaled shakily as three Red Wardens approached, blades drawn. They were slowly making their way toward me.

"Of course you'd find your way out of that prison," one said. "Rangrim said that rats will drag themselves through any cavity they find. And it looks like you've found another hole to crawl into."

The surface of the water tugged at my feet. The darkness tensed.

"She was clear enough," he said. "Kill him."

I dropped into the river.

It took me quickly.

The cold nearly stole my breath.

Plunging into the wild current, I found myself dangling on the end of the rope in a few seconds. It became taut, and I realized I was being pulled back upstream.

And then I saw the stars.

Through the glassy mountain water I saw scattered blue lights, dimmed by distance and the chill assaulting my eyes. But there was no way to get upstream without being plucked from the water by the Red Wardens.

My lungs began to burn.

I reached upward, hoping for hand-holds, and found only smooth rock. I could not simply stay and drown, could not return to the surface.

I pulled numbly on the knife at my hip. It slid from its sheath and found the rope.

I was swept into the tumult of the black mountain void.

THE STONE BIT DOWN INTO THE DARK, A GLUTTONOUS JAW CLOY with the detrital wash of grief. I knelt in tokens left for the dead — waterskins, rotted food, toys, clothes, and gifts were all laid here in forlorn piles. Small prices to pay, perhaps, for peace of mind.

I'd left my torch behind. It would've been soaked anyway. The torches among the piles, however, were not.

I looked up to see the river gushing overhead. I'd been dropped on a ledge that sat beneath a waterfall, a hand cupping water under a spigot. It was incredible luck that I hadn't skewered myself; upon lighting an adopted torch with flint, I'd found my knife wedged between two stones, its blade staring up at the mouth that'd spat me out.

I recognized the pack that Noskre had sent for her sister. If this was the place of exile for enemies of the chieftain, it told me two things. First, that it was dangerous. Second, that if I met Callisgrim in the lowlands, it meant there was a way out.

The torch was an old spruce branch crowned with oil-soaked jute. Easy to light, and a little resistant to water, but I gauged it would only last a few minutes at best. I retrieved my knife and made to assess the situation more fully.

There was a pocket of open space where I'd landed that was about fifteen feet deep and tall enough to crouch in. The water beat heavily somewhere below and curtained the ledge from the space beyond.

There is, of course, no sense of north once you've tumbled through dark water. I had no idea how far down I was, but I knew I'd made a grave mistake — the lights shown in the smoke had been upstream.

I slid myself between the stone wall and curtain of water.

The cavern was massive. Torchlight could not find its ceiling, could not brush its floor or its distant walls. Below me was something between a slope and a wall; too sheer for the former, too angled for the latter.

What I'd do for a ladder...

I briefly considered feeding the flames with a mixture I'd prepared that morning, but the pack was surely soaked, and I wasn't sure I could see the specter clearly anyway.

The only way was down.

I could only imagine that the wall-slope led to deep water; where else would this modest freshet go?

The slide was free of scree, and I was once again glad to be rid of ripgut. I slid from hand-hold to hand-hold, catching with my left and lighting the way with my right. But the spirited shadows cast upon the wall made it difficult to predict the path.

I fell as my fingers groped helplessly on the stone. The torch plunged into the cavern with wild, top-heavy swings. My luck from earlier was gone.

First was my chest against the torch; then came my chin and knee against the stone. The blood was immediate upon my tongue.

My body lurched spasmodically from the flames. My breath was shallow. I'd nearly swallowed a pebble that now rattled between my teeth.

No, I realized. *That* is *my tooth.*

As it happened, the cavern walls did not lead to deep water.

I'D HAD PLENTY OF EXPERIENCE WITH LANTERNS. MOST recently as a means of burning a newly-constructed barn.

It seemed to have enough oil to last a few hours, and as my knee was starting to scream at me, I decided to take a moment in the shallow stream I'd found on the cavern floor. I set the lantern down, ignored the protests from my knee, and laid it bare in the frigid current. If I was going to walk, climb, and potentially fall again, the swelling would need to go.

Perhaps the next time I needed to find a mysterious woman in a foreign land, it would be on a beach.

My eyes surveyed my surroundings but returned frequently to the living wick, wide with greed for the oil it held. I felt the leather circle over my heart. My mother made this shirt over a year ago, and that added layer against my chest may have just saved me from a broken sternum.

I looked toward the small waterfall I'd dropped from. It was held by the darkness in an unseen place.

But its current isn't.

If this small river could escape the cavern, maybe I could too. I only hoped it wouldn't require my half-drowning like the previous route.

I felt my goal melting. The stars were *upstream*. I couldn't *go* upstream. No one knew I was here except—

Something scraped against the floor behind me.

I leapt halfway up. My knee bent more easily, but still it bludgeoned my senses.

There was only the water, whispering into the darkened pockets of the cavern.

It was just loose rock from my slide, I told myself.

But that slope was a smooth surface, made slick with centuries of running water.

A sudden draft pawed warmly at my back.

I spun back toward the water.

Okay, I rationalized, *drafts mean a passage.*

Footsteps.

They pushed through current, heavy, determined.

Then, from my left, the light steps of a child splashing in the shallows.

Now came the wind, blossoming with heat, blistering.

I looked to the lantern and saw its caged flame flickering as if exposed. The strange wind seemed to pass through the glass and attack the light.

It grew bright, grew red, became blood and anger.

And died.

The wind stopped in an instant.

Silence.

Darkness.

Through the paralysis of fear I worked my way forward, crawling to the lantern's unseen place on the ground. The soft press of my hands and knees against the floor felt loud and foolish. My breathing came short and stuttering through the choking silence.

Footsteps again. Slow. To my right, to my left, behind me.

My left hand felt the biting iron of the lantern — it had grown impossibly cold — and my right made to produce the flint from my pack. But in the midst of these strange happenings, it simply wasn't there.

I placed both hands on the lantern as if it were the only thing floating in the sea of this cavern. Soon, I realized the handle was warming. Not from my grip, but unnaturally. Quickly.

The flame returned with a cracking growl. Light spilled upon the floor.

And it revealed the man standing beside me.

I screamed as I jumped away. The lantern came with me, and for a moment it revealed the face of the figure.

I retreated with the staccato of broken floor and fear. I kept the figure in front of me, outlined in the resurrected firelight.

A voice swam forward.

"Be calm," it said. "Control your breathing."

"Get back!" I yelled. My jaw throbbed from the fall.

My hand grasped the handle of my knife, but I could not bring myself to pull. I knew I could not brandish a blade to the ghost I had seen.

It stepped forward again.

"You cannot conquer fear with a half a lung, Rennik. Steady yourself. You need to breathe deeply."

It was his voice that pulled the shade from his face. In it was the sound of fire, the silence of snow, the shivers of self-sacrifice, tears upon laughter and fingers upon string. In it was my childhood, my joy before loss, the world when both feet walked on steady ground.

I ceased my retreat.

The figure stepped forward, steadfast and calm, and in the warm light of the fire came the face of my father.

19

NO LIGHT TO REACH THE GRAVE

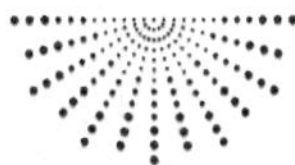

*I try my best not to think about them anymore. I
can't bring them back, and wishful thinking
would only end up hurting myself.*

— MALIK

The Achare don't tell many ghost stories.

I stood in the void of shock.

There was a soft grin — *his* grin, plucked without flaw
from my memories — brushed upon his face.

"What is this..." I asked, not to the figure but to the entire
world. "...What are you?"

He frowned.

"Are you feeling okay? Did you hit your head?"

"No." *Well, yes, actually.* My voice came through a swollen
jaw. I took a breath to steady myself. He looked around as if
studying landscape. I saw nothing to look at. He was wearing
the Sree war bow on his back and a quiver at his hip. Some

feathers were dyed; some were not. He was equipped for a scouting trip.

"...What's happening right now?" I asked him.

He looked past me. I glanced tentatively around and saw nothing but darkness.

"Walga is almost done with the food. We'll eat while we walk. If, by midday, we don't find the phantom herd the Chieftain insists upon, we'll turn around and head home." He shook his head and lowered his voice. "No one else saw the other bison. It's not that I don't trust him, but it doesn't make sense. Why would a second herd live so close to another? And even so, why bother with locating another herd? We have all the bison we need."

"Right," I told him.

"I don't appreciate a fool's errand through the grasses." His face changed, lit up a bit as he glanced over my shoulder again. "Perfect, Walga, thank you." He took something from an invisible hand. "Got yourself together?" he asked me.

"I do," I told him. My heart was starting to tear. The sutures of my closure had settled years ago, but now the dark fingers of the impossible plucked them apart, cut the scar tissue and left me bleeding.

My father turned away and began walking.

He pushed at grasses that were not there. He spoke with companions that did not speak. He shielded his eyes from a sun that would never touch this cavern.

I followed in his steps.

GREEN HERONS WILL DROP SMALL OBJECTS INTO THE WATER below a tree. They know fish often mistake the movement for evidence of insects, and when they come to the surface to investigate, the heron will dive, catch, kill, and devour its victim.

I couldn't shake the feeling that I was being lured. What other bait could be more effective than my dead father?

There were invisible Shivers stalking the grasses, a tree that collected herds like children in the long arms of its influence, people like me seeing impossible things. I was learning to accept that strange magics existed, and they were not always an ally.

But I was trapped in a corner. The only thing to do was to walk into what felt like a snare.

We'd left the large cavern behind. My father and I — and what seemed to be at least seven other Achare — walked through the shallows of the river, pushing through the water as it led through a thinning tunnel.

People have a habit of doing everyday things when their world is upturned, and I was no exception. I was numb in my motion, following this figure because there was no precedence for anything else. As the minutes went by, I regained a bit of my reasoning.

And I began testing the phantom before me.

"Chieftain Moddimok is dead," I told him.

He looked over his shoulder, confused. "How would you know? We haven't heard from the Turin in over a year."

"Avid is twelve years old."

"Avid is *one*."

He can't learn. This is my father strictly as he was in that moment, I realized. *But what moment is it?*

"How old am I?" I asked him.

"Ten, soon enough," he said, "far too young to be doing this."

I searched for an exception in my memory but found none. This is the day he was killed.

He began speaking to me about little things, about the children in the village and the fish I'd caught, about our best hunts and the herds we follow, about everything a father discusses with his son as they wander together.

The tunnel seemed to be descending steadily, albeit slowly. We had to navigate around the occasional stalagmite or squeeze through a tight spot. I'd lost my fear of the mountain since walking with my father. The mix of doubt and love was enough to keep me preoccupied.

"You know," he started, dropping his voice, "I've been meaning to talk to you about something."

"What's that?"

"Gatsi has been speaking to me more often lately. He's expressed an interest in educating you, one-on-one. Says he's noticed a certain cleverness in you that should be sharpened and pointed in the right direction."

"Okay," I answered. After a moment, I asked how he felt about that.

"I'm not sure," he said. "There's nothing wrong with Gatsi, he's shown nothing but care for the Achare — guess I should tell you he isn't quite Achare — but ever since that winter, Rennik...he's looked at you a little differently."

"He's the only one who still looks at me *at all*," I said. "He isn't like the people who won't even talk to me. I wouldn't want to learn from anyone else."

"I just worry...you know, one of the most important things I've ever learned is that there is such a thing as too much knowledge. There are some folk who start to obsess, start to get attached to a lure that leads them away. It's possible to grow fat on knowledge, you know? To fall in love with the chewing, the satiating of curiosity. There's just..."

I could tell he was dancing around something he

wouldn't say directly. I was fascinated; my father had never expressed these things to me before.

"A survivor stays lean. A survivor only carries what he needs. And Gatsi is the only one of us who's never been seen hunting. Do you understand what I'm saying, Rennik?"

"Maybe," I said. "But can't I be both? What's the danger in learning from a storyteller? Can't I learn what Gatsi knows and be Achare, too?"

"I'm not saying Achare can't learn, boy. I just...between you and me — *strictly* between you and me...there's a feeling in my gut that's kept me — well, I guess kept *him* at arm's length. I'm just not sure what his goal is, and it doesn't always sit well with me."

"Okay. I'll be careful."

"It's sort of like walking in the dark. You feel the huts and grasses nearby even if you don't see them. And I feel like Gatsi has a lot in the dark."

"He's never hurt anyone," I said. "But I'll still be careful," I added when he made to respond.

He turned his head and looked at me discerningly. His eyes were dramatic in the light of the lantern, a shade of green that could both see something clearly and see past it all at once.

"There's too much of your grandfather in you," he said with a smile. He looked forward again, swatting at an insect in the ethers of his world.

"Was he hated by the clan, too?" I asked.

"No," he said bluntly. "He had a memory you couldn't pierce. Swear he slept with his eyes open and read the stars each night." He laughed a bit. "I didn't get that from him — I've always been a lot like my mother."

"And that's a bad thing? His memory was a curse?"

My father grew somber and thought for a while. I'd

forgotten how long he'd take to really declare himself about something. "He was spiteful, near the end. There wasn't a mistake he couldn't remember, whether his own or in others. Seemed like he couldn't shake what he knew. Remember that, Rennik. It's hard to unlearn something once you've seen enough of it."

"I'm not sure I have your father's memory," I told him.

"Huh," he puffed out. "We can hope."

I remembered to check the lantern; the flame had already quaffed half of its reserve. Having no idea where I was going, I simply hoped my father would walk me the entire way. A few minutes passed, mine in the black of Ba Turin and his in the sun-soaked grasses of lowland Kalanos.

"I would've starved without you," I eventually told him.

"What? When? Your mother's a fine hunter too, you know."

"Not for long. Her bones will become brittle after a couple years, like her father."

"I don't understand, Rennik."

"The people you've spent your life protecting won't set their superstitions aside. They'll spurn your wife and children. So many nights, I've gone to sleep hoping I'll dream of you, because I'm terrified of forgetting your face. Even if the memory is painful, I want to keep you...I just...don't want to lose you in two ways."

This time he stopped and turned to me. He put a hand on my shoulder. "You're not going to lose me, Rennik. Your sense of direction is far too good for that. Sometimes I think you could find a pebble in a snowstorm. I'm not sure why you're so upset today, but...well, if you're out here with the rest of us, you're going to have to act a little older. Take a breath, get yourself together, and keep your eyes open. You're going to be alright."

There was a hard thump on my back as he slapped me between the shoulder blades. I did not expect him to be able to touch me. He continued walking, but pushed me ahead of him.

A moment later, I looked back. There was only the darkened ascent of the cave, the hum of the mountain, and the empty space where my father had been. He had gone as lightly as the passing shadow of a cloud.

"I suppose there's only one way to go, now," I said aloud.

Another voice came from downstream.

"Only you could manage to get lost on a straight line."

I spun and held the lantern high.

A man appeared, young, scowling, blocking my way.

"I was told you'd already left. What do you want?" asked Ciqala.

He wore a thick hide shirt — the one he wore on the day the Achare were massacred.

He stood looking to the horde on the ridge. He stood between decade-old huts and certain death. He stood with the Achare in a wall that would fight before giving way. His was a world of tension, of furious hearts in the embrace of home.

"Ciqala," I said to him. "I need to pass."

He snorted. "No."

"Please. You don't understand."

"We're preparing to defend our home," he said, pointing behind me, "and you choose to walk away."

I was slow to turn, slow to see the ghosts of a gossamer home I'd left behind. There was, of course, no one else here.

"For once in your life, Rennik, don't be a coward."

"I don't have time for this," I told him, glancing at the lantern in my hand. "Let me pass."

"No." He bristled up and gestured to the people I could not see. "We're counting our advantages. Perhaps you could actually lend a hand for once."

"There are no advantages," I told him. "The horde will swallow this village in one pass. You will die in the chieftain's hut."

He scoffed. "You think I won't die in sunlight? You think, even if I were to die by the horde's hands today, I would cower in a hut? It may be hard to imagine, Rennik, that some of us don't run."

"Ciqala," I said, raising my voice, "Let me pass."

"Why?"

"There's a woman who wants me dead. The daughter of the Turin chieftain. She's destroying her people and she needs to be stopped."

His brow furrowed. "The Turin are here? They're aggressive?"

"Yes," I lied.

He looked downward, then found his familiar criticism.

"And you're going to stop her?"

"Yes."

"You're going to kill her?"

I hesitated.

"Of course," he said, dismissing me and looking back to a table that wasn't there.

"What's the problem, Ciqala? I have business beyond this place and it does not concern you. Let me pass."

"The problem, Rennik? The true problem?" He stood up and threw something at his table. "Your mother is strong, and cunning, and an incredible example of what it is to be Achare. Your father was the fighter I wish every

Achare was. Even your brother is marked with incredible intelligence; I've seen him mentally take apart every construct he's ever come across, and I'm willing to bet he never forgets the process once he's worked it all out. But you... yes, you're smart, you're a good hunter, but *none* of those things manage to work through the mud of your self-pity. *No one* feels as bad for you as you do. And I know what you're thinking: 'that's the problem.' You blame your emotional stunting on everyone else, but for all your cleverness, you haven't criticized yourself thoroughly. Of *course* everyone else is to blame. That means it's not dependent on you to fix it. The only way to solve the problem would be to first forgive your neighbors and then place the onus of your suffering in your own hands, but I don't think you've ever brought yourself to do that. And I don't think you ever will."

My heart was in my throat.

"You can't possibly know how I carry my sufferi—"

"You tried to lead them to safety, but it was guilt that drove you, not forgiveness, not love for your people. *Malik* convinced you. It was sleight of hand. You were the cat's-paw. She pulled the strings of your guilt and she's shaking your pretty colors in front of the horde and in front of me and she'll never get close to the fire herself. 'Only you can lead them', she says, and suddenly you feel responsible. You're attached to your guilt, and so you are led by the nose like an ass when someone handles that guilt. You won't stay to defend our home, and unless you shed the weight of your guilt, you'll never kill this Turin of yours."

"Feeling guilt is part of being human."

"As if there's one sort of human," he responded. "It's also human to weep. It's human to feel anger and hunger. It's human to become sick. It's human to hurt and be hurt. It's human to die, but I don't see you rushing off to do that. Each day you draw breath, you choose what to be."

"I don't want to know what kind of monster I'd be if I shed remorse."

"Call it monstrous if you want. Maybe it's 'human' to decide the traits *you* don't possess make someone else less than human. It's comforting to believe that, I'm sure. But at least it'd be a monster who could take action. At least a monster has spine enough to stand, spine enough to fight for what they think is worth fighting for. If you truly need me to make your decisions for you, Rennik, here it is: if this woman stands between what is right and what is wrong and is willing to die for it, then you must be willing to kill for it. No one else will do that for you."

"Move aside, Ciqala."

"No one else will do that for you."

"I don't understand—"

"Yes you do. You're just as clever as your family and you can't feign ignorance. You're just treading water." He drew his weapon. He shifted his feet and became the pillar of his conviction. "No one else will move for you."

The shadow of my father had slapped me on the back. Perhaps this phantom could actually cut me down. Or maybe...

I tensed, took my knife in my hand, stepped forward, and plunged it into his chest.

He smiled.

"Like watching an infant take its first steps," he said, glancing down as I let go of the blade. There was no blood pouring upon the bison-bone handle.

I screamed in anger, clutched the knife again, and ripped the blade from his heart. I stabbed at him again and did not stop, feeling each time the breaking of taut flesh.

I smelled smoke.

Ciqala's face fell slack, became worrisome. His eyes traveled to the ground.

The lantern seemed to grow in power, but I soon realized the light was not coming from it. There was a fire at his feet, climbing steadily up his legs, the burning earth of his year-old death.

"What's happening?" he asked. Confusion widened his eyes. He grew fearful. "Why…"

I stepped back in horror and watched as Ciqala was immolated, as he screamed in the wild verses of pain, as he turned from phantom to ash and lay down in a bed of char.

And then it started to rain.

INSTINCT TUCKED THE LANTERN INTO MY EMBRACE, FEARFUL that this rain could douse the flame like the wind had before. Each drop carried the proper impact and bite of a true downpour.

The tunnel is flooding, I thought, having no experience with underground waterways.

I ran forward, lantern squeaking on its handle, feet sloshing through the stream. If not for the purposeful current beneath me, I might have lost the sense of descent. It seemed logical that the deeper into the mountain I ran, the less likely I was to get out, but there truly seemed to be no alternative path.

I'd learned that the Delkhi seemed to pull from both the living and the dead. Gatsi said its roots stretch great distances…had I found one such distance? Had I reached the land where the dead are kept and the tree's knowledge is born? And slowly, reluctantly, I wondered if perhaps I wasn't a visitor at all. I fell into a deep underground river...maybe I'd found the land of the dead through its most direct channel. I continued running, trying to withdraw from the cavernous rain assaulting me.

I almost ran over the little girl.

I hurdled past her, and the lantern went out in an instant.

When I'd met the first of the phantoms, the wick had reignited of its own accord, so I hoped it would again. I stood in place and waited for the light.

I felt a cold touch.

A hand slowly worked its way into mine. Small, icy, shivering. The hair on my neck raised.

"Are you one of them?" Her voice was as small as she was.

"I don't know," I said slowly. "Who are they?"

She waited a beat. "Can you take me home?"

"Can you light my lantern?" I asked.

She leaned toward me and rested her head on my hip. "I don't have anything," she said.

"Okay," I told her. "Do you know which way to go?"

"I think so." Her answer was muffled by my shirt.

She led me in a half-turn and pulled a bit. We began walking through the lightless tunnel, careful of the hidden things that tripped and snagged. I refrained from speaking for a while; this phantom was leading me somewhere, so I decided it was wise to let her. Maybe this wasn't a snare at all. Maybe I needed a guide.

"Are you Achare?" she asked.

Alright, so she doesn't know me.

"Yes," I told her. "Are you?" I felt her nod again.

"Have you seen my mother?" she asked.

"No, I haven't."

"Have you seen my father?"

"I haven't seen him either."

"Okay."

"Were they here with you?"

She nodded.

"When is the last time you saw them?"

"Yesterday," she said.

"How did you get separated?"

She didn't respond. Her hand tightened a bit, and her breath came quickly, fluttering with cold. Every few moments, she choked back a sob.

"Has it been raining for a long time?"

"It's been raining for two days. I think."

"How long have you been away from home?"

"I'm not sure."

"What happened to your parents?"

The water became deeper, and I had to pick her up. I held her in front of me. She wrapped her arms around my neck and buried her face in my shoulder. Soon, the water receded from my knees and we could walk easily again, but she made no move to quit my shoulder, and I likewise did not put her down.

"Did the Achare wash away?" she asked.

"No, the Achare are doing just fine."

"Is Kinran okay?"

"Yes, she's fine," I said. I was taken aback to hear her mention someone I knew, but I suppose she could have lived and died during Kinran's lifetime and before my own. "You must like her food."

"She makes the best pumpkin treats," the girl said.

"I don't know that I've ever had one of those." I stepped awkwardly over a rocky obstacle in the dark. "You're sure this is the right way?"

She nodded again.

"Will you tell me something?" I asked.

"Yeah."

"What happened to your parents?"

The girl hesitated for a while.

"You know the storyteller?" she asked.

"I do. His name is Gatsi." I was ready to give up asking.

"He tells stories sometimes of these big birds that make lightning and storms."

"Yes, I've heard those stories. Storms come from the Wahkeen. Their wingspan is wider than the villages we put down, and they spit lightning to the ground."

"They took my parents."

I stopped walking. Her statement was hard to process. "What do you mean? Did the storm...take your parents away?" The rain was relentless; it had not stopped for the duration of our walk together. My clothes were heavy with the weight of water and the child in my arms.

"Kind of."

"Can you give me some more detail?"

"We were sitting under a couple trees, and they said we shouldn't be under the trees, so we walked into the rain and tried to find somewhere else, but then the rain stopped, but only around us. You could still see rain a little ways away, but not over us. And we looked up, and there was this thing above us...it was really big, and it blocked out the rain. It looked back down at us, and then..."

There were people in our clan who worked to appease the Wahkeen and the Dalkhur, who considered them as much a danger as winter and wolves. I was always taught that they had left us, that the Dalkhur finished the world and moved on, that the Wahkeen were somewhere so far away you couldn't see them, like desert scorpions or deep-sea fish.

"What did it look like?"

"It looked like a big bird, like when birds sit in the air

without flapping and ride on the wind, but just right over us. I was watching it, then I looked back and my parents were gone. Then the rain came again, and I couldn't find anyone."

"And then you found me?"

"It took a long time first."

We walked for a while longer.

"You can put me down now. I think I can walk."

I did.

"What's your name?" I asked.

The mountain hummed, the darkness waited, and the girl was nowhere to be found. I knelt and set the lantern on a dry section of stone. I expected a new figure to reach from the void or speak in my ear.

Nothing came.

~

Okay, I thought to myself. *I think that's it. No more phantoms...no more lantern...no more sunlight or fresh air...* I took a deep breath.

I think I'm going to die down here...if I haven't already.

I knew of cultures who buried their dead. Rucost was peppered with graveyards; its cities embraced gaudy mausoleums. Plenty of dead folk wound up in the earth, but that wasn't where Achare belonged. It was a dishonor to die under a roof, whether natural or manmade. It was proper to become one's ashes and join with the soils of Kalanos, not become trapped beneath them. This wasn't where an Achare belonged. This wasn't where I was supposed to die. I looked in each direction and found them empty. This truly was a grave.

Then, from the eternal darkness above, the slow, patient gleam of a star.

It pierced me like an arrow and held me in awe. Forgotten was the frigid lantern, forgotten was the hurt and rain.

Another slowly dwindled into place to join the first. They were a pair of curious eyes studying me from above. I watched them as they watched me — muted, inert.

Soon an entire constellation formed above my head, turning dark into dusk, shedding on stalactites, trailing downstream in its labyrinthine twists. It played upon the surface of the water, and before me came a path of restless starlight.

The stars grew down toward me. They lengthened like icicles, skittering in the air as if crawling with spiders. I reached up and found my arms just short of the luminous thread.

Some sort of plant?

The material was the bright blue of Owasa's paint. She must have gathered the string-like material in the chamber upstream and mixed it with something else.

But why are they twitching?

I retrieved the dead lantern and followed the river again.

THE MOUNTAIN MOTHER

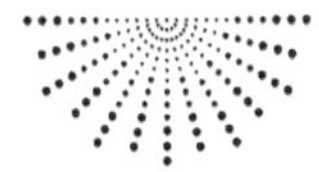

*It is astonishing, truly, the variety of life one finds
in travel, but one must also consider the life we
don't see. There are movements too great and
movements too small to perceive. But always
know: silence is the choir of a thousand subtle
heartbeats.*

— ARCHDRUID VARSAELIA

They were alive.

Or a part of them, at least.

There was a small, worm-like creature roaming the space above each dangling star. When I was finally able to touch one of the threads, it stuck to my fingers and stretched as I pulled. I briefly wondered if I could fill the lantern with the material like fireflies in a jar, but decided against it. The worms were giving me direction; there was no need to disturb them, so I journeyed forward in their gloaming light.

Pitiless stone appendages struck my arms and shins as if to abjure me, as if to turn me from the inevitable end of the these caverns. But I'd beaten bruises before, and I'd come too far to simply relent in the face of the unexplored.

The sky full of worms became narrow, thinned into a long and twisting limb that left the passage in near-dark. I became exhausted with the distance. My eyes were beginning to adjust, however, and I was able to ignore the pain in my knee and push myself forward.

After what felt like hours, there was finally something to see.

When one is journeying the high hills of Kalanos by night — especially a night without stars — even the most distant campfire can command the landscape. A traveler is redirected; the plains shrink with the eye's sharpening focus. A speck of light in a world of dark draws the wanderer near, a moth to the flame of friend and foe.

I did not expect such a light in the mountain. Though it was the same blue glow of the stars above, this was a light that exploded from its source. It sat against the corner of a distant wall.

Because it was, quite literally, seated.

The brilliant light ahead of me was a corpse.

THE BONES WERE HELD IN THEIR PROPER PLACE BY SOME strange phenomenon. They surely should have collapsed by now.

Otherworldly shadows were cast throughout the wide cavern. The glow worms had taken shelter in the cavity of the body, hung in the heartless space and lounged where lungs should be. Its face stared perfectly forward, exactly at the tunnel from which I'd emerged as if this cave dweller died in expectation. The starry threads above ebbed and disappeared.

"Is this..." I spoke aloud to an empty room; the words were meant for Gatsi. "You said...when you said you knew of a Turin woman..." I let out a single crazed laugh, the kind that comes from a long journey turned to failure. Gatsi. The smoke. It all led me here. "...I thought she'd be *alive*..."

There was only the soft blue glow of the tireless bones, the icicle-like threads draped from the jawbone, the ribs, the wrists upon its knees. There was only the soft drip of stalactites salivating in their yawning void, the sound of my breathing filling the vacuous and unforgiving chamber of Ba Turin's earthen heart.

And suddenly, I was not alone.

"Excuse me."

I leapt like a cat and scrambled to the wall. I hefted my knife, drawing a bead on the figure in the darkness.

It was a set of simple gray robes.

If I'd only had a glance, I might not have noticed there was somebody *in* them.

The clothes hung upon boney shoulders. A hard-lined woman put one sure foot in front of the other, approaching with a staggering calm as my heart tumbled through my chest, my fingers white-knuckle on the knife's handle.

"You may have been sent here for *me*."

"You're another apparition," I said after a tense few moments.

"An apparition?" she asked. She wore the tattoo of severe shadows thrown by the bones below.

"They've been coming to me throughout my journey

here. People who have died. You're one of them." I felt as though I was trying to convince myself more than anything.

"Not quite," she said slowly. "I'm afraid the heart of the mother is full of death. But I am not of the dead you've seen. I am alive."

She studied me for a moment.

"Step into the Mother's light," she said. "I'd like to see you clearly."

I hesitated before approaching the bones. The woman looked me over.

"Can you light my lantern?" I asked her. "It's been fickle."

"I can," she said.

I half expected her to flick her wrist and light the fire with some sort of magic. Instead, she left the light and returned moments later with a piece of flint.

My flint.

I knelt down. Keeping an eye on her, I opened the hatch of the lantern and began striking sparks with the steel I still had. The wick caught flame, came alive, and explored. It mingled warmly with the blue of the bones and shared its space with a bouncing flicker. The colors tugged playfully at each other over the crowded remains.

"Are you human?" I asked her.

"I am," she said with a slow nod.

"Are you alone down here?"

"I am not."

"Were the people I saw real?"

"Who's to say?" she asked, shrugging her gaunt shoulders. "May I ask questions now?"

"Okay. Sure."

"Are you hungry?"

"...a little, yes."

"Are you hurt?"

"Yes."

"Wait here."

I did. She left me alone with the body on the ground. With the light of the lantern I began to walk the dimensions of the chamber. The ceiling's height reached what I estimated to be twenty feet. It sloped down in jagged shapes to form the walls, which were far enough apart that I could not light them all at once. After walking a bit, I discovered the chamber to be wider than the throne room in Mother's Hall. The floor was flush, which was surprising given the treacherous canyons that led here.

The woman emerged from a tunnel I hadn't seen. She carried a steaming teapot and a roll of cloth.

"I've brought you some tea. This will abate your feelings of hunger."

She poured the steaming liquid into a clay cup and handed it to me. Having recently been poisoned, I was reluctant to take anything from anyone, but I suspected I'd need to become comfortable here. She said I might be looking for her...I brought the tea to my lips; it was too hot, of course, and the taste was much more acrid than I'd expected. The vacant spot in my teeth ached with the heat.

"It's mostly made with bleeding bonnets."

I spit the tea back into the cup.

"It's a type of fungus," she clarified. "The tea also contains cavern oysters. And chamomile."

"I've never heard of oysters in tea."

"It's another type of fungus."

"What is your name?" I asked after a few moments. The warm tea relaxed me, though I wasn't sure it was possible to feel comfortable this far underground with a stranger in the dark and luminescent bones on the floor. She began to wrap my knee tightly, and for a moment I was worried she would offer another hot drink to soothe my tooth.

"My name is Tsavi," she said, smiling for the first time, mild as it was. Her hair was long, pulled into a braid that ran the length of her back. "What is yours?"

"Rennik. I come from the Achare."

"I've never met an Achare," she said.

"Alright. You claim you're not dead, Tsavi. But I don't see how anyone can live here."

Her smile grew a bit.

"The heart of the mother is full of dead things. It's true. But it's also full of life. Look upon her bones and see the colonies within. Look upon the ground and see fungal forests. Look within the arteries of the mountain and see us, its blood, traveling — thriving, in our own way. It's interesting, the things people can see in the dark."

"So I've been told," I said. There was the sound of someone walking from elsewhere in the tunnels. "This..." I turned to the star-draped skeleton. "Is she the Mountain Mother?"

"She is." She turned reverently to the figure. "This is the explorer to whom the mountains were gifted. This is the first of the Turin and the last of our wandering ancestors. She was invited to die in the heart of the mountain, and in turn has been dressed in its love. It is in the nature of mountains to envy the sky. They exist in immortal reach. This is the only mountain to have reached the sky and gathered its fruit. It swallowed the stars and kept them for her. Many on the surface consider her the first mother, but they are mistaken. Ba Turin adopted Senna, took her in as its own. In our older tongue, Ba Turin means 'mother of people.' Senna is just one form she takes."

"I learned some of this a bit differently. I was told Senna

was the daughter of the woman who founded Ba Turin, not the Mountain Mother herself."

Tsavi shook her head. "It's been many years. Certainty becomes fragile."

"Okay," I said. "I understand the history. I understand your reverence and I understand the light. But I just saw people who are *dead,* Tsavi. I saw my father burned on the pyre — I was *there,* and I was the one to scatter his ashes, but he was *in this cavern.* I saw a man die in the charred remains of my village and he spoke to me in that tunnel just a few hours ago. There was a girl..."

Tsavi listened patiently and seemed to be waiting, making sure I was finished.

"Just as the mountain can foster," she said, "just as it can weep and blush, it can show us what we need to see. Senna is a bridge. Here she sits, one foot in our world and one foot in death. People learn best through familiar things. Perhaps the images of your past are exactly that. Living things speak with what they have. We use words. The Rucosti use theirs. Birds sing and wolves howl. But when something speaks using the faces of the dead, I find it's best to learn their language."

"Images?" I asked, setting the tea down. "My father couldn't seem to learn anything new...but there was something real in that figure. If the phantom knows what my father knew and remembers what my father remembered..." My eyes began to water. "How do I know that wasn't really him? How do I know I didn't just see him for the last time all over again?"

Tsavi looked at me for a long while, then turned her attention to the bones of Senna. She seemed to be meditating as she sat and stared.

"I don't think we can know, Rennik."

"Who else would know but you? How long have you been down here at the threshold of death? *You* should know!"

"And I don't."

I put my head in my hands. I felt a hand on my back — not my father's, but the hand of a stranger who lives in the dark.

"It can be difficult to leave the ones we love, even when they leave us first. Having the chance to say goodbye allows you to end the thread, to understand the weave of their tapestry as something complete. But when people leave us suddenly...it is not just an incomplete tapestry, but a cause to wonder. For to wonder is to have no knowledge. Truly, imagination is a curse we share. The thoughts dwell on what could have been, perhaps what *should* have been, if we feel the lack of justice in it all. We love life because it contains always the chance to reach a beautiful end. Only in death is that chance truly taken from us.

"How beautiful it would be to see a person become their full tapestry...in truth, none of us will see ourselves complete. Everyone has a tear in the fabric. An empty stomach. An empty heart. No creature reaches their end without a hole or two. The trick, Rennik, is to stop waiting for closure that isn't coming. Your father is dead, whether you saw him here or not."

"Why would the mountain, or Senna, or whomever — why would they do this? What interest is it of theirs to present me with horrors like this?"

"What did they tell you?"

I thought back. My father seemed to tell me that I should learn to forget. He told me I'd need to grow up a little...and he told me to be wary of Gatsi. Ciqala provoked me until I killed his ghost. The girl...told me that the Wahkeen are more present than not, I gathered. But what was I meant to do with that?

"I suppose they wanted me to move forward. Shed baggage, steel myself, and do what I need to do."

"And do you know what you need to do?"

I nodded. She did not ask for details.

"You told me you weren't alone down here," I said. "Were you referring to the images as well?"

"No. There are others like me. We are meant to stay here and tend to the mountain."

"Where is it you come from? How many of you are there?"

"We are Turin." She chuckled. "What else would we be? There are twelve of us. The others were all Red Wardens, once. Taken young and given strict purpose. Ours is not to shield and to harm, but to watch, tend to, and learn from the mountain's heart."

"What does that mean? 'Tending' to the heart?"

"Our most sacred duty is to maintain the order of this chamber. Everything must stay as it is exactly, else the Mountain Mother cease to speak."

"And she speaks to you?"

"Sometimes."

"What does she say?"

"She gives, and she asks. Sometimes she tells me where my people are to mine. She wants the fruits of the mountain to go to us, of course."

"How does the mountain mother feel about Rucost mining in Ba Turin?" I asked. "About Moddimok's selling the steel?"

"She hasn't expressed an opinion," she said, grinning. "But...she has, perhaps, pointed us to fewer iron roots in the past few years."

"And did you say she *asks*?"

"She does. The mountain can only paint in broad strokes. She speaks in falling boulders, flooding rains, and plummeting snow. So she asks of us the things she cannot do herself. The precise movement of a pebble in the caverns beyond. The draining of a pond on the surface. The transplanting of a vulture's nest."

"So you do visit the surface?"

"Of course we do! Not even Turin should live in perpetual darkness."

"When we're done here, when we've finished...whatever this is...could you show me the way up?"

"Up?" She sighed patiently. "I'm afraid there are many more surfaces than those above our heads. But I can lead you out of the mountain when the time is right."

"There was a...tree. Where my people lived, there was this tree that influenced other living things. My mentor called it the Delkhi. He said it pulled herds of animals to it, pulled my people to it...then repelled us when we were in danger. He said it saved me from death as a child, and that's why it could give me visions and the ability to read smoke... You said that Senna exists in both life and death, and I think the Delkhi does, too."

"And so you've come with questions," she said.

"Yes. But I'm not sure how to ask them yet."

"We have time, Rennik. Be patient with yourself. Let's walk."

We stood and began walking, sipping the awful tea as we went.

"What about you?" I asked her. "You say she speaks to you. You've been here for years. What surprises have you seen come through the dark?"

She smiled again.
"Just you."

21

NESTS

There comes a time, Rennik, when you find the end of a thread. Sometimes there just isn't more of something.

— RAISHA

Avid had spent the last year trying to pry any information he could from me.

"I think there are bears nearby," I'd told him while we were riding through some deserted countryside.

He'd looked quickly from side to side. "Where? Wouldn't the horses have smelled them? Should we go?"

"Not *nearby*," I clarified. "I meant this far south. I haven't seen one in person yet."

"You saw it in the smoke," he asserted, grinning confidently. "How do—?"

"No, Avid, I found some hair I didn't recognize in the nest of a chickadee. They don't fly very far to collect building materials, so it was from an animal in this area. They don't dream of granite walls like you do."

"So how did you know it was bear hair if you haven't seen one? Did you burn the hair? That means you used the smoke to find out!"

"No, Avid. I didn't use the smoke. It was a long, coarse, black hair. I know it wasn't bison because the herds have learned to stay away from Rucost. And there's not much else it could be based on what I've heard."

"Then how did you know the nest belonged to a chickadee? You had to have—"

"Because I *saw* the birds, Avid."

"Oh, well, then you must have used smoke to *find* the nest, right? How could you possibly have found something so small and useful? Wouldn't it be convenient for *both* of us to—"

"Because I saw it, Avid! With my eyes! My real, physical eyes!"

"Oh, well...then how about the kind of bird? How did you *know*, without smoke, that it was a chickadee nest—"

"Because I saw the birds in it!"

"Reach for a blanket."

"Right. The Mountain Mother, like any living thing, has needs that must be met. If your Delkhi drew the bison, the oryx, and the Achare to it, it was out of necessity. You were a blanket, in some figurative way, for something that needed it."

"But what did we do for it? The bison just...roamed around. The oryx were a little more restless, but didn't *do* much for the tree. And I suppose we were similar."

Tsavi thought for a moment. "When the Mountain

Mother requests that a stream be diverted or a fir be pruned, I don't know *what* it does. I just know it must be done. Does your dog know why it's asked to sit, or does it simply obey?"

"But I don't think anyone listened to the Delkhi. The Mountain Mother has you and the others to act for her...the Delkhi didn't request anything."

She shrugged. "Maybe the creatures it kept were enough. Maybe it influenced your people in ways too subtle to see. Maybe it, like us, simply craves company."

"...But what is it?"

"You mean to ask what they *all* are? What is the creature we call the Delkhi or the Mountain Mother?"

"Yes."

"I don't know. I just know to tend to its needs."

"How many are there?" I asked.

"Who's to say?"

We'd ended our walk in a furnished room — "room" being used in its broader sense. It was, like everything else here, a cavernous space. There were cushions at the feet of stalagmites and a table stretching along the wall. It was lit with candlelight and worms.

"Gatsi mentioned a 'Turin woman'. There are a dozen of you down here. Why was I meant to find you specifically?"

She smiled into her tea. "I suspect it's because we have a similar past. A specific experience. Did you, Rennik, nearly die of frost as a child?"

I was about to sip more tea, but brought it back down. "Yes," I told her. "How could you have known that?"

"Tell me what you've deduced already about your relationship with the Delkhi."

I told her of the river, of my childhood and visions, of the smoke and the pale man. She listened patiently as I tried to explain the funeral of the chieftain, when I'd felt as though the roots of the Delkhi were pressing the air from my lungs and stealing my voice. She was not surprised when I told her that a dark figure seemed intent on finding me time and time again. She confirmed that creatures such as the Delkhi exist in two worlds at once, and that they seem to have a limit to their territory, hence my dependence on the smoke once I'd left Kalanos.

"All these things..." I began. "They've happened to you, too?"

"In some ways, yes. When I was young, I was taken on a pilgrimage to a peak nearby, just east of Katabat Col. It's one of the highest in all of Ba Turin. My parents took turns carrying me on their backs in a sling, took the time at each resting point to let me adjust to the altitude as we went.

"It was a storm that came suddenly. To make a long story short, my parents and everyone else were killed by that storm. They say I walked into the Hanallta a week later, but I have no solid memory of these events. The chilblains and the frostbite should have killed me, of course. If not that, sky blindness could have led me down a cliff face.

"Chieftain Moddimok and her advisors told me I was blessed. They made a place for me here in the heart. Because I'd been touched by her hand, I was to listen to the will of the Mother. And I still do."

"So we really are similar...do you read smoke as well?"

She shook her head. "No. The Mother has taught me a few things, but never that."

"Do you know my mentor? His name is Gatsi."

"No," she said quickly. Her grip tightened on the cup as she brought it to her face.

"Are there many like us?"

She thought a while. "I think there are plenty who are saved by the Mother. They may never know it, or if they do, they may not act upon it or receive her other gifts. Which is a blessing in its own way. The world in which we are placed is a rather dangerous one, Rennik."

"Why's that?"

"Consider the figure that follows you. Both of our peoples would likely call it a Shiver, since that is the word we know. As you clearly have learned, this figure is not a benevolent one."

"It took a companion of mine named Macha. The first night I saw it, we made eye contact, and I felt like I was dying again. When I came to, Macha was just...gone. No marks on the ground, no bent stalks. Just gone."

She paused for a long moment, searching for an explanation. "You are familiar with snakes?" she asked.

"Of course."

"Then you surely know that they need not eat so often. They consume their prey whole and are sated for weeks or months."

"It...it ate him?" I asked. I felt sick.

"That is likely, yes. Your friend Macha is certainly gone. But I do not think the same will happen to you."

"But it stalks me."

"Yes, but you are not the same as Macha. The Delkhi has elevated you into a different world — no, not a different world...the Delkhi has revealed a new layer of our world. Not by choice, I think. Simply as a byproduct of your saving. That's why you can see more of its people than others can."

"Does that mean Macha was like us?"

"No. The creatures of the higher world can interact with all peoples. Only a few can *see* them."

"Does each person the Delkhi saves earn some sort of Shiver like this? Is Av...are you and I *both* in danger?"

"It would not surprise me, but I've been safe all my life."

"How do I end this connection? How do I rid myself of this hunter?"

"It seems one way to do so is for the host to die, but that's...clearly not ideal. Truly, Rennik, I don't know if these things can be harmed."

"So what does this thing want with me? Why is it stalking me if not to eat?"

"There are...other byproducts of our saving, Rennik. When the Mountain Mother saved me from death, it made a connection. By necessity, it created a bridge between the world of the living and the world of the dead. Doing that does not come without consequences. In our case, we become targets of a strange sort of people who absorb the light around them and who feed on our emotions, on the energies we exude. They each affect their targets differently."

"But it ate Macha. It eats two different things?"

"And for different purposes, I believe. Perhaps it has both a physical and spiritual sort of stomach."

"It feeds on emotions..." I thought aloud. "That explains why Rangrim and Moddimok were instilled with such rage and suspicion. It was feeding on them."

"I tried to warn Moddimok of her shadow, of the influence she could not see, but that influence was already too strong. Well...there's something I don't know, exactly. Did it incite the feelings of paranoia and anger so as to feed on them, or were those feelings all that remained when it had finished?"

I thought on this for a while. "That begs the question, then...what does my Shiver feed on?"

"I think that's something only you can discover. And only when you experience it again."

"Rangrim saw it," I said after a few moments.

"She saw her shadow?"

"Is that what you call them?"

"For lack of asking them, yes."

"She told me she listened to its whispers, and she made it seem as though she'd seen it," I said. "She called it a 'person of shadow'. I wonder if she's seen it her whole life..."

"Rangrim always kept too many secrets," thought Tsavi aloud. "She considered their sharing to be a weakness."

"But Marmot described that Shiver in *detail*, as a person with certain clothing."

"...Marmot?"

"The boy in the Hanallta. Only a few people can see him. He waters plants all day..." Even in the midst of a fantastical conversation, I felt delusional just saying the words out loud.

She looked confused for a moment, then burst out loudly. When she had wrestled her laughter, she apologized. "I just didn't know he was going by 'Marmot' these days."

"You knew him?"

"Yes. Of course."

"He...Rangrim's shadow killed him."

She grew somber and nodded slowly.

"So how do I stop it?" I asked.

Just as I feared, she had no solution aside from Rangrim's death. She only knew that she'd never seen a shadow in close proximity to the heart. Perhaps it was my proximity to the Delkhi that had kept mine away for so long.

"I thought perhaps that there was one of these entities for each region," I said, "but both the Delkhi and the Mountain Mother are in Kalanos."

"Kalanos is a circle we've drawn in our minds, Rennik. They likely don't obey the maps we've made."

"Fair enough."

"That makes a bit of sense, though. One in Ba Turin, one in the lowland plains...perhaps regions have consistent qualities because of these creature's influences. Like a bird who keeps its nest a certain way."

"It's as if they're vestiges of the world's creation," I said. It felt good to be in this sort of company. Someone who'd been through what I had been through, someone who could wonder and philosophize over a pot of tea. "You're sure you're not dead?" I asked her.

"No, Rennik. I was born fifty eight years ago, and nothing's killed me yet. Why are you so doubtful?"

"Because each phantom that appeared seemed to want me to grow or move on. And meeting you, hearing my mysteries reflected in someone else...it makes it easier to do the things I'm supposed to do. The solidarity makes me feel... stronger, I guess."

"I'm glad of it," she said.

"But there's something I don't understand. If you and I are alike, why haven't you seen these dead spirits in the dark?"

She smiled the excited smile of a child at the cusp of discovery.

"I don't know. But now I wonder; you've learned much about this Delkhi of yours. Do you intend to return home? Will you listen to the Delkhi as I have done here?"

"No." I was surprised to hear myself answer so readily. "I watched my home die. There's nothing there to return to, and it's not in the nature of the Achare to settle."

"So where will you go?"

"My chieftain, Malik, is leading the new clan through the areas bordering the Marchland. I'll find them there, and travel with them until I know what to do next."

"But specifically, Rennik, when you leave this mountain in a few days, what will you do?"

"A few days?" I asked incredulously.

"You've knocked out a tooth and your knee is swollen. I bet you were hurt before coming here, too. Yours seems to be the pride that makes your wounds worse. You're going to stay here and rest, and I'm going to tell my companions not to speak to you. You *need* to rest your jaw."

She wasn't wrong. But there was conflict in the Hanallta above, and I couldn't let innocent Turin get hurt.

Maybe Ciqala was right. I feel responsible for everything around me. A certain kind of guilt.

"It's bad enough I came down here before helping the people above," I said. "I need to return."

"You don't need to return," she said bluntly. "There are wars being fought as we speak, thousands of miles away. There is a murder in Rucost every day—"

"Tsavi, we're talking about *your* people!"

She looked at me a long while.

"I'm going to leave," I said. "I'm going to do what I need to do, and when I'm done, I will return to heal."

She did not change. At this point she was staring, as if trying to discern something at a great distance. She picked up an assertive tone as she spoke.

"Come with me."

THERE WAS A ROOM FULL OF RUNNING WATER, BUT NOT LIKE the river that brought me here.

It was like a scaled-down version of Mother's Hall. There were small waterfalls pouring from the walls, some into crystalline pools, others into minuscule flumes that circled the room before disappearing into the stone.

There was a garden, organized beautifully, on one end of the room. Each flower, stem, and seedling were perfectly healthy, despite there being no sunlight. Juniper spread its fingers, chamomiles grew in abundance with lupines and yarrow, sage bustled behind the flowers, and sweetgrass stuck up wherever there was space. The plants twitched now and then, rustled as if animals and insects capered among them. A man was quietly looking over the garden.

"This is a sacred place," Tsavi told me. "A nursery of sorts. It is another facet of the mountain we must nurture."

"It's as if each element of the mountain were placed here in miniature," I said in amazement. "How can they grow without light?"

"There are countless small miracles in our world. The Mother has gathered a bouquet of them here. I'll be happy to discuss more when you return." She looked to the man leaning over the garden. "Any better?" she asked.

"A bit restless for a while, but calm now."

"Restless?" I asked. "Do the plants feel stuck?"

Tsavi gestured me forward, reached a hand into the cavern's oasis, and parted a taller bunch of lupines.

In the garden was a baby.

He slept upon sweetgrass that'd been woven like a bed beneath him. His hand, even in slumber, was wrapped around a bit of juniper. His cheeks were round, and he was as comfortable as could be in his rooted repose.

Tsavi told me that he was expected to sleep for the next few weeks. He would rest until he was ready and grown, and he would enter the world in which he belonged.

"We call him Sil," she said. "But I believe you know him as Marmot."

TO BURN WHAT WAS BUILT

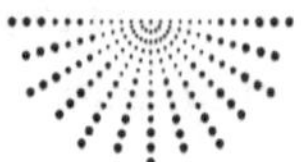

*It takes a while for blackwood to really light — it's
very dense. But once it does, it'll burn hot, and
it'll burn forever.*

— EXCERPT FROM *RUMINATIONS ON
SURVIVAL* BY MARTINOR THE
UNTETHERED

The trail back to the Hanallta was cleverly-hidden and brief, and I received the impression it was only one of several secret ascents.

I traced a circle around the leather guard over my heart. It was damaged from my fall, but I hoped it'd stop an arrow or a knife if needed.

An echo sounded from the south, a shout from the Hanallta above.

I wracked my mind for some other solution, for some dim memory of Gatsi and Tella and the strange things they did. Maybe some herb or metal could be used to purge Rangrim of this shadow. Maybe the papers above our door, the ones Tella made, would turn the shadow back toward its own world.

Words fell violently to me, shouts, curses, commands, the bestial sounds of life and death.

I had to focus.

My only goal was Rangrim. This was not my war — just a war my enemy happened to take part in.

I climbed a final stone and dropped into the bloodshed.

THERE'S A CERTAIN KIND OF PERSON WHO DESTROYS BEFORE giving in.

These are the people who see an impending defeat in a card game and throw their hand on the floor. The people who, when they feel they're losing an argument, begin to verbally attack the other speaker rather than defend their point.

Rangrim was losing her card game.

There were shouts from elsewhere on the Hanallta, the telltale percussion of neighbor fighting neighbor, of sickles striking swords. The conflicts were small and separated; this was the end of a larger skirmish, when its embers are scattered and left to die in their own time. My concern did not land on any of these minor feuds.

I was concerned with the smoke billowing from the mountainside.

The sachas are burning.

A brief scan of the Hanallta told me Hegira, Kheze, and Owasa were not in immediate danger — not here, at least. I hoped they were hiding somewhere. There was no sign of the Rucosti traders, and it seemed likely they'd found their own hiding place in which to weather the storm.

I quickened my pace as much as I could, giving ample distance between myself and the violence. By the time I'd reached Hegira's home, I'd passed several wounded and several dead. I whistled. Karay came bounding out of the door.

"Down!" I told him, fearing he'd worsen my swollen knee. He was clearly nervous; he'd had probably been listening to the sounds of panic and pain for far too long.

I stopped at the door. It suddenly occurred to me that this is the perfect place to lay a trap. Rangrim said I'd always find an escape. This is where she'd expect me…

My ear tilted to the space inside. I heard nothing. I hurried to my room, and in that instant, the figure concealed in the corner launched toward me.

I struck reflexively with my fist. There was little power behind it since I was mid-step, but I managed to find the assailant's nose.

He reeled back.

I lunged forward and pinned him against the wall, his blonde hair—

Blonde hair?

"Vivonno?!"

"Rennik!"

"What are you doing?" I let him go.

He turned, cradling a profusely bleeding nose and blinking through the tears that came with it.

"We thought we were safe here!" His voice was muted a bit. "We thought Rangrim wouldn't look here!"

"We?"

Two more Rucosti stuck their heads into the room.

"This is *exactly* where she would look for me!" I shouted to Vivonno. "Your instincts are terrible!"

"I'm sorry!" he wailed bloodily.

I grabbed my axe, bow, and quiver.

"Hell, Vivonno. *I'm* sorry."

"No, I deserve that," he managed as I rushed out of the room. "Six silver for a night was robbery."

I RAN MY FINGERS ACROSS THE SHAFTS OF MY ARROWS, PUTTING pressure on the ends, testing the spine of each and confirming their future precision.

I placed my hand on the handle of my axe. Its leather wrap knew my grip like rain to a river.

I looked for any separation or cracking in the stave of my war bow, hewn of my home's strongest mulberry. There were no imperfections.

Hegira's fifth and fourth terraces were destroyed, and the fire was fast approaching.

It made mountains out of smoke and impelled the wounded howls of man into their final crescendos. Many of the Turin must have run to the sachas to protect their crop.

Strangely, and despite the obstacle it presented, the seven-foot maize felt a bit like home. It was easy to hide in tall grasses like this, but advantages tend to work both ways. I strode a hundred feet down one row, hesitated, and realized I could wander for hours without finding someone first — though it seemed the flames would find *me* before then.

I thought of Hegira on the day of my arrival.

"We are a people of craft."

There were Turin in the soil, in blood and in armor. The high craft of Rangrim was red vengeance and fear.

"When I realized the Mountain Mother blessed me..."

The crops that were meant to feed hundreds fed only the flames of her fury. My stinging eyes searched for movement.

"...the Hanallta became my table..."

I strode upon an acres-long chopping block. I stepped over the dead and departed as I searched for the blight of the raven-feather crown. The smoke hid the distance of Ba Turin's mighty heights and kept my vertigo at bay. It would have been wiser to walk with my knife in a place like this, but I fell into the familiar groove of nock and string.

"The fact that she turned out so incredibly kind is a miracle."

The flames cracked and seized at the air. I stepped out to the ledge.

A Red Warden stepped into view, just beyond the lip of the second terrace.

I put an arrow through his arm. His screams were swallowed by the conflagration, and I retreated deep into the stalks.

"My help would be irrelevant if not for her hard work."

There was the crashing of man and maize as one of Rangrim's guards leapt from overhead. We tumbled, then separated. I ducked under his sword. Karay leapt at him; I stepped behind and put an arrow high and to the left of his shoulder blade. His arm would swing no more.

An upward wind pushed the curtain of smoke more heavily against the sacha. It carried the smell of Kalanosi wildfires — the ash of plant life and the stench of animals caught in the blaze. I knew, however, that there were no mountain creatures wandering the terraces. The true source of the animal-char smell revealed itself to me, and I stifled the coming sickness.

Of course, I was aware of the fourth ingredient. I could focus the scope of my augury by selecting properly-prepared sage, hair, or bones. But there existed another degree of this sorcery that I kept far out of mind. It is the bloody gem that sent the pale man prowling. It is the reason, as I stood in my smoldering home, that I witnessed his journey through Kalanos, heard strange voices and found my mother and Malik alive.

I could not stifle the words of my enemy. The pale man spoke from deep in my memory.

"They are the door through which I welcome my knowledge... your death has meaning."

If the living are brought to death by fire, the smoke produced opens a limitless door of discovery. One can reach to the furthest limb of the world and see what it clutches, if one has the strength to direct it.

No, I thought. *I will not become him.*

But Rangrim could be hiding anywhere. She could destroy another terrace in a moment's notice or kill more of her own people. The Achare couldn't stop the horde, but maybe I could end this horror if I found just their leader. Somewhere above me were tradespeople fighting for their lives, for their homes and their children. I had no home. I had no children.

And I rarely missed.

Now spoke Ciqala.

"...unless you shed the weight of your guilt, you'll never kill this Turin of yours."

I smothered the stone in my throat and did what I had to.

"...Malnostos."

I breathed deeply of the smoke, leaned in an ethereal direction, felt the presence of something much larger than me, and searched for Rangrim.

~

HER FACE WAS ASH AND ANGER.

Air came into her lungs uneasily, scraping and burning

as it traveled. She pulled herself over a terrace ledge. The fire licked at her boots from below. A Red Warden stood beneath her, pressing on his wounded leg. He was unable to climb the ledge on his own and held his free hand up to his chieftain.

Rangrim pushed into the next sacha without him. The torch she held had long lost its fuel and was now burning to its core. She wielded this searing brand as if it lit her way. She began to laugh.

Then, something pushed through a solid flame beneath her. An invisible shape.

The Shiver.

The terraces traced miles of mountainside; I knew which of them she was on, but I needed to see something more if I were to locate her.

She tilted her head as if listening.

"Hegira's," she said. "Of course he is."

At the same time, I saw the jutting awn, the place where Rangrim threatened me before.

She was close.

And she was looking for me.

~

I snapped from the vision and searched my immediate surroundings.

"Ready?" I whispered to the dog.

We rushed through the stalks, one after the other. I knew Karay's nose couldn't be depended on in the haze of dead crops. His eyes would be no better than mine, screened by maize and stinging from the smoke. We hurdled dead fighters, withstood the cutting leaves, breathed deeply as though each breath was our last.

"If this woman stands between what is right and what is wrong..."

I saw her.

The dread form of Rangrim pounded forward, became draped in the low tide of smoke, and was revealed again as it lifted. Her eyes were wide; her mouth worked as if speaking frantically. She was bent forward, as if the weight of the crown and the falling ash pressed her shoulders toward the earth.

"...then you must be willing to kill for it."

She looked up to see me in the same row of hissing maize. She pivoted swiftly into the next row, and I saw her draw a long knife. I produced my axe and stepped into her row.

I didn't expect her to have reached me so quickly.

The edge of the knife whistled, a sound that cut through the roar of the nearby inferno, and I pulled my neck back just far enough to avoid its bite. It was followed by her burning brand, which largely missed but briefly licked at my arm.

I tried to use the momentum of my evasion to swing my axe down, but she twisted nimbly away.

"You've never been taught how to fight," she growled as she stabbed forward again. Her knife came up and I stepped back with my right leg to catch myself. "Or you would know not to favor a knee."

Her foot slammed into my left leg, just above my swollen knee. She had aimed a bit too high and missed her mark, but her grin told me she thought she's succeeded. In an instant, she'd dropped her knife, wrapped her fingers around the arrows in my quiver, and plucked them from their place.

Where's Karay?

She was off-balance from her overreaching maneuver, so

I brought my axe across in an attempt to take advantage of her poor stance.

The stalk to my right fell as I cut cleanly through it.

She'd rolled away and leapt to her feet. Two of my arrows fell to the soil unnoticed.

"Don't try to follow, Crow" she shouted as she ran north-ward to the next terrace. She brandished my arrows in her hand. The flames in her grasp touched at the maize around her and managed to spread their disease to one of the hearty stalks. "Savor your one good knee before the flames reach you."

I sprawled forward and retrieved my fallen arrows.

I stood.

The feathers hit my cheek.

She looked back and froze. An animal in its final moment.

The stalks to my right began cracking, pushed in rapid succession by something big.

I released, but the arrow flew wide as the Shiver's weight threw me down.

Karay was close behind it, snarling as I swung desper-ately with my bow.

It caught my wrist; the massive hands of Rangrim's shadow pressed into my skin, pulled my arm high like an executioner's axe. My feet left the ground.

I felt its breath against my face.

Karay leapt forward, and the invisible vise released me.

Hand to quiver; nock to string.

But Rangrim had moved, careening like a drunkard through the tomato crop below.

I began running on my swollen knee. The snarling sounds behind me turned to yelping.

I pushed through the spear-like maize, coming closer to

the lip of the terrace — the Shiver launched me from the edge as soon as I'd found my footing. I hit the ground hard.

Without a second's delay I sprinted toward Rangrim's location. She was perfectly visible over the stems of tomato plants, but I knew the Shiver was on my heels.

Rangrim reached the edge of the terrace and could not go further. She turned to me, her back against a wall of flame. The heat only amplified the upward wind of the mountainside. Embers took to their flocks. The earthen shell of the world was roaring beneath us, and one of us would fall to meet it.

I took the one chance I had.

She was screaming wildly, brandishing the fire in her hand.

There were pounding steps behind me.

I stopped running and drew.

The arrow whistled—

And punched into her chest.

The black heart of Rangrim poured forth as if to douse the coming flames. She fell back into the torrid earth below, lain lower than her mother, lain lower than the food that feeds her people, lain in the limbs of the fire that grew to consume its maker.

The sacha exploded behind me.

STONE UPON STONE

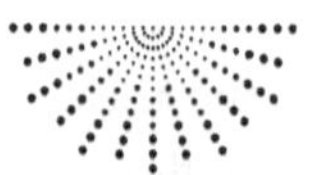

*There's something beautiful in the whole cycle of it
all. It's empty, it's growing, it's flourishing, it's
gathered, it's empty...it feels like the whole
world is breathing in and out, and I get to
breathe with it.*

— HEGIRA

My ears were ringing.

I was covered in tomato.

Leaves were fluttering in wild acrobatics, riding the rising heat and falling back to the earth in their own time. One of them rose, flipped, and alighted on an inhuman shape. It took a moment for me to process.

"Karay?"

I looked back at where the Shiver had been and tensed, waiting for another onslaught. But nothing came.

Sound was returning.

There were people yelling, people running east on the edge of the Hanallta. They hefted various containers filled with water. Fighters in the trappings of Red Wardens, children, people with the hard aprons of iron workers. Each sort of Turin, it seemed, was coming together in the creation of a massive waterfall. Buckets, waxed baskets, pots and cups were upended into the maize.

"Karay?" I raised my voice at the figure.

His head moved, rotated a bit to rest his chin on the ground and look at me.

I dropped at his side and saw another wound, similar to the one he'd received before, had appeared on his right shoulder and cheek. He managed to stand, but I could tell he wouldn't be able to climb the stone stairs between each terrace. I tried once to lift him, but a Kalanosi dog is no small creature. Even if I managed to lift him to my chest, I wasn't confident I'd be able to see over him. He twitched painfully each time I reached for his head. I sat with him and pet his back leg.

The ported water was soaking the tallest step of the mountainside. It was apparent they feared the fire would rise to the Hanallta proper and were turning damp earth into their defense. They'd formed a new line, and people were passing containers to each other in rapid succession, as if they'd cover the entire length of the terrace.

Just like the pulley-and-bucket system in their mines, I thought dazedly.

My eyes were blurred with biting smoke, and for a moment, I saw my mother.

She was running toward me, covering her face with her hand. Behind her was my father. He pointed past me.

But it was Hegira and Kheze who ran by, each with a damp cloth tied behind their heads. I knew I'd be coughing a long while after running so much in the smoke. It scraped from me now in a sigh of relief at the sight of their faces.

They each placed their hands under one side of Karay and lifted. He wriggled uncomfortably — and when a dog his size wriggles, it's more of a tumultuous boulder — but they managed to keep him up and between them. Hegira knew I was hurt and exhausted; she would not allow me to help. I thought Kheze looked as though he'd been crying, but perhaps the smoke had bitten too viciously at his eyes.

As they carried Karay back to the Hanallta, I looked at the space where the Shiver had been.

There was a crater in the terrace.

In its sides I could see the layers Hegira told me about. At its deepest level, the terrace contained palm-sized stones, and the substance of each successive layer grew smaller and finer until it reached the topsoil. Much of what was underground was now settling back to the surface, having been thrown into the air.

Azmi, Kheze's friend, had come down a distant set of stairs and was walking the long curve of the crater toward me.

"What happened?" she asked. "What was that?"

I opened my mouth before I realized I couldn't reasonably tell her the truth. "I'm not sure," I said. "Rangrim was burning everything, screaming like she'd gone mad. Then the ground just...exploded."

"Is that what killed her?" she asked, looking from the crater to the flames that were losing their fuel in the next terrace.

"I think so," I lied.

"It only seems right," said Azmi, "that she fall to her own actions."

I took Azmi's hand, got to my feet, and pushed painfully in the direction of the stairs.

❧

WHEN THE TURIN BUILD A TERRACE, THEY DO SO WITH obsessive precision.

Hundreds of ashlars were stacked together, placed with purpose to ensure a proper fit. Once there, the stones distribute the weight of the earth evenly, each neighbor sharing the burden with those around it. It is a communal effort for which each individual is needed.

Hegira and her neighbors worked the entire next day to repair what the crater had destroyed. I thought she would be stricken with heartbreak — and perhaps she was the day before — but she wore the face of passionate toil, the signature grin of the builder in the midst of their work. It was the mien of my mother when she produced a flawless leather pauldron, or Avid's face upon disassembling some new contraption.

I sat with Karay on the edge of the Hanallta.

"You know," I told him. "We might be the saddest saps on the mountain. Feels pathetic to sit in the sun while others labor all day."

"Shed the guilt," I imagined him saying. "Rest is the reward for hard work."

"Fair enough," I said, scratching behind his ears. His nose began to twitch in the air.

A boy no older than thirteen approached with something wrapped in cloth.

"It's from my uncle," he said, unwrapping a roasted goat's leg. "To thank you for your help. He said he saw you try to stop the fire. I'm supposed to tell you... 'the greatest actions are sometimes invisible'."

"Hm. Words to chew on."

The boy nodded. Karay was salivating wildly and panting

like the mountain's updraft. I tore half the meat from the bone — it fell apart beautifully and steamed in the air — and fed him his portion. The boy smiled.

"You know," he said. "I haven't seen Hegira this happy in years."

"Some people are happiest when they can watch their progress. I know the type."

"Sure, but it's not just today. You probably noticed that she was happy to talk to you when you were around. But before you came, she hadn't really looked like that for a while."

And, banal as it may sound, I felt a warmth that did not come from the goat. There was a tear in my eye, and my shoulders melted a bit.

This is what it feels like when someone wants you around.

The boy saw the tear roll down my cheek and looked confused.

"It's just...*really* good goat."

"Okay! Well, if you need more, come find me!"

"Thank you. I will."

～

Hegira was maniacal.

Sprouting from the soil of her sacha were dozens of mushrooms the rain had spawned and grown to age in the span of one night. Poking their proud, pallid fingers up through the damp earth like dead flesh, spreading in necrotic plentitude between every middling stalk of maize and juvenile tomato plant, their very existence was a sleight upon Hegira's ego that could not be borne with any of the social graces indigenous to a Turin adult. I wondered if her hands were jealous that the fungi looked more like they belonged perpetually stuck into the dirt. In my imagination, she courted her late wife with roots on her wrists; she watched her daughter grow up with a trowel in tow; she slept with clods of cobble and clay up to her neck and descended into a dream-state of stalk and stem in the passing of each night.

I'd asked her once if she'd defend her own home. Now, after combat had sprouted in the Hanallta, we knew that she was not a fighter. But when war sprouted in her sacha...

"Plenty of mushrooms are good for crops," she explained between over-the-shoulder tosses of disinterred fungi. "But these — these *Nightfeeders* — every time they come up, the crops go bad. Can't for the life of me figure out what it is they do, but I'll be damned if they're going to sully my sacha."

It'd been three days, and my knee was nearly back to normal. I hoped someone in my clan could help me strengthen it when I returned. I'd asked a few people to gather ingredients for me, and I read the smoke yesterday. I asked it, very simply, if the Hanallta would prove to be a danger in the coming week.

I was relieved to see the shoulders form warm, playful wisps.

The ankles told me nothing.

"Hegira," I started casually. "How will the Turin choose their next leader? And who will determine when the Red Wardens can be released from their prisons?"

A piece of Nightfeeder slapped me in the forehead.

"To be honest," she said, lowering her voice, "no one's really talked about it...we've all just been doing what we need to do. Peacefully, too. No chieftain, no wardens...I think the Turin are quietly hoping we just go on like this forever. But I assume the discussion will come up any moment, and some young woman will kill some big beast and some new chieftain will sit on the throne."

She sat up and looked at me more squarely.

"You seem to be better," she said.

"I am. Knee's not swollen, jaw isn't...awful."

"You'll be taking off soon, then?"

"Sometime today, I think."

"Well," she said, taking a moment. "If you ever find your-self coming up the mountain again...you have a place to stay."

"Thank you for giving me everything I needed."

"You'll always be welcome at my table," she said, gesturing to the Hanallta.

~

IT WAS IMPRESSIVE, REALLY, HOW MANY THINGS VIVONNO could put on a mule.

There were the necessities of travel: waterskins, dry rations of fruit and jerky, a blanket, a sketchbook, and the precious few wine bottles left that still sloshed with their sweet-smelling contents. His tent was packed with the others and pulled in a cart by the small team of oxen in the back of the caravan.

Then there were the fruits of his industry: heads for picks and mattocks ("no one makes 'em like the Turin!"), a tightly-packed bundle of stone-carved figurines ("I've got a rich contact who'll buy *anything* from these folk!"), and even though their guild's main carts were full of high-quality iron and steel billets, he had a few of his own stored away ("the trick is to hold your steel until winter, when the caravans aren't running!")

"Are you sure your mule can handle this?"

"Ol' Cardamom's faced plenty worse," he said, patting the animal lovingly. "This downhill trip is basically a vacation!"

Cardamom didn't looked convinced.

He turned to me and grew serious, his nose still swollen from a few days before.

"I'm not sure how to proceed, Rennik. Unless you can find out where Noskre's secret iron was, I think the idea's a bust."

"Not quite," I told him. His face lit up and immediately reacted to the pain of his nose. "I have a few tricks of my own. Just tell me where to find you in Rucost, and I'll meet you there someday."

"Someday?" he asked. "When an opportunity like this hits you, you need to act quickly, Rennik. 'Strike while the iron's hot', as your people say."

I realized that Vivonno thought I was Turin. I grinned.

"I'll find you soon, then," I told him. "But there's something I don't understand," I said. "The mountains are red due to the iron...why are iron veins so difficult to come by?"

"Well, they aren't found every nine feet, but they aren't rare, either."

"Then why—"

"For a few reasons. There's good iron and bad iron, and the Turin have a knack of pointing right to the good stuff like a dowsing rod. Good Turin iron is single-minded. Iron from elsewhere needs to be *convinced* into steel. Theirs jumps into the charcoal like it belongs there. The steel is near perfect every time. And also...because the Rucosti aren't just mining for iron," he said. He looked down and seemed to second-guess sharing his next words. "There's something else, something far more valuable to extract from the veins of Ba Turin. I don't think many in Rucost are privy to it, but...Well, we might be rich, Rennik. And I'll tell you more when you come see me."

Vivonno detailed the route home, told me of a caravanserai that's good for "travelers like me" to stop at, and explained the location of the city in which he lived.

We shook hands as all Rucosti are wont to do. I gave my farewells, wished Cardamom luck, and left them to their journey.

THE MAN WITH TWO NAMES

A great actor will never appear an actor at all.
They are as they are in each moment, a closet
of masks on an empty head.

— PHILIPUS CROWNE, CRITIC OF
THE ARTS

"What business does a lowlander have here?"

The crowd quieted.

The thin man was right to question my presence. Hegira had invited me along, and I came simply out of curiosity.

We stood, a few dozen Turin and I, in the throne room of Mother's Hall. Since the Turin were discussing what to do about a new chieftain, Tsavi had emerged from the mountain and was haunting the gathering patiently.

"A fair question," Tsavi said, "but he and I are familiar. Rennik is an ally."

The Turin took her word and continued discussing.

"I have been living near Moddimok for my entire life," continued a woman named Bandoray. She was a courtier, based on her attire, and had been interrupted by the thin man's question. "I know the politics of the Rucosti well, and the nuance in our sale of iron. I know many among you may distrust us who worked closely with Moddimok and Rangrim, but I assure you...the evil influence that plagued our leaders is gone."

"She speaks honestly," said Tsavi. She held a clear, quiet weight with her people. "I can personally confirm that the disease in our mountain has been cut out. Now that it has, we will be acutely watchful for its potential return."

Voices became layered.

"I find it concerning that your priority centers around relations with Rucost."

"Its *return?*"

"Why don't we choose from the farmers?"

"Most of our wealth comes from Rucost — of course she's prioritizing their politics!"

The discussion proceeded.

No one was looking for ravens.

Aside from the throne room, Mother's Hall was a barren place, the shadowed grave of Moddimok's reign. The torches were days dead. The histories painted on the walls were hidden in the dark. The only sound was the echoing persistence of falling water, drowning all that remained therein.

There was no one to see the warning written in a hasty hand and brought by bird.

It was foolish, in hindsight, to leave it all unattended. But the Turin had seen their chieftain and her daughter die in the span of a few days. They were resting, rebuilding, reconciling with one another.

No one knew what stood at the Sentinels that very moment.

~

HOOFBEATS ON STONE PUSHED FORTH AND DRUMMED US TO silence.

We looked to one another. Bandoray's face grew livid; it was surely an offense to ride into a sacred place such as this. She passed through the crowd to stand at the forefront of her people.

The smell of horse pushed into the hall.

A young Kazel man appeared beneath the giant hands. He sat astride a beautiful horse, a blood bay with a caparison of red, gold, and soft purple brocade. His armor, a bright breastplate inlayed with a copper-colored material, picked up the pattern from the cloth below and became an extension of the horse. He held a feathered helm in his arm. The horse's stride was proud and powerful.

He was flanked by two other riders. The feathers of their arrows fanned widely behind them in their saddle quivers, and their gaze scanned the pasture of the room predatorily.

"The Rucosti may be coming...the Crooked King's men will surely be here sooner."

The smoke had promised me a peaceful week. But I began second-guessing the form of my question. I'd asked if the *Hanallta* would prove to be dangerous. Perhaps the smoke didn't consider these newcomers to be part of that.

But it wasn't the pale man. The three riders before me were one Kazel, one a Rucosti, and another who was possibly Ilgo from the Inkwood.

"Which of you is Chieftain Moddimok?" he asked. His voice was controlled and even.

"Moddimok is dead," said Bandoray, pointedly omitting the title. "And you, cur, trod your beast upon hallowed ground."

The decorated man passed his helmet to one of his riders and leaned forward on his horse, looming over Bandoray.

"Am I to understand that you're the authority here?" he asked.

"Indeed I am," she said. It wasn't a declaration to her people; I think she didn't want the Turin to appear weak and disorganized. "You will address me as Bandoray."

The man scanned the room and its people again. His eyes found each far corner, as if to note the lack of armed guards.

"I am Calaman. My people received a raven from Chieftain Moddimok. It was to inform us that a wanted criminal is imprisoned in your mountain. We've been invited to take this prisoner into our possession."

I heard someone whisper to my left. "Has anyone been down to the prisons since the fight?"

"Where are your Red Wardens?" Calaman asked.

"Attending to business in the Hanallta nearby," Bandoray replied. "Why did the Rucosti send a Kazel man? Where are the usual envoys?"

Calaman raised an eyebrow and didn't respond. I wondered if this man would recognize Rangrim's name.

One of his riders spoke up.

"Malnostos."

Everything else faded at once. Only his name remained.

Calaman turned to the speaker and listened to his quiet comment. He nodded and dismounted his horse.

"Please. Take me to this prisoner, Bandoray" he said.

She turned, motioned for a few others to follow her, and led Calaman Malnostos from the throne room.

My mind was spinning. The resemblance was there.

It seemed like Corde was too delirious that night at the overhang, the night I'd read the smoke and spoken the name. But then there was the chance he'd heard, the chance he knew I was the person the pale man sought and the man who'd killed Calaman's kin. And the words I'd spoken in anger just a few days ago...

There was a hand at my back.

"Follow me," said Tsavi.

THERE WAS A TUNNEL.

Of course there was a tunnel.

It was hidden in a room used to store dry goods. Tsavi and I descended into the mountain; she produced a candle, lit it, and led the way.

"Does this lead back to Senna's—"

She put a finger to her lips.

We strode, slid, and ducked through the various shapes of the mountain's veins. At one point I thought we'd reached a dead end, but Tsavi passed the candle to me, slid on her stomach into a minuscule gap in the floor, and thrust her hand back out for the candle. I begrudgingly followed suit.

I wanted to whisper and ask her how many people knew of these tunnels, but I decided to wait.

I tried to reason with the situation. If Corde was more conscious than he seemed that night — and he was never as he seemed — he might tell Malnostos about me. Calaman would surely want me dead, in the name of both his family and this "Crooked King." But how far were they willing to go for one man?

Or maybe, if no one had attended to the duties in Mother's Hall, Haston Corde had been forgotten, too. Maybe the insects proved too little to feed a healing man. Maybe he'd been dead for two days, and there'd be no danger in his being a loose end.

A few minutes passed, and I began to hear voices.

Tsavi stopped me and put a finger to her lips again. She blew out the candle.

"...will not be allowed back in this mountain, or anywhere in Ba Turin. To direct your beast into Mother's Hall is tantamount to spitting on the throne!"

"My sincerest apologies, Chieftain Bandoray," said Calaman. "My army will quit the mountains once we have Giligas Crattle."

"Army?" I heard the waver in her voice.

"Yes. My accompaniment."

"How many of you are there?"

"Now? At the feet of your Sentinels? Forty fighters, forty-one horses."

"And elsewhere?"

Their voices trailed away. Tsavi lit the candle again and waved me forward. I saw, after two steps, the small opening in the stone that overlooked one section of the long stairway to the prison cells.

The path shrank continually until we had to crouch to move forward. My knee groaned at the chore of it all. We came to a place where torchlight flickered through another small opening, and she dismissed our light once more.

"...We were told he was alive," Calaman said. My heart leapt.

"He is. I saw him breathe, just now."

The jingle of metal keys. The creaking of iron hinges in motion.

"Get up," commanded the Kazel man. When a few

seconds passed, I heard what sounded like a man being shaken. "Speak, Crattle. Your hour has come."

The man named Giligas Crattle produced a few incoherent mumblings.

"Get some water," Bandoray instructed someone. "And some bread."

When the water and bread had reached the sparrow and his manstomach, he spoke more clearly.

"Zamri," he croaked. "You've been absent for days longer than expected."

"Clear your eyes, you dolt. I am the son of Zamri Malnostos. You speak to Calaman."

"Cala...Calaman! Your father..."

"Is dead," he finished. "Can you walk?"

There was a pause in conversation.

"I'll need your assistance in bringing him to the surface," said Calaman. "Once there, we will tie him to a horse and relieve you of his presence."

"You," stated Bandoray. It sounded like she was getting someone's attention. "The Turin above have begun to repair the damage you and your kind have done. Have you seen the errors in your blind loyalty?"

"Yes! Please! Let me see my home!" responded a desperate voice. I assumed it was that of a captured Red Warden.

"Bandoray," said Calaman with a lowered voice. "There was something else mentioned in the letter. It implied that the chieftain had something for me that couldn't be expressed in writing. Do you know where this daughter is?"

"Days away, I'm afraid. Traveling south with haste per the late chieftain's orders."

"Have you any idea what this other interest might be?"

An Achare refugee sitting in a stone twenty feet above you.

This confirmed to me that Calaman had not been contacted by Moddimok, but by the letter Rangrim had sent our first day here. She'd curried favor with the pale man's people while letting her mother think the prisoner was to gain favor with Rucost. I wondered how long it would take me to unravel all of her machinations.

"I'm sorry," she said after a moment passed. "I truly don't know."

Calaman made a resigned noise as Bandoray spoke again.

"Assist in bringing this man up the staircase," she told the Red Warden. "We need not dirty ourselves with his filth. Do this, and we will discuss the finer details of your return."

"Yes, of course...chieftain," he finished uncertainly.

"From the outside, the mountain looks like solid stone. I never would've guessed it to be all stilts and scaffold."

Tsavi grinned. "There are many pores in the mountain, yes, but you underestimate its size and strength."

We stood on a rocky outcropping, overlooking the Hanallta in its entirety. I could see for miles.

The horde of Calaman Malnostos was leaving. There was an occasional glint of sunlight from a helm or cuirass, the delayed cacophony of chatter and hoofbeats, and emptying space beneath the Sentinels. It was as if the Hanallta had been holding its breath and finally expelled the riders with its exhaling.

I felt I needed to do something about Giligas Crattle. Should his memory find itself upright, should his voice find the right words, I might find the fury of the horde coming quickly. But what was I to do now, when he had the protection of dozens?

Before I left Ba Turin, I had a promise to fulfill. I was wanted in the heart of the mountain, and I felt I had a thousand small questions to ask if I were to put the pieces cleanly together. It seemed the Turin were on their way to repairing the damage done. If Bandoray were chosen as chieftain, or even if some other took her place, I knew the Shiver would not burden their decisions.

With one last look, I saw the Hanallta through Owasa's eyes. The great sienna dais of the mountain rose high above the Kalanosi lowlands. The sprawling green grasses and twisted, sun-bleached bristlecones shifted patiently in the highest winds of the world. The people, the true crop of Ba Turin, were the colors of clay and iron, of friends and family, of food shared and memories held. And I hoped my own memory would stay as vivid as Owasa's art, would glow like stars in a blackened night when I sought for rosy comfort.

I shouldered my bow and walked.

GOING HOME

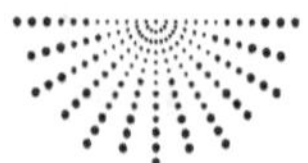

There is a grandness that cannot be properly
summarized. There is a depth too great for the
ropes of written word. So to the critics of my
explorations, I say only this:
Take a walk.

— MARTINOR THE UNTETHERED

I'd spent three days healing with Tsavi.

But now, as the miles passed, I felt the true euphoria of lowland air. After so long in the choking altitudes of the Hanallta, at heights no Achare is welcome, my lungs gorged themselves on the honeyed breezes below. I bathed in desolate solitudes and felt myself cleaned of the blood of Ba Turin.

An overcast evening. The dog shared in my lively pace. A hairless strip ran from his right cheek to his shoulder. It matched the scar on his back with its strange black coloration. Karay had proven to be my fiercest companion, and I remembered what Ikoda had said last spring.

"They like the idiots. They want 'em safe."

"I'm glad one of us has brains," I told him. I stopped to rest against a lone oak. It was young, thin, and grew without competition for the sun. "Spoiled." I rubbed his head. "Just like you."

A BREEZY MORNING. THERE WAS WARMTH FROM THE WEST, suffusing the surprisingly crisp air with the threat of a storm. I thought back to the horde. I could only hope Giligas Crattle would die before he spoke.

We walked in the writhing paths of dry hilltops left by the rainy season. The pools here were not as deep as those further north. The effort of keeping dry added distance to the journey as straight lines became impossible to walk. Few journeys, I reminisced, are ever so simple.

A STORM IN THE NIGHT. WICKED WINDS. I'D STRAYED FROM MY path to find the caravanserai Vivonno had mentioned; once I'd found the road, I simply followed what I assumed were his guild's cart tracks in the dirt. The place was impressive; it was a wide-ranging stone structure surrounded by a great mass of wooden addendums. In it was music, warm food, and a dry place to sleep. It smelled heavily of horse and beer. The air was full of Rucosti chatter. I purchased a small, light tent made of rawhide that'd been rubbed with some sort of cactus — or maybe something *from* a cactus. My proficiency with the Rucosti Language did not extend to inebriated slurring, but I caught enough to know that it was sufficiently waterproof. The dog slept anxiously at my side.

A HUMID MIDDAY. I WONDERED IF THE SHIVER WAS BEHIND ME. When I asked Tsavi, in the day or so I'd spent with her, if the Shiver I'd destroyed could come back like Marmot did, she told me it was likely. Unless there is a way to cut its ties to this "lower" world completely, it would find its way back someday far in the future. I asked if there were a way to cut *my* ties with the "higher" world. She didn't know that either. I told her that for someone who listens to a magic mountain speaking through a magic corpse, she didn't know as much as I thought she would. She laughed. I was only half-joking.

I told her about the power I'd used, the smoke I'd breathed to find Rangrim in the fire. I told her about the pale man and his horde. She said people like me can do all sorts of things, but that I must be careful with what those things do to *me*.

"There are abilities some have learned that I consider evil. A connection to the dead is not always a comfortable one to initiate, as you well know. But power can be tantalizing. I believe this man you've seen is caught in the snare of knowledge. You have a heart, Rennik. Be sure you keep it."

A CRICKET-FILLED EVENING. I THOUGHT AHEAD TO MY HOME. I'd find Avid making something small and complicated. He'd been toying with some sort of two-part buckle when I left. Apparently it'd make our packing, unpacking, tacking, and untacking of the horses quicker. When I find him, he'll have one end of a strap tied around a tree, the other end in his hand, and pulling with all his might to test the stress of the buckle under weight.

"Maybe if you weighed more than a hundred pounds," I'd say to him.

And he'd say, "I'd have you try *your* weight, but I don't want to break my only model."

We'd laugh, embrace, and tell stories late into the night. And now that I'd learned about Shivers, I might never leave his side again.

My mother would welcome me momentarily before noticing the tear in my padded shirt. She'd ask what happened. I'd tell her I fell down a wall like an idiot and landed on a torch.

"You're not an idiot," she'd say. "But if it happens twice..."

Malik would be patient while I spoke with my family. After Avid fell asleep, I'd find her next to a campfire a small distance from the others, as is our tradition. She'd ask if anyone tried to kill me.

"One or two people, yeah." And I'd tell her the entire story, with Barim and Callisgrim, with an immortal boy, everything from Hegira to the Sentinels, from painted walls to hidden rivers.

And I'd be home.

A TEPID AFTERNOON. DRIZZLING. I DECIDED I WOULD FIND two poplar seedlings. I would find a strong, stony outcropping — stubborn, even — and plant them near it. I'd kneel down and speak to the women for whom they were planted. I'd apologize to the both of them that they died working with me. I'd apologize that it was ultimately me that led to their deaths. I'd apologize to Noskre for never telling her that Callisgrim lived beyond the Shadowlands, and that she died just a week before returning. I'd tell them that I couldn't fix any of it now, but I could at least plant something in their honor.

I'd tell them that I knew we were all impatient as hell, so I found the fastest-growing trees I knew of.

A GRAY SKY THAT STRETCHED OVER AN ENTIRE DAY. Unremarkable grasses. It felt as though we were walking the same acres over and again.

I would return one day to visit with Marmot. I have much to thank him for — and a bit of criticism as well.

"Hey," I'd tell him. "If it's a matter of life-and-death, maybe drop the cryptic games."

"What games?" he'd ask with a cheeky grin.

Perhaps he'll remember his previous life. If not, Karay will get to tackle him again.

A CLOUDLESS MORNING. NO WIND. WE PASSED BY A FIELD OF wheat. At this point in the summer, it'd grown to a few feet tall. It was bound for acres by a low stone wall that told the world, "this is the property of just one family. Stay out. This land is not your land."

EVENING. THERE WERE MANY MILES TO GO, BUT I'D STOPPED IN my tracks. The wind had picked up. It pushed the low grasses in the patterns each traveler knew by heart.

The blood left my face. The hairs stood high on my neck. The dog was staring at him.

Gatsi was waiting for me.

26

REUNION

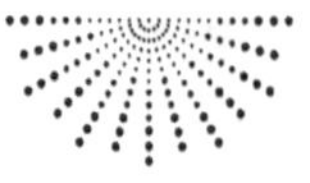

*We are creatures of the day. All that we see is
what seems in the light. Our deepest bias is a
blindness to what we look like in the dark.*

— ARCHDRUID VARSAELIA

He stood like a stone in my path.

Upon his shoulders were hung two hares, freshly killed, skin cut at the ankles. With no weapons to weigh them down, he held his hands outward as if to present himself.

"Come, Rennik." He spoke as if we'd been talking just a minute before. "The evening is young, and we have much to discuss."

He turned and walked a short distance to a campfire. Karay put his nose up, and it quivered at the presence of meat. He marched cautiously forward. So did I.

Next to the fire sat two blankets in wait. He hung the hares over a stick held up by a pole and the end of a small tent.

"Sit," Gatsi said genially, gesturing to one of the blankets.

He produced a few strips of jerky and fed them to Karay. I couldn't bring myself to sit.

"So," he began. "What have you learned?"

I found my voice.

"Did you know I was alive?" I stood squarely.

"I knew you had a good chance, Rennik. But I did not truly know."

"You left me."

"And you did just fine—"

"They're all dead!" I raised my voice. "So many of your neighbors, so many of the people you saw born and raised, they're nothing but ash in the earth and you did nothing!"

"I did everything I needed to," he said calmly. "Have you divined who it was they were after?"

"I didn't have to read the smoke. Zamri Malnostos told me as he threatened Avid's life."

Gatsi's mouth twitched to show the slightest amount of pride. "Your reading is going well, then?"

"Avid's alive, by the way."

"Good. And Zamri Malnostos?"

A moment passed. He registered my hesitation and grinned like a jackal.

"So it is his name you speak...Hmph. There are worse men to stitch into yourself."

"And who did you kill?" I asked, trying to rein in my anger.

Gatsi seemed to notice it anyway, and he looked into the fire. "It was a long time ago, Rennik. Some things are best left as they are in this moment. And in this moment, those people are nothing but names."

"People? How many have you killed?"

"Something tells me your list has grown as well," he said.

I took four steps away from the light and looked out over the grasses.

"You're angry," he said. "And you deserve to be."

"I thought of you as a father."

"I know, Rennik. But I feel I need not explain myself."

"Yes, how *exhausting* it must be to explain your abandonment," I said bitingly.

"You confuse me for something else." His voice scraped steadily from him. "Despite your feelings, I am not your father. I came to the Achare as a means of reaching the Delkhi. But when your parents brought you to me...I felt a kinship. Not the noose of fatherhood, but *kinship*."

"You had no such noose."

"You are familiar with story, Rennik. You know well the rotating cast of whom they consist. We tell legends for a reason."

"To teach," I said shortly.

"To teach." He nodded. "There is the Hero. Dauntless, merciful, loyal."

"To make us brave in hard times." The rote response fell from my mouth.

"To make us brave..." he repeated. "There is the Child. Curious, blameless, pure."

"To put value in our young, in our future. To protect them is to make our people stronger." I hated that I was finding a familiar groove in our conversation.

"There is the Wise Elder. The old man on the hill. Patient, ready to depart his knowledge to the hero." I saw his face tighten. It was the most he'd moved in minutes, so I stayed quiet. "Well, Rennik? What do stories teach us of the Elder?"

"It teaches us to respect the lessons of the past."

"No."

"It teaches us to depend on him." I found my voice rising.

"No, Rennik."

"Teaches us that he is family, *that he's a father—*"

"*No!*" He shouted, standing to his feet. He looked to me from across the fire. "It teaches the young to dispose of the old! It teaches us that the oldest among us have only to dispense what is useful before they are a nuisance, a weight on the story of the young that must be cut loose!"

"That's not true—"

"Think, Rennik! Think back to our legends. What fate befell Wheltsun of the Stone?"

"He sacrificed himself to give his son time, but—"

"And Uldren? Lady of the four crows? What became of her?"

"Gatsi, I don't understand!"

"Answer, Rennik! What hell was brought upon her?"

I felt something pull at my stomach. "She was swept into the seas after revealing the truth she knew. To bring courage to Kivik after—"

"Koskomon. The old chieftain."

"Abandoned by his grandson. He himself decided that he was one stomach too many. He modeled sacrifice to his people so that the hero could move them on."

Gatsi turned and scanned the grasses. I smelled something burning that was not wood. Rage was in his eyes, in the clenched muscles of his jaw. "We keep these tales to show each other how life must be. Value the children. Value the hero. *The old must die.*"

"You left us."

"I was no dog." He spat the words at me. "I was not leashed to you or your people."

I began to shout again. "*My* people?"

"Yes, Rennik! *Your* people!"

"You were no such weight to me," I said. "You were not disposable."

"Time turns us into knaves, each of us a rogue of our own design. There are survivors and there are the dead, Rennik. I will not wait for that killing sea! I am no Uldren!"

"Nor I the ocean!" I yelled up at him as I got to my feet. "You act as though the laws of our lives were written by our ancestors—"

"Our stories reflect *real values*—"

"You say they taught us to sacrifice the old, but I say they only taught you to be a coward, Gatsi." The air in my chest was all anger, my lungs a bellows. "You learned only to fear, and it is *you* who cut *me* away."

" 'Coward' is a tool of the ignorant and the hypocritical. I didn't think, Rennik, you'd manage to become both." His voice had grown teeth. "You call me a coward, but when the Achare were attacked, you took your brother and ran. When things seemed hopeless, you fled into the earth itself—"

"That was not my intent! The Delkhi did something, it pulled me away—"

"And now you seek another on whom to stack the blame. What a courageous leader you've become, Rennik. What a noble shape you've assumed, leaving your brother to die at the feet of the Delkhi."

"I..." Grief plucked at my stomach. I fought the urge to be sick. I didn't care to ask how he knew about that. Tears rolled steadily down my face. "I thought that's what it wanted!" I shouted. "I thought it might save him, but you weren't there to tell me any different! What could I have done?"

"The mistake," he said slowly, "is in valuing what it wants above what you know of yourself."

"And what should I have known of myself?"

"That you are no leader of men," he answered. "You should have run."

"You condemn my running and suggest it all at once."

"I suggest you stop running in *fear* and instead make intelligent decisions."

"I should have been the rogue you foresee in us all?" I asked him.

"Yes."

"Your cynicism consumes you."

"The Hero, the Child...There's a reason we've both survived, Rennik. The only way in which to atone for the past is to learn. The great powers of this world have put you in motion, have set you — just you, not your people — on a shelf so as to see a privileged distance only few can."

"You're no Achare." It had been meant as an insult.

"No," he said flatly. "I'm not."

"Then what are you? What sort of person abandons those who gave him a home?"

The strange substance in the fire caught a proper flame. It grew and brightened.

Gatsi looked toward it. "Pity," was all he said. "Yes, Rennik, I am a criminal by every definition legends put into your head, but I was not raising you to be a storyteller. You must understand that you are something more than a forlorn Achare hunter. We survive by existing away from the others. They were not long for this world, but *we*—"

"Do not place me next to you! *We* are nothing! I am *nothing* like you."

"You are *exactly* like me, Rennik. You are a man reborn, a speaker of the greater beast, of the tree on the riverbank."

"Then the Delkhi keeps you too?"

Gatsi shook his head. He looked younger, somehow, than

I remembered him. "No," he said. "Not the Delkhi. I am tied to another."

"Another? The Mountain Mother?" I felt the waters of the river around my head. I was there again, without any idea which way was up.

"The plains of Kalanos have but one mind, as all bodies do. A single organ by which to move its limbs, to manipulate the world around it." Gatsi's eyes wandered to the distant north. "There are other minds, coexisting in one world alongside their siblings. In the Inkwood, in the deserts of the Kazel, in the mountains of Ba Turin. Each is a body with a mind and a will, and we are but a hand of that body. Those you abandoned, Rennik, those you left behind were small, replaceable bits on the flesh of Kalanos. It is an awful truth. It is a simple truth. It was both terrible and right to save yourself."

"I don't understand what you're saying."

"Wake up, boy! You are no simple Kalanosi man — that life was taken from you the day the Delkhi pulled you from that river. You are lifted, you are something *transcendent* among the plains." He shouted as I walked away. "You are a beetle become man, a mud figure made flesh!"

I pounded into the grasses. I needed distance.

"WERE YOU CERTAIN I WOULD FIND TSAVI? THE WOMAN IN THE mountains?"

"No. But curiosity will always be the hook for the animal in you. I thought it likely."

I had taken a long while to wrestle with myself and think calmly. He was waiting for me near his fire, unmoving. I decided he knew what I needed to know. He was right. Curiosity will forever bait me.

"Your approach is so different than that of the Turin," I told him.

"How so?"

"They serve their...creature. Gatsi, is there a name for this sort of thing?"

"Of course the Turin live in servitude to their heart," he said with a scoff. "And I tend to call them just that, Rennik. A Heart."

"How does it choose its shape? Theirs is an actual ancestor. Her bones."

"The 'Mountain Mother' is no more a mother or a corpse than the Delkhi is a tree. People project what they need to see in order to serve. A justification for compromise. Know, Rennik, that one need not bend to the will of the Delkhi. One can work *with* it. An alliance rather than grinning subjugation."

"And these Hearts live in two worlds."

"In a way, yes. That's one way for us to understand it."

"How did the Delkhi affect me in the mountains? I had a vision while I slept, I used the smoke from the Turin bodies to..."

Gatsi smiled wide. "So you've discovered a greater power than even sage, hair, and bones provide. When did you first do it?"

"When the pale man came," I told him.

"Kesevirot."

"When the attack started, when the fires had come through already and..."

"Who was it?"

"...Ciqala. Banar. Chaska, Kinran, Teneran, Liril, Mudre, Tella..." I choked on the last few names. "I learned to do it with the burning of my home, Gatsi. They were what let me find my family."

The absent choirs of Ba Turin were gathered here, filling the windy night with a thousand chirping voices. It truly was easier to breathe down in the lowlands.

"To answer your question," he said after I'd collected myself, "The Delkhi may not have affected you at all. I do not doubt the Mountain Mother would reach out to you. You, who were already familiar with creatures like her. And what did she have you do?"

"...what do you mean?"

"Understand, Rennik, that the Delkhi *encouraged* our coming and going. It decided these things should happen."

"She showed me signs to follow, I suppose. Some stars that ended up being a cave-dwelling creature...she showed me my father, and Ciqala, and a small girl in the rain. She wanted me to overcome my guilt and..."

"And?"

"And kill Rangrim."

"And did you want to kill her, too?"

"I had no choice. She was going to kill me."

Gatsi nodded. "They tend to not be entirely selfish. The Delkhi did save you, after all."

"Who was the girl?" I asked, as if he'd know the secrets of all my experiences.

"I don't think, Rennik, that something so intelligent would use a word you didn't know. Perhaps this will become clear in time."

"In time...Is this going to last the rest of my life, Gatsi?"

"Yes, Rennik. This has given you a *new* life."

"I do not want this." I said it firmly. But Gatsi merely shook his head.

"You already have this."

"Do people like me…do *we* get something out of their deaths? The people we kill?"

Gatsi nodded. "And Kesevirot has killed hundreds."

"And what does he get? A list of names to choose from?"

"No, Rennik. Something far more powerful."

"Is that what those are for?" I asked as he stood to retrieve a hare. I realized then that the hare left hanging from the line was alive. Its chest beat a rapid and silent tattoo at the precipice of death.

He laughed a pleasant, unburdened laugh. "This will be another layer to peel back. It will be uncomfortable at first. Jarring. But in time, it may just convince you to prefer having been saved by the Delkhi."

The fire crackled. The dog slept.

"What is it, exactly?"

"It's something that will allow you to render information from others."

"…from those I've killed?" I asked, putting the pieces together.

"It will take time. It's what I've used for years to learn much of what I know."

He gripped the hare by the ankle and stripped it of its skin.

"And it's what I'm going to teach you now."

Ben Merrick's childhood was defined by the stories he read and the worlds he created with building blocks. Now that the impulsively creative child has become an impulsively creative adult, writing books seems like a natural outlet. He independently published his first book, the award-winning *Where the Valley Meets the Sky*, in 2021. The sequel, *Where the River Goes*, was published in June of 2023.

Ben Merrick attended the University of Iowa and earned his BA in English and Certification in Secondary Education in 2016. He teaches various high school courses in Iowa, where he was born and raised. When he's not teaching or writing, he's running a D&D campaign, playing music, working in the woodshop, or spending time with his wife and dog.

Check out his website at benwritesbooks.com for expanded lore and announcements!

@BenLikesBooks on X

@_benlikesbooks on Instagram

www.ingramcontent.com/pod-product-compliance
Lightning Source LLC
Chambersburg PA
CBHW051132190726
48290CB00006B/1809